A MURDER UNDER THE BRIDGE

DONALD L'ABBATE

DEDICATION

To my wife who makes my life complete and to my children and grandchildren who make it interesting and fun.

TABLE OF CONTENTS

DONALD L'ABBATE

A MURDER UNDER THE BRIDGE

DONALD L'ABBATE

CHAPTER 1

My name is Jake Carney I say that because the last time I told you about my life and how I managed to get it back on the rails after being a drunk for some years, I never mentioned my name. So now you know my name.

Anyway, I was in court, and I was bored as hell and not paying too much attention because the Assistant District Attorney was just babbling on and on about the gun he was holding in his hand without actually making a point. Judge Goldstein, a very patient man, had a glazed look in his eyes, and everybody else in the courtroom was on the verge of dozing off. That's when it happened. It sounded like a shot echoing through the high-ceilinged courtroom startling the hell out of everyone and sending us all ducking for cover.

Soon everyone realized the ADA had dropped the gun, and the noise we heard was the gun hitting the tile floor. The gun was a Desert Eagle 44 magnum semi-automatic pistol, a huge gun that's more like a cannon, and weighs four-and-a-half pounds. The ADA was apologizing like crazy. The rest of us were pretending we hadn't had the crap scared out of us, which obviously we had, or we wouldn't be climbing out from under the tables.

Even my client Joey Bats, who allegedly owned the dropped gun, had been under the table alongside me. Joey Bats, whose actual name is Joseph DiFalco, prefers being called Joey Bats. It's a nickname he acquired because he likes to use a Louisville Slugger as a business tool. Ironically we were in court arguing over the admissibility of a gun allegedly in Joey's possession. Frankly, he would have been better off if he had stuck with the baseball bat, but that's neither here nor there.

Joey Bats is what you call a "wannabe gangster," a throwback to the days of the old "Godfather" type Mafia. Unfortunately for Joey, but fortunately for the rest of us, the days of that Mafia in New York City are long gone. That was thanks mostly to Rudy Giuliani when he was the United States Attorney for the Southern District of New York. Today organized crime in New York City is more like disorganized crime run by gangster wannabes like Joey Bats.

Even the old Mafia hangouts on Mulberry Street in Little Italy are mostly gone. Take, for example, the social club run by the Teflon Don, John Gotti. It's now a high-end shoe store. Gone also are the high-priced mob lawyers. Nowadays the wannabes rely on small-time lawyers like me, which explains how I got to be Joey's lawyer. But I wasn't always a small-time criminal defense lawyer.

A lot of years ago I was a hotshot in the District Attorney's Office in Manhattan until too much booze got me fired, and I ended up practicing law out of the backroom of Shoo's Chinese Restaurant on Mott Street. Eventually, I got my life back on track, and now I have an actual office on Mott Street and a decent practice to go with it. I'm still a recovering alcoholic and a card-carrying member of AA, but I'm okay. At least I think so.

Getting sober changed a lot of things in my life, but one thing remained the same. I'm still a criminal defense lawyer with a small practice, which is okay because that's what I want to be. However, since getting sober, I don't have to rely on court-assigned cases to survive. Today, I have more clients than I had back then and some of them can even afford to pay my fees.

On occasion, I have been known to represent a few so-called Mafia-associated clients, but I'm no Tom Hagen or Bruce Cutler. If you don't know about Tom Hagen, watch the "Godfather" on Netflix or pick up the book by Mario Puzo. If you don't know who Bruce Cutler is, I don't know what to tell you.

Back to Joey Bats and Judge Goldstein's courtroom. Joey was charged with violation of Penal Law § 265.01-b, criminal possession of a firearm, a Class E felony which could net Joey one and a half to four years in jail. Naturally, Joey didn't want to go to jail, and he was paying me good money to see he didn't.

The gun Joey was charged with possessing had allegedly been found sticking out from under the passenger seat of Joey's Cadillac during what the arresting officer claimed was a routine traffic investigation. Since there was no evidence connecting the gun to any other crime, it was strictly a possession case. It was small-time stuff, but as I said, Joey was a small-time criminal.

Apparently satisfied he now had everybody's undivided attention, the ADA put down the gun and finally called his first witness, Officer Collins. According to Officer Collins, a twelve-year veteran of New York's Finest, he was on foot patrol on Mulberry Street when he observed Mr. DiFalco's Cadillac illegally parked. On approaching the vehicle and checking for passengers, he saw a pistol "in plain sight" sticking out from under the passenger seat.

Officer Collins said he was in the process of retrieving the weapon when Mr. DiFalco arrived on the scene. Knowing Mr. DiFalco's criminal association and having found the gun in the vehicle, Officer Collins feared for his own safety and placed Mr. DiFalco in handcuffs. Once Mr. DiFalco was securely in handcuffs, Officer Collins proceeded to retrieve the subject weapon. After that, he placed Mr. DiFalco under arrest and read him his Miranda rights. A sector car was called, and Mr. DiFalco was taken to the 5th Precinct Station House.

With the background details out of the way, the ADA had Officer Collins identify Exhibit 1, the gun. Just to make sure we all heard the keywords, the ADA had Officer Collins repeat his claim that a full half of the pistol had been "in plain sight" sticking out from under the car's passenger seat.

The gun was Joey's, and naturally, it had his fingerprints on it. There was no doubt about that, but it wasn't on the floor of the Cadillac, and it wasn't "in plain sight." It had been in the Cadillac's glove box. Officer Collins found the gun when he opened the glove box, and since he didn't have a search warrant allowing him to do so, he had conducted an illegal search and seizure. Under the Fourth Amendment of the Constitution that was a no-no, and a "get out of jail free" card for Joey if I could prove the gun wasn't "in plain sight."

That's what brought us all together that day in Judge Goldstein's courtroom for a hearing I hoped would result in the gun being excluded from evidence. Without the gun in evidence, there was no case against Joey, and we'd all eventually go home.

But I still needed to prove the gun wasn't "in plain sight" on the floor. Joey, not being the brightest member of the gang, suggested he'd just tell the judge the gun wasn't on the floor because he kept it in the glove box. Once I explained to Joey his testimony would constitute a confession of guilt he agreed it wasn't a good idea, or as he put it "that ain't good no way."

It all came down to discrediting Officer Collins and his claim the gun was in plain sight. As it turned out, it wasn't a difficult job. As I said, the gun is huge. It's twelve inches long. But more importantly, the passenger seat in Joey's 2007 Cadillac CTS-V with eight-way adjustable front seats and heated cushions has less than three inches of floor space under the seat before you bump against one of the seat motors. There was no way the Desert Eagle 44 magnum cannon was going to fit under the seat, even a quarter of the way.

Officer Collins had dutifully recorded the Cadillac's vehicle identification number in his Arrest Report, which made it easy for me to introduce the General Motors spec sheet for Joey's 2007 Cadillac CTS-V into evidence. Next, I added a couple of pictures of the passenger side seat taken from different angles and with a ruler showing the space under the seat.

I hadn't asked Collins a single question, but the photographs proved it was physically impossible for the gun to be sticking halfway out from under the seat and in plain sight. Collins knew he was done and he was sitting in the witness box red-faced as the judge studied the photos, glanced at the gun and then looking at Collins, shook his head.

I love cops. When I was at the DA's Office, I worked with cops all the time, and I still have some friends on the force. I think cops have an unbelievably tough job and they're underpaid and underappreciated. But, when they take shortcuts or try to pull fast ones I have to draw the line. That's my job as a criminal defense lawyer.

It was time to drop Collins into the deep end of the shit pond. It was pretty clear the gun hadn't been in "plain sight" so if it wasn't on the floor of the car, where had it been and how had Officer Collins found it? You don't have to be Einstein to figure that out. The gun had been hidden somewhere in the car, and Collins found it by illegally searching the car. But why would Collins target the Cadillac for an illegal search? You know I had an answer to that question, right?

Collins reluctantly admitted he had a history with Joey DiFalco. He had arrested Joey twice in the past, and both times the charges had been dismissed. He, of course, knew Joey went by the nickname "Joey Bats." And Joey, being Joey, his license plate was "JOEYBATS 1." So when I asked Officer Collins if he knew the Cadillac belonged to Joey when he first approached it during his "traffic investigation" he could hardly say no. I was done, and so was Officer Collins.

The ADA made a feeble attempt to rehabilitate his witness, but at that point, Judge Goldstein was counting the holes in ceiling tiles, and all Officer Collins wanted to do was get out of there before anybody thought about charging him with perjury or something worse.

With Officer Collins gone, the hearing moved quickly. The gun was excluded from evidence because it came from an illegal search and seizure. Since the gun was a necessary element in the crime, the case against Joey "Bats" DiFalco was formally dismissed.

Standing outside the courthouse, Joey kept slapping me on my back telling me what a great job I had done. He promised to recommend me to all his associates and said whenever I was near Napoli Trattoria I should stop in, and the meal was always on him. Then he asked when he'd get his gun back, and he wasn't very happy when I said never. The gun was illegal, and the cops would destroy it. That, of course, prompted Joey Bats to ask "what the hell kind of country are we living in?"

I knew the answer, but I wasn't about to tell him. He didn't have the gun anymore, but I was pretty sure the Louisville Slugger was in the trunk of the Cadillac..

CHAPTER 2

You may remember from the last time we met I don't have a lot of sympathy for my criminal clients. Well, some of that's changed. Not entirely, but somewhat. What's changed is I don't hate all of them, just some of them. The rest I can tolerate, and there are some I even like a little bit. Joey Bats fit in somewhere between tolerated and liked a little bit.

Before you start judging me, let me explain something. I've spent a lot of time dealing with career violent felons who have no consciences and no remorse for the pain and suffering they've caused. Those people I hate. I defend them, and I do the best I can for them because that's my job as a lawyer and as a sworn officer of the court. But there is nothing in any oath I took saying I can't hate the bastards. I just want you to know that.

You might think my years of alcoholic drinking have something to do with my attitudes, and you could be right. God knows there are a lot of people who think that. But after five years of sobriety with three to four AA meetings a week, my attitude hasn't changed when it comes to the repeat violent felons. But why dwell on it? It is what it is.

I was on my way back to the office when Connie, my secretary, called my cell phone. Mr. Benjamin needed to speak with me right away. He hadn't said what it was about, but he said it was important.

Joe Benjamin is the Administrator at the 18B Panel who assigns criminal cases involving indigent defendants in Manhattan and the Bronx to private attorneys when Legal Aid can't handle them. I've been doing 18B cases ever since I got booted from the District Attorney's Office many years ago. Back then I was drinking heavily, and 18B cases were my only source of income. Some lawyers do 18B cases for charitable reasons, but back then I did them strictly for survival. Things are different now because I'm different now.

My relationship with Joe Benjamin hasn't always been amicable. In fact, for a while back in my drinking days, it was downright hostile. Particularly when Joe suggested I attend Alcoholics Anonymous. Actually, it wasn't a suggestion, it was more like I either go to AA or lose my law license. But to be honest, that may have saved my life. I don't drink anymore, and Joe and I are on good terms. You might even say we're friends.

A MURDER UNDER THE BRIDGE

Even though I was only about ten minutes from my office, it sounded important, so I called Joe on my cell phone. He had a new case for me, and he wanted me to get on it right away. A homeless man living under the Manhattan Bridge and the FDR Drive had been arrested and charged with killing a young man with a hammer. The police found the homeless guy sitting near the body, still holding the bloody hammer in his hand. The problem was the homeless man refused to say anything, so the police didn't even know his name.

Apparently, when the cops showed up at the scene, the guy wasn't violent or incoherent, so they hadn't treated him as an EDP, or emotionally disturbed person, just as an uncooperative suspect. If he had been categorized as an EDP, he would have been taken to a medical facility for psychiatric evaluation, but instead, he was simply arrested and booked.

He was going to be arraigned in Criminal Court in about an hour, and Joe wanted me there. The case sounded a little crazy to me, but I like crazy stuff, so I said I'd be there, and I'd take care of it. The initial Arrest Report was the only paperwork Joe had on the case, and he promised to fax it to my office right away.

Joe asked me to keep him posted and gave me his home phone number, which was unusual. Normally he'd assign me a case, and unless there were problems I needed to discuss with him, I wouldn't report back until the case was over. So it was obvious Joe was taking a special interest in this case, but he didn't tell me why and at that point, I had no way of knowing why. Besides it was none of my business. My job was to represent this character the best I could, which is what I would do.

CHAPTER 3

I was supposed to have dinner that night with my longtime female companion, Gracie Delaney. Gracie doesn't like me calling her my girlfriend because for some reason she doesn't think the term accurately describes our relationship. I must admit our relationship is a bit offbeat, but it works for us, and that's what matters. So I don't call her my girlfriend, and she doesn't call me her boyfriend. My suggestion she introduce me as her sex god didn't go over so well.

By way of background, Gracie is a Senior Deputy District Attorney in the Manhattan DA's Office, and we've known each other for more than twenty years. We got together romantically the first time when we were both working at the DA's Office. I say, the first time because the relationship was interrupted when Gracie concluded my growing love for Scotch dropped her into second place in my life. Never one to be satisfied with second place Gracie ended our relationship. To be honest, when we split I didn't care except I missed the sex.

About five years ago Joe Benjamin forced me into AA, and I finally got sober. That's when Gracie and I picked up again. This time around Gracie is back in first place in my life, and I do care.

When I got back to the office, I called Gracie and explained why I couldn't make dinner at seven. Being a lawyer herself, Gracie understood the situation and said she'd pick up some takeout on her way home, and we could eat at her place when I was done in court. That's the type of relationship we have, and it explains why we're still together and having sex after all these years.

With the phone call to Gracie out of the way, I read the Arrest Report on John Doe. It didn't have much information about the crime and even less information about my new client. The victim was identified in the report as William Johnson, a 17-year-old African American who had lived in a New York City low-income housing project not far from the crime scene.

According to the report, a sector car was dispatched at 8:12 AM to the location in response to a 911 call from a bicyclist who believed he saw a dead body. When the sector car arrived at the scene, the responding officers found Johnson dead with his skull bashed in and my client, identified in the report simply as Suspect No. 1, seated in a cardboard hovel a few yards away holding a bloody hammer. The cops arrested Suspect No. 1, and since he refused to speak and had no identification, he was booked as John Doe.

It wasn't much to go on, and I was hoping John Doe would give me some details which might put the situation in a better light. Holding a bloody hammer in your hand while sitting near a body with a bashed-in head does make you the prime suspect in the case. It also doesn't leave a lot of room for reasonable doubt. Not if you're sane and thinking rationally. But that remained to be seen.

CHAPTER 4

When I got to the Criminal Court Building on Centre Street, I checked in with the bridge clerk in arraignment who confirmed my client was in the holding cells downstairs. As far as he knew, John Doe was still refusing to talk. That wasn't necessarily a bad thing. I always tell clients not to say anything to anybody but me, so John Doe's refusal to talk was okay, provided he'd speak with me.

It's never easy picking your client out from the many fascinating denizens occupying the holding cells but when your client is named John Doe and refuses to speak it's just about impossible. I was walking around calling out "John Doe," and the only responses I was getting were a lot of laughs and some smart-ass comments, but no takers. Finally, one of the Corrections Officers, who I knew was a friend of Bill's, which is code for a fellow member of AA, took pity on me and offered to bring John Doe to one of the attorney meeting rooms.

When John Doe was brought into the meeting room, he was wearing a Department of Corrections jumpsuit, not his own clothes, so I asked the officer why that was. He said the NYPD Crime Scene Unit had taken his clothes as part of their investigation. He added it was a good thing, too, because the clothes were filthy and smelled like shit. Then he added, John Doe had been offered a chance to shower, but he refused, so even in the clean jumpsuit he still stank. I thanked him for the warning and braced myself for what was to come.

Having lived in Manhattan all my life I've seen more than my share of homeless people. At one time the Bowery, in lower Manhattan, had been the place where most of the city's homeless drunks hung out. But that was before the area was gentrified. Back then there were cheap "hotels" called flophouses, where for a buck or two, a drunk could flop on a bare mattress in a small room he shared with a bunch of cockroaches and maybe a couple of rats.

Nowadays the homeless are no longer limited to the drunks and drug addicts. There are still plenty of them, but they've been joined by the mentally ill and people forced from their homes by economic hardship.

Whatever group John Doe fell into I knew what to expect, and believe me, John Doe didn't disappoint. His hair was long and mattered and apparently hadn't been cut or washed since God knows when. He had a long and tangled beard that began high on his cheeks and covered most of his face. Except for the ends of his fingers, the rest of his exposed skin was caked with dirt.

I suspected his fingertips and fingernails were cleaned when he was fingerprinted during the booking process. Even though the NYPD no longer used ink for fingerprinting if the dirt on John Doe's fingers was too thick the technician might not have been able to get a clear scan without washing it off.

John Doe looked to be maybe six feet tall and weighed about 180 pounds. For someone living in the streets, he seemed remarkably fit. His hands were big and looked like they were strong. Between all the hair and the dirt, there was no way I could tell how old he was. I mean he could have been anywhere from forty to seventy years old.

What mostly caught my attention were his eyes. They were dark and penetrating. They weren't the eyes of a stone-cold killer. I've seen lots of those eyes, and they're always the same, blank and cold. John Doe's eyes were far from blank and cold. They were dark and intense, but I couldn't tell if was from anger, fear or something else.

The Corrections Officer sat John Doe across the table from me and shackled his handcuffs to a big iron ring anchored to the table. Truthfully I was glad he was restrained because he was scary looking.

I tried to get him to talk, but he wouldn't say anything. I told him I was his lawyer, and I was there to help him but still he wouldn't talk. He just kept staring at me with those very intense dark eyes.

A MURDER UNDER THE BRIDGE

After about fifteen minutes of my talking and not getting a response, it was time for me to go upstairs.

CHAPTER 5

Inside the courtroom, I caught up with Shayna Washington, the ADA handling John Doe's arraignment. I hadn't dealt with her before, but I'd seen her around the courthouse a couple of times. From what I could tell, she knew what she was doing which isn't always so with the ADAs handling arraignments, especially at night. The Deputy District Attorney who hands out work assignments usually sends the newest lawyers to the Arraignment Part to cut their teeth. Arraignments are simple, by-the-book procedures so the newbies can't get into any real trouble or do much harm. The problem is some of these newly minted lawyers turn out to be arrogant assholes who give defense attorneys a hard time for no reason. Fortunately, Shayna Washington wasn't one of those asshole attorneys.

Even though the arraignment calendar was relatively light, the courtroom was crowded. Word had gotten around the courthouse some crazy prisoner was refusing to talk, and everyone was waiting for him to appear to see what was going to happen. Some of the courtroom regulars were making nasty jokes about John Doe, and I think ADA Washington was feeling a little sorry for him, and maybe for me as well. I say that because she gave me some information she wasn't required to share. At least not at that point and not without a formal demand.

She told me they had finished running my client's fingerprints through the New York State and FBI criminal databases and hadn't found a match. They were now running them through the FBI's military and civil databases, and that was taking longer, but so far there was no match. It seemed John Doe didn't have a criminal record, and that was a good thing, but the next bit of news wasn't so good. According to the initial crime scene Forensic Reports, John Doe's fingerprints were on the hammer presumed to be the murder weapon. There was nothing good in that news but then again I wasn't expecting good news.

I admit the situation with John Doe was new to me, but it wasn't unique. Under the Criminal Procedure Law, a criminal defendant like John Doe who is incapable of understanding the proceedings or helping in his defense can be committed to a mental hospital for up to 30 days for mental observation. I told ADA Washington since John Doe wasn't saying anything, I intended to ask the judge to commit him. Washington thought that was a good idea, and agreed to support my application.

When John Doe's case was called, the first thing the judge wanted to know was why he was listed as John Doe. I explained the circumstances and asked John Doe be committed for a mental evaluation. When the judge looked to ADA Washington, she offered no objection. The judge asked John Doe some questions, none of which John Doe answered and then the judge ordered John Doe committed to the Kirby Forensic Psychiatric Center, a maximum security facility on Ward's Island in the East River.

I wouldn't see John Doe again for a day or two, but in the meantime, I needed to learn more about him and about the crime.

As I was headed over to Gracie's place for our late dinner, I called Joe Benjamin at his home and told him about the arraignment. He was pleased the judge had ordered a mental evaluation and told me to keep him posted. I said I'd call him the next day to discuss hiring an investigator and probably a psychiatrist. Then, even though it was none of my business, I asked him why he was taking a special interest in this case. All he would say was he had a hunch about John Doe, but he wouldn't tell me what his hunch was.

CHAPTER 6

The morning after John Doe's court appearance I asked Connie, my secretary, to call the Kirby Forensic Psychiatric Center to find out who was handling his case and when I could visit John Doe. While Connie was doing that, I called Joe Benjamin who gave me formal approval to hire a private investigator. The 18B Panel has a list of PIs I could choose from, but my man is Tommy Shoo. Tommy is old man Shoo's grandson, and we shared the backroom at Shoo's Restaurant when my office was there.

Back in those days, Tommy sold knock-off Rolex watches, and there were times he required my legal talents. In exchange for my services, he did some investigations for me. He was good at it, and eventually, I convinced him to get his private investigator's license. Once he did, I got him on the 18B Panel's approved list, and now I use him on many of my cases.

Tommy still operates out of the back of his grandfather's restaurant which is about half a block away from my office. So when I called him that morning and said I had a job for him, he was in my office fifteen minutes later. I explained to Tommy I needed a full-scale investigation into the case, including a complete survey of the crime scene, a dossier on the victim and most importantly anything he could find out about our client, John Doe.

The Arrest Report described the crime scene as an abandoned construction storage area along the East River, under the FDR Drive and the Manhattan Bridge. I didn't know anything else about the crime scene, but I did know the neighborhood was called Two Bridges because it's between the Manhattan Bridge and the Brooklyn Bridge. Obviously, it didn't take a great deal of imagination to come up with that name, did it?

Two Bridges has always been home to immigrants, and it still is with a large population of Latin Americans and Chinese. The housing is a mixture of low-rise tenements and high-rise housing developments with a New York City low-income public housing project thrown in for good measure. It's not a bad neighborhood, but there are some areas you'd do well to avoid if you're alone, especially at night. The housing project is one of those areas.

I asked Tommy to canvas the area around the crime scene to see if he could find somebody who saw something. It was a long shot but what the hell, I had nothing else to go on. Also, I wanted him to hunt around and see if he could come up with any clues as to John

Doe's identity. If John Doe wouldn't talk to me and if the doctors at Kirby couldn't get him to talk, then John Doe's future was looking grim.

I had to handle an arraignment in another case, but after that, I was going to the 7th Precinct Station House on Pitt Street in Two Bridges to talk with a Detective I knew there. The 7th Precinct is the second smallest precinct in the city covering an area of just over half a square mile. You may not believe it, but the precinct's address is 19½ Pitt Street. Like it's not even big enough to have a full address number. Even though it's small in area, it can get busy at times, but not usually with murders. For that reason, I was sure this case was getting plenty of attention, and fortunately I had a contact in the 7th Precinct.

My contact was Detective Simone, a twenty-year veteran and the Senior Detective on the 7th Precinct Squad. If anybody knew anything about the John Doe case, it would be Simone.

But before I could get to Simone, I had to deal with Mr. Cho Wen.

CHAPTER 7

After I had finished briefing Tommy on the John Doe case, I grabbed my file and headed to the Worth Street Coffee Shop and Deli to meet Mr. Wen who was due to be arraigned that morning in Criminal Court. The Worth Street Coffee Shop is just around the corner from the Criminal Court Building, so it's a convenient place to meet with clients before going to court.

Over the years I've done favors for the owner, and in return he lets me use a booth in the back whenever I want. In my drinking days, when my office consisted of a desk in the back room of Shoo's Chinese Restaurant, I used the place all the time, but now it's just a convenient spot to hook up with clients before going to court.

I was early, so I was drinking a cup of coffee while I waited for Cho Wen. Mr. Wen wasn't an 18B assigned client; he was a friend of old man Shoo. Mr. Wen was in a bit of a jam over a high-stakes Mahjong game he operated in the basement of his novelty shop on Doyers Street.

A MURDER UNDER THE BRIDGE

In Chinatown, there are at least a couple dozen high-stakes Mahjong games going on at any given time. If you're ever in Chinatown, look at the shop signs. Most of them are in Chinese characters and a lot them have one or sometimes two phone numbers prominently displayed. Those are the numbers you call to find out if there's an open seat at one of the games. Everybody knows about the games, even the police who don't usually bother with them because they have more important things to do.

Unfortunately for Mr. Wen, one of his clients recently took exception to losing and went to the police claiming the game was rigged. The sergeant at the 5th Precinct discouraged the man from filing a complaint, knowing from experience the guy was unlikely to show up in court, and the whole exercise would be a waste of time. The sergeant went so far as to threaten to arrest the man for participating in the game, but the man wouldn't change his mind, so the complaint had been filed. Now Mr. Wen was about to be arraigned on charges of violating NY Penal Law § 225.05, promoting gambling in the second degree, a Class A misdemeanor. Generally, that's not a big deal.

With a Class A misdemeanor, the maximum sentence is one year in jail, meaning Rikers Island, but nobody usually gets jail time on a gambling charge. That is, unless like Mr. Wen you have a prior situation, then things can get sticky.

Mr. Wen had been arrested a year ago for having slot machines in the basement of his store which, unlike the present charge, was a big deal. After some artful negotiating on my part, Mr. Wen was granted a conditional discharge which was a "get out of jail" card with a condition. The condition being Mr. Wen stays out of trouble for two years. But we were back in court one year later, so his arraignment this time wasn't going to be a walk in the park. Frankly, I wasn't very optimistic about where this case was heading.

Mr. Wen arrived at the coffee shop right on time and over another cup of coffee I explained to him what he was facing. My strategy was simple. I'd try to get a plea deal that involved a fine, but no jail time or at worst ninety days. I explained even with a sentence of ninety days, he'd probably do no more than sixty days at most because of time off for good behavior. If Rikers got overcrowded, he might even be released earlier. If I couldn't get a good deal, we'd plead not guilty and hope the complainant wouldn't cooperate, in which case the DA would have to drop the case.

Mr. Wen listened intently, nodding approvingly as I explained things to him. That was until I mentioned going to jail, then Mr. Wen informed me if there were any jail time involved he would be heading back to China. I told Mr. Wen I hadn't heard that and I didn't want to hear it. He was free to do whatever he wanted so long as he didn't tell me about it. Attorney-client privilege only goes so far. It doesn't cover a conversation in which a client advises his attorney he intends to commit a crime and fleeing the jurisdiction is a crime.

You might think a guy who for nearly fifteen years practiced law drunk most of the time wouldn't be too concerned about ethics, but then you'd be wrong. It's true when I was drinking, I didn't give a shit about a lot of things, but as strange as it may sound I always tried to behave ethically, not always respectfully, but ethically. I might not show up in court on time, or I might call a judge a smuck now and then, but I wouldn't lie or allow a client to lie under oath. In a sense, I held my profession in a lot higher regard than I held myself. Don't ask me to explain why or how, because I can't explain it, so let's get back to Mr. Wen.

Having cleared up the ethical point with Mr. Wen, we headed over to the courthouse where I met ADA James Monroe, one of the newly minted Assistant District Attorneys. As I mentioned, some of the newly appointed ADAs are assholes and Mr. Monroe fell neatly into that category.

What makes them assholes is their superior attitudes and their tendency to overreact in most situations. Mr. Monroe was doing just that, treating Mr. Wen's misdemeanor like it was the crime of the century, and from what I could tell he wasn't even aware of the conditional discharge which was the only real issue in the case.

I got nowhere trying to reason with him, so we had to wait for the case to be called. Judge McKenna who was sitting on the bench that day is a no-nonsense jurist who prides himself on clearing up the court docket. When the charge against Mr. Wen was read, Judge McKenna wanted to know why the case hadn't been disposed of with a plea. I just looked over at Mr. Monroe who started saying something about the demands of justice. But Judge McKenna apparently wasn't concerned with the demands of justice and cut Mr. Monroe short, ordering him and me to approach the bench.

When we got there, the judge said, "Junior," that's what the judge called him, "should cut a deal and make the case go away." Then he sent us away, and he called the next case.

It was all rather embarrassing for poor Mr. Monroe, but it was good for Mr. Wen. Mr. Monroe couldn't go back before Judge McKenna without a plea deal and that, of course, gave me an upper hand. And believe me, I know what to do when I have the upper hand.

In short order, Mr. Wen went from looking at possible jail time to walking out of the courthouse a free man. He was twenty-five hundred dollars poorer, but it was a small price to pay for his freedom. The fine was five hundred dollars; the other two thousand dollars was my fee. Justice is a good thing, but it doesn't come cheap.

It was mid-morning when we left the courthouse, and I said good-bye to Mr. Wen. I took a chance and called the 7th Precinct Detective Squad hoping to catch Simone at his desk, and I got lucky. Simone was there and had time to see me if I got there right away. I said I'd be there in fifteen minutes.

CHAPTER 8

It was a short taxi ride from the Criminal Court Building to the 7th Precinct on Pitt Street and even with traffic, I was there with time to spare.

My relationship with Richie Simone goes back to when I was a rising star in the DA's Office, and he was an undercover cop looking to make Detective. That was back in the 1980s when New York City was going through some hard times. The city was barely recovering from its economic problems of the 1970s and its near bankruptcy in 1975, when crack cocaine, a new cheap drug, hit the streets. Before long crack cocaine use became an epidemic. It was, what some would call, a perfect storm. Crime rates reached new highs at the time budget cuts were forcing the NYPD to reduce its ranks. The number of cops went down, and the crime rate soared. Drug use and drug-related crimes were out of control.

To meet the crisis, a lot of patrol cops were moved to undercover and were in the streets doing buys and busts. Richie was one those undercover cops, who like all the other undercover cops, was looking to make Detective. But his buy and bust drug arrests weren't getting him noticed by the brass.

I was prosecuting most of Richie's cases at the time, and I took a liking to the guy. He was always on time, did a good job and never bitched if he had to come to court on his day off. So when I got a tip about a big drug sale going down in Richie's precinct, instead of giving it to the Precinct Captain which was what I normally did, I gave it directly to Richie. Richie got credit for the bust and shortly after that he was promoted to Detective.

I didn't expect Richie to give me any information I wouldn't eventually get from the DA's Office once John Doe was arraigned. I was only trying to shorten the process hoping if I could get a little more information about what had happened, it might help me get through to John Doe.

Richie had no problem talking to me about his role in the investigation since it pretty much followed standard procedure. As the ranking Detective at the crime scene, he had been in charge of the investigation. Following the protocols in the NYPD Patrol Guide, he had made sure the area was secured and enclosed with the appropriate barrier tape. Then since it was a homicide case, he requested assistance from the Crime Scene Unit and the Office of the Chief Medical Examiner.

Once the Detectives from the Crime Scene Unit arrived, he directed their attention to certain areas and items he wanted them to examine and collect. Richie wouldn't elaborate, other than to say they did collect blood samples and the bloody hammer the patrol officers had taken from John Doe's hand. The bloody hammer had already been examined at the police lab, and it was the murder weapon with John Doe's fingerprints on it. That was no surprise as ADA Washington had told me the same thing.

Richie confirmed William Johnson's body was examined at the crime scene by a Medical Investigator before being sent to the OCME, the Office of the Chief Medical Examiner, where it was to be autopsied. The preliminary finding by the Medical Investigator was homicide by blunt force trauma. Johnson had been hit three times with an object the Medical Investigator believed was a hammer.

The estimated time of death was between 6 PM and 8 PM the prior day.

Richie let me look at the crime scene photos. He confirmed it was an old construction storage site. I was more interested in pictures of the victim than the pictures of the site because the site would still be there when Tommy went to investigate, but the body would be gone.

Johnson's body was lying on an old mattress next to a pile of trash. Visible in one of the pictures was the cardboard shelter, where the arresting officers had found John Doe sitting holding the bloody hammer.

There were a number of pictures of Johnson lying face down on the mattress, which was how the cops had found him, and a couple of pictures of him lying on his back, obviously taken after he had been rolled over by the Medical Investigator.

Looking at the pictures, two things struck me. Johnson's pants were open and pulled partially down, and he had long scratch marks on the left cheek of his face. I asked Richie what he made of the pants being down, and he said maybe Johnson was taking a leak when John Doe attacked him. As for the scratch marks, Richie offered no opinion.

That was about all Richie would tell me about the crime scene, but I did want to know more about the victim. According to Richie the victim, William Johnson, age 19, was a member of the TB Gangsters, and his street name was Lover Boy. He had no record of recent arrests, but he did have a long juvenile record including an adjudication when he was a juvenile delinquent.

Juvenile cases are handled in the Family Court where to be politically correct, they use the term adjudication instead of conviction. As if what you called it makes a difference. In Johnson's case, it didn't matter what you called it, he was sent to Rikers Island, the largest of New York City's jails.

The record was sealed and if Richie knew anything about the underlying charge he wasn't saying. But I knew the only time a juvenile is sent to Rikers is if the crime is a felony and a serious one. One thing was for sure, Johnson wasn't a good law abiding citizen. Of course, it didn't mean he deserved to have his head bashed in, but it did add a bunch of possibilities as to why it happened.

The police had canvassed the area looking for possible witnesses, but they had come up empty. That was all Richie had for me, or I should say it was all he was going to share with me. To him, it was an open-and-shut case. He'd work with the DA's Office on prosecuting the case, but the investigation was complete as far as he was concerned.

John Doe's fingerprints had been run through all three of the FBI databases, and no match was found. Apparently, John Doe didn't have a criminal record, he hadn't been in the armed services, and he hadn't been fingerprinted during a private security check. If the doctors at the mental hospital couldn't get through to him, we might never find out who John Doe is.

I thanked Richie and headed back to my office. It was a beautiful day, so I decided to walk back instead of taking a taxi. Along the way, I got hungry and decided to grab a couple of Sabrett hot dogs from one of the street carts. You don't have to go very far in Manhattan to find a street food vendor.

I have a weakness for any kind of street food, but my favorite cart food is Sabrett hot dogs with sauerkraut and deli mustard. I'd probably eat them three or four times a week except Gracie is on a crusade to get me to eat healthier food and Sabrett hot dogs are not on the healthy food list. But occasionally, I need a Sabrett hot dog, or two, and Gracie is okay with that. Actually, that may not be true because most of the time I don't mention it to her. What she doesn't know can't hurt me.

I walked over to Seward Park, bought two Sabrett hot dogs, a Dr. Brown's Cream Soda, and found a bench in the sun. It was about as close to heaven as I figure I'm going to get.

When I finished eating, I called Connie to see what was up. Connie had spoken with someone at the psychiatric hospital and learned that a Dr. Vijay Najari was treating John Doe. She had called Najari's office and left a message asking when I could speak with him and when I could see John Doe. So far she hadn't heard back.

After talking with Connie I called Doug. He's my AA sponsor, and I talk to him just about every day. I met Doug five years ago at my first AA meeting. If it hadn't been for Doug, I might not be sober today. To be honest, I might not be alive today, and I'm pretty sure I wouldn't still be a lawyer.

I'm an only child, so I don't know what it's like to have a brother, but I think it must be like having Doug as my sponsor. I count on Doug for his advice and, believe me, he's seen me through some tough times. Anyway, I called Doug to say hello and remind him I was speaking at an AA meeting that evening, and his attendance was mandatory. He didn't really need to be there, but I always liked it when he was, and he hasn't disappointed me yet.

It was nice sitting on the bench, and I didn't want to move, but I had things to do, so I dragged my ass off the bench and headed for my office.

CHAPTER 9

I was halfway to the office when it hit me. The scratch marks on Johnson's face and John Doe's clean fingernails might be related. It was possible the Crime Scene Unit had scraped John Doe's fingernails figuring the scrapings would be a DNA match with Johnson. If that was the case, it might be strike three and the game might be over unless John Doe hadn't consented. If he hadn't consented, it might be an illegal search and seizure. If he had consented or given the cops another reason to check for evidence under his fingernails, we had a problem.

The bloody hammer in John Doe's hand was strong circumstantial evidence, but only circumstantial proof he used it to kill Johnson. I could always argue John Doe had picked the hammer up off the ground after somebody else had used it to kill Johnson. It's not a great argument, but it's an argument, something I could use in trying to cut a plea deal. But Johnson's skin found under John Doe's fingernails would be positive proof of physical contact, and I can't argue my way out of that.

If John Doe hadn't consented to have his fingernails scraped, which I doubted he had since he wasn't speaking to anyone, I would definitely have to claim it was an illegal search and seizure. As I thought about it, I remembered an old United States Supreme Court case holding fingernail scrapings could be collected from a defendant without his consent if done during a valid arrest. But that was an old case so if the issue did come up I'd have a lot of research to do. But I was getting way ahead of myself. There were a lot more issues that needed to be addressed before that one if it even was an issue.

I wasn't sure if John Doe qualified for an insanity defense. I needed to talk to Dr. Najari, and I also needed to hire our own psychiatrist to evaluate John Doe. But the most important thing I needed to do was to find out who John Doe was.

I was thinking about that when my cell phone rang, and it was Gracie. She wanted to make sure I was free for dinner at seven o'clock because she was making a reservation at this new sushi restaurant in Soho.

Gracie had gotten me into eating sushi which I admit took a bit of doing. I love to eat, and I love trying different foods, but I don't see why we need to eat raw fish. It's not like we're in a hurry or anything. I'll wait until they cook it. And wrapping it in seaweed doesn't make it more attractive to me. But Gracie likes it, so I tried it and while I can't say it's one of my favorite foods I will eat it for Gracie's sake.

My eating habits are mostly the result of my upbringing. My dear Irish mother, God rest her soul, was many wonderful things, but a good cook wasn't one of them. Her version of Italian spaghetti and meatballs involved ketchup, American cheese and chopped mystery meat.

I shouldn't blame my mother for her bad cooking because she didn't have much to work with. She was raising me alone after my no-good father abandoned us when I was four years old. Even with her working two jobs money was always tight, and so our diet consisted mostly of potatoes and cheap cuts of meat cooked until they were unrecognizable.

So you might be asking yourself, with that upbringing how did I grow up and become a good eater? The answer is simple. I grew up in Hell's Kitchen which was predominately Irish and home to the Irish Mafia, but also home to a lot of Italians and Germans. Some of my best friends growing up were Italian and German and very often I'd be invited to dinner at their homes. That's how I found out what Italian spaghetti and meatballs was supposed to taste like, and how good Vienna schnitzel and bratwurst could be. It was in my friends' homes I found out how good food could taste and why today I eat just about anything, including sushi when I need to.

But I digress. The sushi place Gracie wanted to go to was just a couple of blocks away from where my AA meeting was being held at nine o'clock, so I told Gracie to make the reservation. I'd meet her at her office, and we'd taxi to the restaurant together.

A lot of people who hear my story want to know why I still go to AA meetings. The answer is simple; I go because I'm still an alcoholic. I'm not drinking, but I'm just one drink away from being a drunk again, so I go to meetings, I call Doug and I read the big book. I don't have any intense physical cravings for the booze, but I can slip back into alcoholic thinking, and if I stay there, I'll probably pick up a drink. So I just keep going to meetings and working on my thinking. I'll die an alcoholic but hopefully a sober one. And hopefully not too soon.

But right then my thoughts weren't on drinking; they were on John Doe.

CHAPTER 10

When I got back to the office, Tommy was waiting to see me and Connie had a message from Dr. Vijay Najari. He was available to talk with me after four o'clock, so it gave me time to talk with Tommy.

Tommy had canvassed the crime scene area trying to find out something about John Doe, but unfortunately, he didn't have much luck. He had shown John Doe's booking photograph to people in the neighborhood near the crime scene and while a few recalled seeing him around, none of them knew his name or anything about him.

We've seemed to have gotten to a point where homeless people and the mentally ill no longer register in our consciousness. Maybe it's because we don't want to see them, or maybe subconsciously we think if we don't see them, they aren't really there. I know some of the people living on the street put themselves there because they're drunks or drug addicts and I have no pity for those

41

people. But there are some out there who deserve help, and we shouldn't mix them up with those that don't. At that point, I didn't know what group John Doe fell into, but it didn't matter because my job was to defend him no matter what.

After canvassing the neighborhood Tommy went a nearby homeless shelter, the New York City Rescue Mission on Lafayette Street, and showed the booking photo to people there. Two of the volunteers said he looked familiar, but he wasn't one of the Mission's regulars. It was the same story at the Coalition for the Homeless over on Fulton Street. It seemed no one knew John Doe or anything about him.

Tommy planned on going to the housing project where William Johnson had lived to find out what he could about the victim and see if there might be a connection between him and John Doe. I told Tommy to be careful because it's dangerous being in the housing projects if you're an outsider. Besides, since Johnson had been a member of the TB Gangsters, snooping around asking questions about him could bring trouble. Tommy said he didn't snoop, he investigated, and he was always careful, which I didn't believe because I knew how Tommy operated. On that note, he left the office.

Tommy had taken some photographs of the crime scene and the surrounding area, including the cardboard hovel where John Doe was probably living. He left a copy of the photos on something he called a thumb drive.

I'm a very old-fashioned guy, or maybe I'm just lazy or stubborn, but I have very little interest in anything electronic or digital. As a result, I had no idea what a thumb drive was. In the past, I probably would have gotten frustrated and just thrown the damn thing away. But now I had a better way of dealing with this sort of thing. I called Connie. I told her to do something with the thumb drive so I could see the pictures. She sighed, one those "you're just pathetic" sighs and shoved the thumb drive into a hole in my computer, pressed some keys and that did the trick.

When I thanked her, she gave me one of her "you're so pitiful" head shakes and went back to her desk. Connie has a unique way of communicating with sighs and head shakes I've now come to understand. Not like, mind you, just understand.

You should know by now I always want the last word, so I yelled out to Connie that someday when I learned how to do all the computer things I'd fire her. She just laughed knowing she had job security. Why? Because Gracie liked her and there was no way I was going to fire her while Gracie was around. At least not if I expected to continue having an active sex life.

Tommy's pictures were pretty much the same as the police pictures, and I didn't see anything that looked different except Johnson's body was gone. Tommy had taken more pictures of the area than the cops, and looking at the additional pictures gave me a better understanding of what the place was like.

Clearly, it was an abandoned storage lot for construction material enclosed by an eight-foot-high cyclone fence. Four of the pictures showed holes in the fence close to where the murder occurred. So getting in and out of there wasn't a problem. Other pictures showed some leftover two-by-fours, pieces of lumber and a lot of trash scattered about. There were five or six pictures of the mattress Johnson's body had been on. Then there were pictures of the cardboard hovel that was probably where John Doe lived.

The cardboard was propped up by some of the old two-by-fours and partially covered by an old plastic tarp. Inside there was a dirty mattress and a pile of newspapers. I didn't see any liquor bottles or any drug paraphernalia.

The police Inventory Report didn't list any personal property belonging to John Doe, and Tommy's search of the place didn't turn up any clues as to who John Doe was, or where he came from.

I was totally in the dark and my only hope at that point, was Dr. Najari, the psychiatrist treating John Doe at the psychiatric center, if he could get him to talk.

CHAPTER 11

I was still looking at the crime scene pictures when Connie reminded me it was four o'clock and time to call the Kirby Forensic Psychiatric Center and speak with Dr. Najari.

Kirby is a maximum security hospital run by the New York State Office of Mental Health. It's where the New York City Courts send mentally disturbed prisoners for evaluations and treatment. I've been there a couple of times to visit with clients, and I can tell you it's not a bad place at all, at least as far as mental hospitals go.

From what I could tell talking with Dr. Najari, he seemed to be a decent individual genuinely interested in John Doe's well-being. Unfortunately, he hadn't been able to get John Doe to talk yet. He spent close to half an hour talking with me asking a lot of questions.

Dr. Najari believed John Doe was physically able to speak, but chose not to, a condition he referred to as selective mutism. Except for not talking, John Doe was otherwise mostly cooperative and possibly suffering from a dissociative disorder. There was no physical evidence of current drug or alcohol use, although Dr. Najari wouldn't rule out the possibility John Doe had used drugs or alcohol in the past. Without more information about John Doe, Dr. Najari was unable to make a positive diagnosis although he strongly suspected a psychotic disorder was in play.

I asked the doctor when I could meet with John Doe. He said anytime between 8:00 am and 8:00 pm so long as I had a New York State Attorney Identification Card. He added if I wanted him at the meeting, I'd need to make an appointment, but he was available most days, except weekends.

I figured I should see John Doe as soon as possible, so I arranged to meet with Dr. Najari and John Doe the next morning at ten o'clock. I still had to hire a psychiatrist to do an independent evaluation of John Doe, but before I could do that I needed Joe Benjamin's approval.

When I called Joe, he agreed we needed an independent psychiatrist and recommended David Goldman who, according to Joe, had extensive experience dealing with criminal defendants with competency issues. I wrote down Goldman's telephone number and told Joe I'd give Goldman a call after I saw John Doe and talked with Dr. Najari.

John Doe was being held at Kirby on a simple thirty-day evaluation hold. But if he continued to refuse to talk we'd be looking at a different situation. If the man doesn't talk to me, there is no way I can know his side of the story, and without knowing his side of the story, I can't prepare a defense. So how can the case go forward under those circumstances? The answer is it can't, and while the law recognizes it as fact and has a provision covering the situation, it doesn't work in John Doe's favor.

If we didn't get John Doe to talk, the judge would order two psychiatrists from the Department of Mental Health to determine if John Doe could consult with me with a "reasonable degree of rational understanding of the case." If they found he could, the case would go forward, but if they believe he can't, then John Doe will be kept locked up in a maximum security mental facility until he can assist in his defense. Which meant he could be locked up for the rest of his life.

The first thing the two doctors had to determine was if John Doe was faking his condition. If he was, the case would go forward even if he continued refusing to talk. I'd be left with no real defense, and a conviction would be just about guaranteed. That was one reason I needed a psychiatrist on our side, to give us an independent evaluation in the event the state doctors thought John Doe was faking.

I wanted to make damn sure John Doe wasn't railroaded by a couple of shrinks who'd spend an hour with him and then throw him under the bus. To be truthful, after talking with Dr. Najari, I didn't think he was that type of guy, but I wasn't taking any chances.

I have never believed in psychiatry. I subscribed to the belief psychiatrists did nothing more than describe a human condition, give it a name, call it a disorder and then charge to cure it. That was how I felt about psychiatrists until I met Dr. Najari. I'm still not entirely convinced psychiatry can do everything it claims it can do, but now I'm open to the argument. Not that I ever intend to see a shrink. I get all the mental health treatment I need from Doug and AA.

I know some people say I'm judgmental because I jump to quick conclusions about people and things. But I'll say this in my own defense:

After years spent dealing with criminal defendants, I can look into somebody's eyes and know a lot about them. Not everything, but enough to know if they're guilty or not. That was why I needed to see John Doe and look into his eyes again.

When I looked into John Doe's eyes in the holding pen room, I didn't see the eyes of a stone-cold killer. But I saw something in those eyes that told me this man had a story to tell, and I wanted to hear it.

CHAPTER 12

I picked up Gracie at her office at One Hogan Place, and we took a taxi to the sushi restaurant. Gracie is one of the smartest lawyers I know, so when I have a difficult case I like to get her take on it. You probably think that could be a problem because Gracie works for the District Attorney's Office and you'd be right if she were involved in handling the case. But Gracie is the Chief Deputy in charge of the Special Victims Unit. That unit deals with sex crimes and crimes against children and I haven't defended one of those cases in years. It's not that I haven't been offered that kind of case by Joe Benjamin; it's just I won't take them.

I already told you I used to hate all my clients, and I still hate some of them. I can't stop hating some of the violent scumbags I represent, but I do the best I can for them. But with a rapist or a child molester, I'm not sure I'd want to do the best I could, and that's why I turn those types of cases down. I hope the guilty ones get hung, but

I'm not the one who's supposed to do the hanging. By now Joe Benjamin knows how I feel about those kind of cases, so he doesn't bother sending any of them my way.

But back to Gracie and the sushi. I told Gracie about John Doe and his refusal to talk. If I remembered correctly, Gracie had some experience with that situation and I was right. A couple of years ago, when Gracie was still with the Major Crimes Unit she had handled two similar cases where the defendants refused to talk. In both of her cases, the defendants had been playing possum hoping to pull fast ones, but it hadn't worked. I didn't know why John Doe wasn't talking, but I didn't believe it was a scam. Either way, it didn't seem to matter. If he continued not talking for whatever reason, he faced being locked up for a long time.

I couldn't seem to wrap my head around the problem, so I asked Gracie what she thought. It seemed to me if John Doe was faking and the judge forced us to trial without John Doe speaking, he was going to be convicted and sentenced to twenty-five years to life. On the other hand, if John Doe were found incompetent to go to trial because he legitimately wasn't speaking, then he'd be locked up in a mental institution for God knows how long. So with that analysis where was I going?

As usual, Gracie put me straight. If John Doe was mentally ill, then having him committed to a mental institution was a lot better for him than living in prison or on the streets. I agreed with that. Besides, either way, he wouldn't hurt anybody else. It made sense, but I still wasn't comfortable with the thought I might not be able to help this guy.

All the talk about insane defendants and odd situations brought to mind Vincent "the Chin" Gigante. The Chin was a Mafia gangster who for thirty years wandered the streets of Greenwich Village in his bathrobe and slippers mumbling to himself hoping to convince law enforcement authorities he was crazy. The newspapers labeled him the "Oddfather." When push came to shove during the Giuliani era, the ruse didn't work. Eventually, despite his psychiatrist's claim he was legally insane, Gigante was found guilty on numerous charges and sent off to prison, without his bathrobe and slippers.

After our dinner of raw fish, I helped Gracie find a taxi, kissed her goodnight, and promised to call her after my AA meeting. Then I wandered on down to East Houston Street where I met up with Doug. Doug is also one of the smartest people I know and one of the most patient. Of course, he had to be patient to deal with me for five years.

That night, I was speaking at an open meeting where I'd be getting up in front of a room full of strangers and telling them all about my life as a drunk. How I ruined a promising career, lost all my friends, wound up living in a tenement and nearly lost my license to practice law, all due to booze.

Unless you're a recovering alcoholic yourself, you probably think doing that is crazy. I'll tell you I figured it was crazy the first time I attended an AA meeting. I also vowed I'd never do it. But in the five years since then, I've done it many, many times. I do it for two reasons. One, I hope it will help somebody with a drinking problem come into the program and, two, to remind myself of what my life was like when I drank. It's important I remember because I'm just one drink away from going back into that life. But enough about that.

After the open meeting, Doug and I attended the closed step meeting. I won't bore you with the details. I'll only say when you're an alcoholic, and you're serious about staying sober, that's what you do. You go to meetings, and you don't drink. It's simple, not necessarily easy, but simple.

CHAPTER 13

Getting to Kirby Forensic Psychiatric Center from my apartment downtown is challenging. As I mentioned, the hospital is on Ward's Island and being on an island access is limited. Probably the easiest way to get there is by car, but I don't own one.

I've lived in Manhattan all my life and never had a need for a car. In fact, I don't even have a driver's license. Never needed one of those either because I rarely leave Manhattan. I used to take an occasional trip out to Queens, which is technically part of New York City, to watch the Mets play baseball. But with the price of tickets now, who can afford to go to a baseball game? The same goes for the Yankees. I used to jump on the subway and hop up to the Bronx, another borough of New York City, to see the Yankees play ball. But thanks to the ticket prices those days are over.

Anyway, if you're not driving or going by taxi, you can take a subway and then a bus to get to the hospital, and that's what I did. I should mention for all of you New York City dwellers, there is the pedestrian bridge from Manhattan at about 103rd Street which crosses over the East River to Ward's Island. But then it's a hike to the hospital, so that's why I took the subway and bus.

Being a great believer in punctuality, at least since I stopped drinking, I was seated in a reception area waiting for Dr. Najari at nine-forty-five. When I drank, being on time wasn't important to me, and I was often what I called fashionably late. Sometimes that meant twenty minutes or so late. Sometimes it meant a day or two, or even maybe a week late.

My "fashionable lateness" didn't play well with the judges who are real sticklers when it comes to showing up on schedule. I once had a judge ask me if I thought my time was more valuable than his time. I'm sure you realize that's not a good question to ask somebody who's been drinking heavily. Not surprisingly, the judge didn't care for my answer, and he slapped me with a $500 contempt citation.

Dr. Najari was apparently a punctual man as well, because at ten o'clock on the button he arrived and introduced himself. He suggested we talk before we sat down with John Doe and he led me down a long corridor to his office.

He was of average height and weight, had dark curly hair and what I would say were average facial features. But there was something in his eyes and his smile that was commanding and, at the same time, comforting. If appearances were any indication of competence, then Dr. Najari was a damn good psychiatrist.

His office was large, and the walls were covered with diplomas and plaques. I'm one of those nosey people who likes to know whom I'm dealing with, so I had a good look at his diplomas. He had an undergraduate degree from NYU and a medical degree from Yale University. He had done his psychiatric residency at the Cleveland Clinic, and he was a Fellow of the American Psychiatric Association. It was all top notch which meant his opinion would carry a lot of weight with any judge hearing John Doe's case.

Once we were comfortably seated, Dr. Najari said the hospital staff had gotten John Doe cleaned up and he was eating regularly. All of which was a good sign. Other than not talking, John Doe had been cooperative and exhibited no violent behavior. They had him on a course of very mild sedatives and anti-psychotic drugs, and they were doing a mental evaluation.

Still, no one could get him to talk, and Dr. Najari wasn't optimistic they would. He believed John Doe suffered from some emotional trauma and not knowing what it was made it difficult to deal with. He wanted to know if I had any luck in finding out anything more about John Doe and I told him I hadn't, but I was still trying.

Dr. Najari suggested we visit with John Doe, then come back to his office and talk some more. I agreed, and the doctor arranged to have John Doe brought to a conference room.

When we walked into the conference room, John Doe was sitting there, but I hardly recognized him. He was clean shaven, his hair had been cut, and he was neatly dressed in a white short-sleeved shirt and a pair of white pants. Cleaned and dressed, he looked from a distance to be completely normal. When I got closer and looked at his face, the fire in his eyes I had seen the last time was still there, but not quite as intense.

Dr. Najari estimated he was in his early to mid-sixties, but he could have been younger. I was pretty sure living on the street would have aged him.

We sat at a table across from John Doe, and I introduced myself and told him I was his lawyer. He said nothing and there was no change in his facial expressions. I asked him some questions but got no response. Dr. Najari tried to talk with him, but John Doe said nothing.

Then I noticed he had a tattoo on his upper right arm, most of which was covered by his shirt sleeve. I asked John Doe if I could take a closer look at his tattoo. He made no reply, and he made no effort to move when I stood and walked around the table and stood next to him. Looking at Dr. Najari for any sign I should stop, I told John Doe I was going to lift his shirt sleeve so I could look at his tattoo. There was no response from John Doe, and Dr. Najari nodded his approval, so I lifted the shirt sleeve.

Tattooed on John Doe's right upper arm was the U.S. Marine Corps insignia, the eagle, globe, and anchor. I then told John Doe I wanted to look at his other arm, and I lifted his left sleeve. On his upper left arm were the words *Semper fi* over the letters "U S M C."

I sat back down in my chair and asked John Doe if he had been a Marine. He didn't answer, but I thought I saw something change in his facial expression. I may have been imagining it, but I didn't think so.

For another twenty minutes, Dr. Najari and I tried talking with John Doe, but he refused to respond. Then Dr. Najari called an attendant who took John Doe back to his room and the doctor and I returned to the doctor's office.

Dr. Najari asked if I thought John Doe had been in the Marine Corps. I said it seemed likely because of the tattoos, but a fingerprint check through the FBI database which includes military personnel hadn't turned up a match. Still, why would a guy have Marine Corps tattoos if he hadn't been in the Corps? It didn't make sense to me, and it didn't make sense to Dr. Najari.

I told Dr. Najari I'd follow up on the possible Marine Corps connection, but in the meantime, I was going to send over an independent psychiatrist to examine John Doe. Dr. Najari thought that was a good idea and when I mentioned it was probably going to be David Goldman, he said it was a good choice. It seemed he knew Goldman and thought he was an excellent doctor.

I left the hospital and decided it was time to stop in at the 7th Precinct and chat with Richie Simone again.

CHAPTER 14

I lucked out once again. Richie Simone was sitting at his desk in the Detective Squad Room when I got there. I told him about my visit with John Doe and about the Marine Corps tattoos. If John Doe had served in the Marine Corps, the FBI fingerprint search should have turned up a match. Simone assured me there had been no match found, but agreed it was strange a guy would have Marine Corps tattoos if he hadn't been in the Corps.

Simone had nothing new to report on the case, at least nothing he was going to share with me. I hadn't expected to hear anything new because as far as Richie and the NYPD were concerned their job was done. They had arrested the suspect at the scene of the crime holding the murder weapon in his hand. What more did they need? The DA was happy, Richie's boss was happy, and Richie was happy. Case closed. I was the unhappy one, but that didn't matter to Richie and the NYPD.

As far as Simone was concerned, the suspect having Marine tattoos, but no record of serving in the Corps, was curious, but it had no bearing on the case. As for the fingerprint check, Richie suggested I talk to the FBI since it was their database. It was clear I wasn't going to get any help from the NYPD in sorting out this mess, but calling the FBI was a good idea.

When I got back to my office, I gave my old buddy Special Agent Michael Chang a call. I met Michael five years ago on a case, and we've kept in touch ever since. Michael had moved up in the command chain since our earlier business together, but his office was still in Federal Plaza in lower Manhattan. Since this wasn't official business, I didn't want to put Michael in an uncomfortable position by meeting in his office, so we agreed to meet at the Worth Street Coffee Shop at four o'clock.

After talking with Michael Chang, I gave Dr. David Goldman a call. For the third time that day I got lucky; he was at his desk and free to talk with me. How often do you call a doctor's office or a Detective, and find them at their desks and willing to talk to you? In my experience, hardly ever. It could be just me and my lovely personality, but I don't think so.

Anyway, Dr. Goldman spoke with me, and after he heard the facts he was very interested in the case. He wanted to see John Doe as soon as possible, and he suggested I follow up on the possible Marine Corps connection because it might be critical. When I asked him why, Dr. Goldman explained if John Doe was in his mid to late-sixties, and served in the Marines, it was very possible he was in combat in the Vietnam War and could be suffering from post-traumatic stress disorder.

To move things along, I faxed Dr. Goldman a retainer letter so he could examine John Doe as soon as possible. I still needed to find out if John Doe had a connection to the Marine Corps and for that, I was counting on Michael Chang being able to help.

I called Joe Benjamin to fill him in on what was happening and when I told him about the Marine Corps tattoos he gave out a little sigh. That's when I figured out why Joe was so interested in this case. Joe had suspected all along that John Doe had been in the military and had served in the Vietnam War and now it was looking like he had. I asked Joe if he had fought in the Vietnam War and he said he had. It all made sense, but it would still take some time for me to appreciate the bond that exists between war veterans.

CHAPTER 15

It was just after four o'clock and Michael Chang and I were enjoying a cup of coffee and chatting in the back booth at the Worth Street Coffee Shop. We hadn't seen each other in a couple of months, so we were just sort of catching up for a while. Then I brought up John Doe and the fingerprint matter.

Michael confirmed the FBI fingerprint database was supposed to contain fingerprints of all military personnel, but he understood some records had slipped through the cracks. As Michael explained it, in 1989 the FBI began a program to upgrade its fingerprint database and by 1999 had launched the IAFIS or the Integrated Automated Fingerprint Identification System. As a part of the new system, the FBI included fingerprint databases for military personnel and individuals fingerprinted during routine security checks. The task of putting all military fingerprints into the system was enormous, and some may have been missed or misidentified.

I asked Michael to run John Doe's prints again and maybe, this time, we'd get a hit. But he explained since the system was automated the results would be the same no matter how many times the prints were run. But Michael, being a good friend and a good guy, offered to have John Doe's fingerprints run through the Marine Corps database. If there were a hit, Michael would do what he could to get the guy's military records.

As much as I wanted the information, I didn't want Michael getting into trouble on my account, so I said if it was a problem he should just forget about it. Michael assured me it wasn't going to be a problem, then he added a condition. If he delivered the information I needed, I'd have to buy him dinner at Ruth's Chris, an excellent but expensive steak house.

Five years ago, I had to buy Michael dinner at Ruth's Chris to make up for my client nearly costing him his job. I remembered two things about that meal, how much Michael ate and the amount of the bill. I went for my lungs that night, and I'm sure the prices have gone up since then. But if Michael got me the information on John Doe it would be worth it.

After leaving the coffee shop, I headed back to my office. Gracie had a staff meeting and wouldn't get home until after ten o'clock, so I decided to get some work done, grab a quick bite to eat, then go to her place after that.

As I walked up Mott Street, I passed the Chinatown Fair, an arcade that's been there on Mott Street for more than fifty years. It's funny, but when I look at the place, it doesn't seem to have changed in all the time I've been on Mott Street. But it has changed a lot. It used to be famous for its tic-tac-toe playing chickens, but the last of the chickens, a bird named Willie died during a hot spell in July 1993. The New York Times actually printed an obituary for Willie; that's how famous the chicken was. Now the place is just a plain arcade. Arcades are okay, but tic-tac-toe playing chickens are something else.

I don't know how he did it, but Willie always won. Of course, Willie went first which gave him an advantage, but what the hell? He was still a chicken. I used to stop by occasionally just to watch people play and listen to the excuses they came up with when they lost. I never tried playing Willie because there was no way I was going let a chicken beat me in a game of logic, whether the chicken went first or not.

As I said, Willie is gone, and now the place is filled with videogames.

CHAPTER 16

When I got to the office the next morning, Tommy Shoo was waiting for me. He had spent the last two days at the housing project where the victim, William Johnson, had lived. It turned out Johnson was a real piece of work. He and his gangbanger buddies operated a drug business catering to suburban kids from Long Island, Westchester County, and New Jersey.

They sold crack cocaine in a fire lane alley that ran through the middle of the housing project. The housing project was surrounded by a decent neighborhood, and one end of the alley was just off the main thoroughfare, so the location appeared to be a lot safer than it really was.

Johnson and his buddies used kids as young as eight years old to collect the money and deliver the drugs. That way whenever the cops raided the location the only ones who got grabbed up were the juveniles who'd get a slap on the wrist, and that would be it. After a while the cops got tired of getting nowhere and gave up raiding the location.

So with the buyers never having to leave their cars and little kids collecting the money and delivering the drugs, the suburban kids thought they were perfectly safe. Of course, none of them bothered to notice the nearby gangbangers with guns in their waistbands.

From what Tommy could tell, Johnson's death had little impact, and it was business as usual. But Johnson had been one of the gang's leaders, so the TB Gangsters had sworn to revenge his death. There were rumors that murder contracts were going to be put out on two individuals who were supposedly responsible for Lover Boy's death. But Tommy was unable to find out any more about it.

Other than the gangbangers, the neighborhood people Tommy spoke with were glad to have Johnson gone. Nobody outside of the TB Gangsters was mourning his death.

William Johnson was, by nearly all accounts, a vicious low-life prone to violent outbursts. He earned his street name of Lover Boy because he thought he was God's gift to women and was known to rape any girls who dared turn down his romantic advances.

It was rumored the mother of one of his victims had chased Lover Boy through the project with a butcher knife threatening to cut off his private parts. That woman was later found murdered, her throat cut so deeply her head was almost severed. Johnson was a suspect in the case, but it was never solved.

That got me thinking about the police crime scene photos of Johnson with his pants undone and pulled partially down and the fresh scratches on his face. I mentioned it to Tommy and suggested he check out who Lover Boy had been seeing or had been seen with just before his death. It wasn't much, but it was something, and at that point I had nothing.

I was anxious to find out if forensics had found any of Lover Boy's skin under John Doe's fingernails. If they hadn't, I might have a whole new area of defense to explore. But first things first. I still needed to find out more about John Doe and get him to talk to me.

I wanted Tommy to continue canvassing the area, but he was running out of places to go. I suggested he show John Doe's picture at more of the homeless shelters and other nearby areas where the homeless hung out.

After Tommy left, I got a call from Peter, my pigeon. A pigeon is AA slang for a sponsoree. Why are they called pigeons? I don't actually know, but the general consensus is it has something to do with pigeons being used during World War I to carry messages. I know, it doesn't make a lot of sense, so you're probably sorry you asked.

Anyway, I'm sponsoring Peter who I met at one of the lawyers' group AA meetings. Peter works at a prominent Wall Street law firm. He's an associate trying to make partner, so he works sixty hours a week and does what he can to make the senior partners like him. Peter calls it a career advancement strategy; I call it ass-kissing.

Whatever you call it, it can be very nerve-racking, and like a lot of other lawyers, Peter relieved the tension with vodka and pot. Unfortunately, somewhere along the way, Peter advanced from social drinking and recreational drug use to pretty much full blown addiction.

When his problem started to become noticeable at work, Peter was smart enough to seek help and showed up one day at the lawyers' group meeting. That was nearly six months ago, and I've been his sponsor for the last four months.

On the phone, Peter told me he's upset with one of his bosses, and he wants to get high. It's not the first time Peter has said this and probably won't be the last, but I'm his sponsor, so I must listen to his bitching.

Understand I'm not like my own sponsor, Doug, and my approach to sponsorship is a bit different than his. To be truthful, it's probably a polar opposite from Doug's approach, but it seems to work on Peter.

I told Peter getting high wasn't going to solve anything. It certainly wasn't going to change the way his boss is treating him. If he really wanted to do something that would change things he should get stinking drunk and confront the son of a bitch. That would certainly bring about changes. I know because I did it and look how well it worked out for me.

Peter laughed when I told him that and then we talked for another half hour. Peter knows getting high isn't going to help anything. He just needed to be reminded, that's all. I offered to go to a meeting with him, but he said he was okay and promised to call me later.

Peter is a lot like I used to be, and that's probably why I understand him so well. He started out believing if he worked hard and were successful, he'd find happiness. That's what everyone says, right? I bought into it, but happiness eluded me just as it has eluded Peter. It seemed like happiness was always just one step away. One more promotion, one more big winning case, a little more money, a new girlfriend. But I never got there, and I couldn't figure out why so I drank. If I couldn't be happy, at least I'd get rid of the pain that came from being unhappy. Peter had been on the same trail.

It took a while for me to learn happiness wasn't a destination you arrive at. Happiness was the trip itself. That I learned as I got sober, and not surprisingly, that's when I got happy. I also realized I didn't need to be a hotshot lawyer to be happy.

I'm happy with my life now just as it is. I have a decent practice, a good woman, good friends, and peace of mind. I don't have a great deal of money, but that doesn't matter. Money can't make you happy. It can make you happier if you're already happy, but it can't make you happy to begin with. You can make jokes about money and happiness, but if you want the real hard truth, just ask any rich alcoholic about it.

Peter, being young, still has a chance to be both happy and rich and there's nothing wrong with that, so long as he gets the happy part first. That's where AA and I come in because there's a lot more to AA than just not drinking.

A MURDER UNDER THE BRIDGE

I'm not going to preach to you about AA, but I want you to understand when you're an alcoholic, you're an alcoholic for life. There's no cure. You have to work at staying sober, and that's why AA becomes a part of your life. It's a good part of my life, and so I talk about it a lot just like I talk about Gracie or the cases I'm handling. If you don't like it, don't listen.

CHAPTER 17

The next afternoon Dr. Goldman called. He had met with Dr. Najari and visited with John Doe. He felt the visit with John Doe was productive even though he was unable to get him to talk. Dr. Goldman and Dr. Najari agreed John Doe was exhibiting the classic signs of PTSD. If, as we suspected, John Doe had been in the Marine Corps and had fought in the Vietnam War, it would confirm their diagnosis.

Since his arrival at Kirby, John Doe had been given a complete physical examination, and after reviewing the medical findings, Dr. Goldman agreed with Dr. Najari that John Doe's mutism was not due to a physical condition. In other words, he could speak; he just refused to do so. Although mutism was not typically associated with PTSD in adults, both doctors agreed it could occur if the PTSD were severe enough.

Dr. Goldman explained PTSD is a complex disorder most often accompanied with other disorders such as depression, social phobia, dissociative personality disorder, and addiction, to name a few. He described some therapies he used to treat PTSD but said none of them would work unless John Doe decided to speak. In the meantime, the doctors were adjusting John Doe's medications trying to determine which drugs and in what combination they worked best.

The first step in getting John Doe to speak was to win his confidence, and the doctors could best do that if they knew his history and background. Knowing the nature of the trauma that was causing the stress would enable the therapists to offer support.

So long as John Doe refused to speak, the best the doctors could do was to observe his reactions to certain stimuli and build a behavior profile based on those reactions. It wasn't the best way to evaluate a patient, but right now it was the only way they had. So Dr. Najari and Dr. Goldman had worked out a program they would jointly administer over the next week to ten days.

My job was to get as much information about John Doe as I could. I was pondering exactly how I was going to get that information if Chang didn't come through with John Doe's records when Tommy came into the office with a young Chinese woman.

Her name was Joanie Ming, and she needed legal representation. Joanie was Charlie Ming's daughter. Charlie owned the Golden Pearl Restaurant, one of the longest operating restaurants in Chinatown. The Golden Pearl had been opened by Charlie's grandfather who had turned it over to Charlie's father, who had turned it over to Charlie, who was likely going to turn it over to his oldest son. That last turnover is just my guess as to what is going to happen, but it's probably a pretty good guess.

After Charlie's father died and Charlie had taken over the restaurant he moved his then young and growing family from Chinatown to an affluent community in Westchester County. Charlie worried that living in Chinatown, his children would be exposed only to Chinese culture and while Charlie honored his Chinese heritage, he wanted his children integrated into the American way of life. So with that in mind he moved the family out of Chinatown.

So why was Joanie in Chinatown and why did she need a lawyer?

It seemed despite her father's efforts to keep the family out of Chinatown, Joanie liked to hang out there. Joanie also liked to take things that didn't belong to her. Her father called it a bad habit; the police called it larceny. It didn't matter to me what you called it; all that mattered to me was she needed a lawyer and she had money to pay the fee.

I know you probably think I'm heartless, right? Well, I'm not. This woman had two problems, the first was her compulsion to steal, and the second was a pending criminal charge. I'm not a psychiatrist so I can't help her with the first problem, but I can help her with the second problem provided she can pay the fee. I'm not heartless; I'm a realist who has grown accustomed to eating and living indoors.

But back to Joanie. She had stolen a $25 Buddha statue from a souvenir shop on Canal Street. Why, who knows, probably for kicks, but she was spotted by the owner and caught on the security camera slipping the statue into her pocketbook. When Joanie denied taking the statue, the cops were called and eventually Joanie was taken to the 5th Precinct and issued an appearance ticket. Now Joanie sat on the other side of my desk while I took a quick mental inventory of the items on the desk. It wasn't judgmental, just practical.

This was not the first time Joanie had been caught light-fingering merchandise. There were at least a dozen incidents that led to three arrests but no convictions because Daddy always came to the rescue and bought off the charges. But not this time. This time, Daddy said no, and so Joanie faced arraignment on a Petit Larceny charge.

Petit Larceny is a Class A misdemeanor, and if found guilty carries a penalty of one year in jail and a $1,000 fine. The first step in a case like this is to try and get the charges dropped by making restitution. Tommy said that had been tried but didn't work. It seemed Joanie had an affinity for this souvenir shop and had been caught lifting merchandise from there twice before. The owner was understandably fed up and refused to drop the charges.

I explained to Joanie the best I could do for her was to try and get the DA to agree to a diversion program. That's a program that allows defendants charged with low-level, non-violent crimes to escape conviction by making restitution, attending educational programs or getting treatment, and performing public service. If the defendant complies with all the conditions of the program, the charges are dismissed and the record expunged.

It's a good deal, but generally it's only offered to first-time offenders. In Joanie's case, she had no convictions but three arrests, so the diversion program might be a reach. Still, it was her best chance to avoid a conviction and a criminal record.

Joanie wasn't too happy about the treatment requirement, but I told her the alternative was to work out a plea deal that would include a guilty plea and a criminal record. She wanted to know if the guilty plea would involve jail time. I said it wasn't likely, but she should be more concerned about having a criminal record. Besides, Daddy would probably be happy if she went for treatment, and he'd probably agree to pay the therapy bill and who knows what else.

Joanie agreed, so while she sat there, I called the DA's Office, found out who was handling her case and set up a meeting for the next day.

CHAPTER 18

The following morning, I met Joanie at One Hogan Place just outside the doors to the New York County District Attorney's Office. We went together to the cubicle of ADA Tammy Duke-Barrera. I didn't know Ms. Duke-Barrera but I had seen her around, and Gracie said she was good and would probably be fair. Sometimes Gracie can be terribly wrong.

Our meeting didn't get off to an encouraging start when Ms. Duke-Barrera announced she had reviewed the file, and if we were there to talk about a diversion program, we were wasting our time. I'm not one to take "No" for an answer, so I wasn't about to give up.

Playing innocent, I asked Ms. Duke-Barrera why she was taking a hard-line approach when we were talking about such a petty crime committed by a repentant defendant who wanted nothing more than a chance to reform with a clear name. A defendant, who was willing to make restitution, do community service and whatever else it might take to make things right. You see I can be eloquent. It doesn't come to me naturally, so I have to work at it.

Ms. Duke-Barrera laughed, not just a smile or a chuckle, but an actual laugh. That's never a good thing after I make an emotional plea for fairness. Frowning is okay, but laughing isn't good at all. Ms. Duke-Barrera reminded me Ms. Ming was a serial shoplifter.

I admitted Ms. Ming obviously had a problem, but if you totaled the value of everything she was accused of stealing it hardly put her on the FBI's ten most wanted list. Then I suggested justice would be better served if we put an end to Ms. Ming's crime spree by sending her to mandatory counseling. Counseling to be paid for by her and not the taxpayers. After all, what was to be gained by incarcerating her?

As it turned out, Gracie wasn't wrong, and I'll deny I ever said she was if anybody tells her otherwise. After some further discussion, Ms. Duke-Barrera agreed to a diversion program conditioned on Ms. Ming having at least eighteen months of weekly counseling by a Board-Certified psychiatrist. Joanie wasn't thrilled with the idea, but she knew she had to take the deal.

We were sitting there working out the wording, and I was keeping a tight watch on Joanie because Ms. Duke Barrera had some attractive little items on her desk that Joanie seemed to be eyeing. I was pretty sure if Joanie lifted anything off the desk, it would screw up the deal. Fortunately, we got the deal finished before anything went missing.

I think Joanie was lucky. I don't know if her problem is an illness or not, but I know one thing. She hadn't done anything yet to help herself, no pun intended.

Now at least there was a chance she'd get some help, and if she did it would be a good thing. And if she didn't, she'd spend some time in jail and maybe that would force her to face reality.

When we left the DA's Office, Joanie suggested we go over and visit Daddy at the Golden Pearl and tell him the good news. I figured Charlie would be happy, and I could probably get a free lunch out of the deal.

I was right on both counts. It was my lucky day; I just didn't know at that point how lucky it was going to be.

CHAPTER 19

I was on my way back to the office after lunch with Joanie light fingers and her father, Charlie, when FBI Agent Michael Chang called. He had great news. When John Doe's fingerprints were run through the Marine Corps database, they got a hit. Not only did Chang have a name, but he also had John Doe's entire military record.

We were still working on the down-low, so Chang didn't want me coming to his office to pick up the file. Instead, he suggested we meet at the Worth Street Coffee Shop, and I buy him a late lunch. I had just eaten an early lunch, but there was no way I was going to say no.

When we met at the coffee shop, Chang handed me a thick file. It was the military file of Michael Costanza, my John Doe client.

Chang wanted to shoot the breeze over a leisurely lunch, but having just eaten and anxious to read Costanza's file, I dropped a twenty-dollar bill on the table and told Michael to enjoy his meal. As I was leaving, Michael reminded me I still owed him a dinner at Ruth's

Chris Steak House.

You can imagine how anxious I was to read Michael Costanza's file and I'd like to say I ran all the way back to the office. But at 51 years old it was more like a slow trot or maybe even a fast walk. When I finally got there, I told Connie I didn't want to be disturbed, and I locked myself in my office and started reading about Michael Costanza aka John Doe.

Michael Costanza was born in 1948, so he was 61 years old. In 1967, at the age of 19, Costanza enlisted in the Marine Corps. After completing his eight-week boot camp training at Paris Island, South Carolina, and four weeks of Infantry Training Regiment he was assigned to the First Marine Division, an infantry division headquartered at the time in Vietnam. While in Vietnam Costanza was promoted to Private First Class and eventually attained the rank of Lance Corporal.

Costanza served two tours of duty in Vietnam before being honorably discharged from the Corps in 1971. During his service in Vietnam, he was in some of the fiercest battles waged against the Viet Cong and the North Vietnamese Army.

In 1968 he fought in the Battle of Huê' where his unit engaged the Viet Cong in bitter street fighting and hand-to-hand combat. During the battle, Costanza was wounded rescuing civilian medical workers from a hospital being shelled by the Viet Cong. His injuries were minor, but he was awarded a Purple Heart and the Silver Star for gallantry in action against an enemy of the United States.

Before leaving Vietnam in 1971, Costanza fought in the battles of Operation Allen Brook, Mameluke Thrust and Operation Meade River. According to Marine Corps' records, the First Division left Vietnam in 1972 having lost 7,012 men killed in action, many of whom I figured had died fighting alongside Michael Costanza.

There were no disciplinary issues in Costanza's record or any indication of behavioral problems during his time in the Corps. However, after his discharge in 1971, he was treated on three separate occasions at VA Hospitals for post-traumatic stress disorder. Bingo! Now we might be getting somewhere.

Costanza first visited a VA facility in 1975 in New York, and he was diagnosed as suffering from PTSD. He was treated at the facility for a few months but, according to the records, he stopped showing up for treatment.

The next records were medical records from the VA Hospital in Los Angeles where Costanza was treated in 1985 for PTSD. In Los Angeles, he remained in treatment for a longer time than he had in New York but in the end, he once again simply stopped showing up for his appointments. It wasn't clear from the records where he was living at the time, but he did tell the hospital staff he was working.

The next and final records in the file were from a VA Hospital in Arizona. According to hospital intake notes, in January of 2003 the Phoenix Police had found Costanza wandering the streets mumbling incoherently. Somehow the police determined he was a veteran and they brought him to the VA Hospital. Costanza was hospitalized for five days, during which time he regained lucidity. But then he refused further medical treatment and against medical advice, left the hospital.

That was it. There were no records for the last six

years, but at least we now knew who John Doe was, and maybe, just maybe, we had a way to reach him.

I told Connie to make three copies of the files and while she was doing that I called both Dr. Najari and Dr. Goldman and filled them in on what I had just learned. Of course, both doctors wanted copies of the files, and I said I'd send them by messenger as soon as they were copied.

Dr. Najari suggested Dr. Goldman and I meet with him after everyone had reviewed Costanza's files to discuss how best to use the information. Dr. Goldman thought that was a good idea, so we set up a meeting for the following afternoon.

Then I called Tommy and told him about the files, and I needed him to do a complete background investigation on Costanza. Tommy said he'd come to the office first thing in the morning to pick up a copy of the file and fill me in on what he had learned about Lover Boy and a possible girlfriend.

The last call I made was to Joe Benjamin. I told him about John Doe's record and, of course, it didn't come as a big surprise to him that Costanza had been in the Vietnam War. I tried to get Joe to talk about his own war experience, but like so many guys who had been over there, he didn't want to talk about it. All he'd say was that it was bad, and he was one of the lucky ones who came home without scars.

I knew enough at that point to drop the conversation about his war experience and asked instead if he had some suggestions for me. He laughed and said "Don't drink and go to meetings," then he got serious again and authorized me to do whatever I thought was best for Costanza and not to worry about the cost. That gave me an opening to tell him about my promise to buy Chang dinner at Ruth's Chris Steak House, hoping he'd say I should put the bill through as an expense. Joe thought about it for a minute, then said I couldn't put it through as an expense, but he'd split the cost with me. That was better than nothing.

CHAPTER 20

The next morning over coffee Tommy gave me a full report on his investigation into Lover Boy's love life. Tommy had worked the housing project hard trying to find out about Lover Boy Johnson and the girls he hung around with. It took a while, but he finally came up with a name, Latanya Jefferson. Latanya was a fifteen-year-old girl who, her friends said was hassled by Lover Boy all the time.

Latanya lived in the projects with her mother and younger brother, Tyrone, and by all reports, she was a good kid and a good student. But when Tommy went looking for Latanya he couldn't find her. She had disappeared.

The best source Tommy had found so far was Carlos Ramirez, a sixteen-year-old Puerto Rican boy who was Latanya's classmate, and either her boyfriend or at least a close friend. Carlos had been more than willing to talk to Tommy, but he didn't know where Latanya was, and he hadn't heard from her.

According to Carlos, Johnson was always going after Latanya, asking her to go with him to his crib, or to show him some love, always grabbing at her whenever he saw her. But Latanya would have nothing to do with the gangbanger.

On the day Johnson was killed, Carlos had seen Latanya running into her apartment building crying. It was around nine o'clock at night. He had chased after her, but she wouldn't answer the door and he hadn't seen her since. Carlos didn't know where Latanya was and he worried about her.

Apparently, word had been spreading in the neighborhood that Latanya and Tyrone were responsible for Johnson's death and the TB Gangsters were out looking for revenge. Nobody seemed to know exactly how Latanya or Tyrone were involved in the death, but that didn't seem to matter. When the TB Gangsters wanted revenge, they got it and there were contracts out on Latanya and Tyrone's lives. The bounty was ten thousand dollars on each head, and the neighborhood was on edge.

Rumor around the project was that Latanya's mother had sent the children away. Tommy had tried a number of times to talk with Latanya's mother but she refused, and no one who would talk to him admitted knowing where Latanya or Tyrone was.

I knew the situation was tense, but when I noticed Tommy was carrying his gun around I figured it was a lot worse than just tense. His gun was legal; he had a carry permit. But he didn't usually carry it, so if he was carrying it now, that meant the situation was dangerous.

Except for the Latanya connection, Tommy's investigation at the projects hadn't produced very much useful information, and I was tempted to shut it down because I was worried about Tommy's safety. Tommy wasn't keen on shutting down that part of the investigation, so we worked out a compromise. Tommy would keep tight with Carlos, but he'd shift his efforts to find out more about Michael Costanza. We now knew where Costanza grew up so that would be a good place for Tommy to start. Tommy said after he finished with it he intended to go back to the projects and I needn't worry about it.

Tommy always told me not to worry about him because he knew how to take care of himself. He had a black belt in something called Taekwondo, whatever the hell that is, and he claimed his whole body was a lethal weapon. Right. All I could think of was the scene in the Indiana Jones movie where the bad guy pulled out a big scimitar and was twirling it around in threatening fashion getting ready to attack Indy. What did Indy do? He pulled out his pistol and shot him. Taekwondo or no Taekwondo I was glad Tommy had a gun, but I still worried about him.

I spent the rest of the morning dealing with some paperwork, then grabbed a quick lunch at the Worth Street Coffee Shop and headed up to Kirby to meet with the two doctors.

The meeting at Kirby didn't take long. Both Dr. Goldman and Dr. Najari had read through Michael Costanza's military file, and both had reached the same conclusion. Michael's experiences in Vietnam had left him badly traumatized and while Michael had sought treatment, he never remained in treatment long enough to have resolved his issues. As a result, his condition had continued to worsen until it blossomed into a full anti-social personality disorder.

After Dr. Goldman and Dr. Najari finished explaining the details of Costanza's condition, I asked them where it left us. Dr. Goldman answered first and said it left us with a problem, or more accurately, it left me with a problem. According to Dr. Goldman, people suffering from anti-social personality disorder are reckless, often abuse alcohol and drugs, and are prone to homicidal behavior. In other words, Michael Costanza fit the profile of a killer. To make matters worse, Dr. Goldman said it was more likely than not he knew the difference between right and wrong, so we couldn't even plead legal insanity.

On the positive side, Dr. Najari and Dr. Goldman planned to conduct a second battery of tests to help them better evaluate Michael's state of mind and provide them with some insight into the causes of his emotional withdrawal. I was invited to attend the sessions, but I didn't see how my being there would help, so I told Dr. Goldman to let me know when the testing was finished. I figured I might drop in on Michael between tests just to see for myself how he was doing.

CHAPTER 21

For the next week, not much happened in Michael's case. I didn't hear from Tommy, but I wasn't concerned. When Tommy was on a case and I didn't hear from him, it usually meant he was on to something.

I dropped by the Kirby Center and saw Michael twice, both times without either Dr. Goldman or Dr. Najari being there. Physically Michael looked good. The attendant told me Michael was showering daily, shaving, brushing his teeth, and taking care of himself. He was also eating well. But he still wasn't saying anything; he just sat in his chair staring. I stayed for about half an hour each time just talking to Michael, hoping to get some response.

The thirty-day mental evaluation hold on Michael's case was half up, and we'd have to go back to court in two weeks. If Michael still wasn't talking, the judge was likely to order an evaluation by Dr. Najari and a second state-appointed psychiatrist to determine if Michael could assist in his own defense. I know it sounds stupid that we'd have to go through another evaluation process, but that's the law. I don't remember exactly who it was, but some English author a long time ago wrote "the law is an ass." And not a very attractive one at that, I might add.

I know it wasn't Shakespeare who wrote it because he had far worse things to say about the law, or actually about lawyers. It was Shakespeare who wrote, "The first thing we do, let's kill all the lawyers." I never did like Shakespeare, but from the death threats I've gotten from my clients over the years, I'd say he had his finger on the pulse of the criminal class. Of course, my clients were far less eloquent in expressing their feelings. Their intent was the same as Shakespeare's and clearly stated. However, it was typically expressed with words that included reference to motherhood, fornication, my birth status, and deviant sexual activity. I think you get the point.

Anyway, back to Michael. When the mental evaluation hold was over, if Michael was still refusing to talk I had no doubt he'd be sent to Mid-Hudson Forensic Psychiatric Center, another maximum security mental institution. Only there his problems were not likely to be addressed, and he'd probably spend the rest of his life in some prison ward.

On the other hand, if he started talking anytime soon, he'd be going on trial for murder in a case where the evidence against him was close to overwhelming. There was nothing particularly attractive in either situation, but if he was talking and we went to trial he'd at least have a chance to get his life back. But it would take some doing on both of our parts.

I spoke with Dr. Goldman who was now certain

Michael knew the difference between right and wrong, although I don't know how he figured that one out with Michael not talking. But I had to take Dr. Goldman at his word, so that meant a plea of not guilty by reason of insanity wasn't going to work. Under the law in New York, you can be mentally ill and in fact, you can be nutty as a fruit cake, but that doesn't make you legally insane. To be legally insane you must lack the capacity to appreciate either the nature and consequences of your conduct or know that such conduct was wrong.

I don't think you're going to be surprised when I tell you insanity pleas in New York are successful less than 2% of the time. I used the insanity defense once in my career, and it didn't work. The defendant was a nineteen-year-old young man with a long and well-documented history of mental illness. One day while riding on the subway the young man took exception to the way the man across the way was holding his newspaper, so he stabbed him twenty-seven times. Then he took his seat as though nothing out of the ordinary had happened.

I thought the kid was crazy, which he was, only he wasn't legally insane. Why? Because I couldn't prove he didn't have the capacity to appreciate stabbing someone twenty-seven times was a bad thing and would result in the death of the victim. The kid was found guilty and was sentenced to twenty-five years to life, but I was able to have him sent to a prison that provided some mental health services. As far as I know, the kid's still in prison and given his mental state that's probably a good thing.

Michael wasn't legally insane, but I was beginning to think we might have a different defense to the murder charge. My working theory was that Lover Boy was attempting to rape someone, presumably Latanya Jefferson, and Michael stopped him by hitting him with the hammer. So far all I had to go on were Lover Boy's pants being partially down, the scratches on his face, his reputation as a rapist, and my own intuition. I needed a lot more than that to prove justification. First, I needed Michael to talk to me and hopefully confirm my theory. Then I needed to find the victim and get her to testify.

I was counting on Tommy for help, but I still needed Michael to talk to prove a defense of justification. In New York, the use of physical force, even in some cases deadly physical force, is justified if used in defense of yourself or someone else. In the situation where you kill somebody to protect someone other than yourself, you must prove that you reasonably believed that the person you killed was attempting to kidnap, rape, or rob the person you were trying to protect.

I called Richie Simone over at the 7th Precinct and pitched my theory to him, just to get his reaction. He wasn't impressed. He agreed it was possible, and certainly the Lover Boy's pants being down suggested possible sexual activity, but to Richie, it didn't prove anything. As for the scratch marks on Johnson's face, he gave me some good news. There were no DNA Reports on anything from under Michael's fingernails. Michael wasn't the one who had scratched Johnson's face. My theory had a life but it wasn't breathing on its own, at least not yet.

Then things started to break and break for the good.

CHAPTER 22

I hadn't heard from Tommy in a while, and I was starting to wonder if he was still working on the Costanza case, or if he'd gone on vacation. Then as often happened with Tommy, he showed up in the office unannounced, all smiles and carrying a file filled with papers.

It seemed Tommy had spent the last week and a half out in Queens County, where Costanza was born and lived until he joined the Marines.

Technically Queens County is part of New York City. It's a complicated thing involving New York City boroughs and state counties, but all you need to know is true New Yorkers live in Manhattan, and regard Manhattan and only Manhattan as being "the City." The other four boroughs of New York City, which are called the "outer boroughs" are just that, and as far as I'm concerned, they should never be referred to as "the City." I know technically I'm wrong, but I don't care.

Anyway, the reason I brought this whole thing up to begin with is when you're a New Yorker like me, and

Tommy is a New Yorker like me, you don't want to leave Manhattan. So going to Queens is like going to the dentist. For Tommy, spending a week and a half in Queens was like spending two weeks in Philadelphia. The best you could say in either case was it wouldn't kill you to be there. That is, if you didn't die from boredom.

Tommy had survived his time in the hinterlands and returned with some useful information about Michael Costanza. Michael was born and raised in Flushing, Queens, a solid middle-class neighborhood. He had a younger sister, Claire, who was married to a guy named Arthur Molinari. The last anyone knew Claire and her family were living in Los Angles, which might explain why Michael had sought treatment at the VA Hospital in Los Angles.

Tommy had located the house where Michael spent his childhood and lived until he joined the Marines. It was a small Cape Code style house on a quiet street around the corner from St. Kevin's Church, the local Catholic Church attended by the Costanza family.

Michael's parents were both deceased, and ownership of the house had turned over twice since it was occupied by the Costanza family. Most of the people now living on the block had moved in after the Costanzas were gone. However, Tommy did find two couples who were longtime residents on the block and remembered the Costanza family.

Initially, both couples were reluctant to talk with Tommy, but Tommy has a way about him that makes people trust him and given a little time he can win over just about anybody. That's what made him so successful at selling knock-off Rolex watches back in the old days before he became a private investigator. Don't get me wrong, Tommy's not a con artist at heart. He was a decent kid who was put in a tough situation when both his parents died in the 911 attack, and he went to live with his grandfather in Chinatown.

Anyway, Tommy used his charms, and the old timers opened up to him. He found them to be very nice and, as he put it, "seemingly lucid." The "seemingly" qualification bothered me a little, but Tommy assured me the stories they told were accurate. He said there was enough consistency in the details of the stories to make them trustworthy.

Both couples painted the same picture of the Costanza family. Good people, hardworking, church going and good neighbors. Michael's father was a very outgoing man and an usher at St. Kevin's Church, and Michael's mother was a member of the Church's Rosary Society. They recalled Michael as a good kid, respectful, and a well-behaved nice boy. That was until he came back from the war. They all said the war had changed him. He was withdrawn, always angry, got drunk a lot, and wound up in quite a few fights.

No one could remember exactly when, but sometime around 1976 or so Michael disappeared and they hadn't seen him since. They all commented that after Michael left, the family was never the same. Michael's father became withdrawn and even stopped attending church. He died in 1980. Michael's mother, then alone in the house, became more and more reclusive until her death in 1993. Both couples reported sadly that Michael hadn't shown up for either of his parents' funerals.

As for Michael's sister Claire, everyone recalled her

as a wonderful girl, very friendly. A lot like Michael until he changed after coming home from the war. They said after the father died, Claire was a big help to her mother and very devoted. Everyone was extremely sad when Claire moved to California. As for Michael, well he was a lost soul.

I was just a kid during the Vietnam War, but I have vivid memories of those days and the impact the War had on our neighborhood. I remember what it was like when word spread one of the local guys was killed. The whole neighborhood mourned. The women, including my mother, went to all the wakes, the funerals and prayed for the dearly departed. The men mostly went to the bars, cursed and got drunk.

Of course, when one of the guys came home safe and sound from Vietnam there was always a big party, with potluck dinners and late hours in the bar. The women went home early, and the men stayed, cursed and got drunk.

Most of the guys came back in one piece, the same way they had left. But a couple of them came back changed. It wasn't that they were physically injured; it was just that they were always angry and quick to pick a fight. They weren't like that when they left. Something had made them change. My mother said they suffered from shell shock or battle fatigue which she knew about from World War II. It was only when I got older that I learned about PTSD and what it did to combat veterans.

Between what I had learned from the Marine Corps records and what Tommy had discovered about Costanza's life, I was starting to understand how Michael Costanza wound up as John Doe, and it was making me angry. Michael had volunteered to fight for his country and had done so, not only with honor but with courage that earned him the title of war hero.

But the war had taken a terrible toll on him, eventually reducing him to an almost sub-human existence, and nobody had done anything to help him. Yes, the VA had tried to help him, and it looked like Michael hadn't cooperated, but somehow everybody lost track of this man. It wasn't right, and I vowed that I wasn't going to lose track of him. Michael Costanza's case became my top priority.

I called Dr. Goldman and passed on the information I had gotten from Tommy. Dr. Goldman said it was helpful, and he'd pass it on to Dr. Najari when they met the next day. We needed to meet soon to discuss the next legal steps and unless there was a breakthrough with Michael our options were limited.

CHAPTER 23

I hadn't seen a new 18B case in a while which was okay because I wanted to concentrate on Michael's case but I called Joe Benjamin anyway just to make sure everything was alright. Joe was fine, he said he hadn't sent me any new cases because none had come across his desk that needed my talent and he wanted me concentrating on Michael Costanza's case.

Joe didn't know Michael, had never met or seen him, yet the fact they were both Vietnam vets formed a natural and immediate bond. I could understand that happening because in a lot of ways that's what happens in AA. In AA, there's an intimacy that comes from sharing experiences, some very personal and very painful. When you realize, you're battling the same demons as the people, you're sharing your thoughts with, you bond with them. For me, it wasn't easy to do. I didn't trust anyone, and I certainly wasn't going to open up my gut to a bunch of strangers.

Fortunately, I met Doug, my sponsor, and he gave

me the strength and courage to trust and share. What I went through as an alcoholic pales in comparison to what Michael went through as a soldier in Vietnam but in some ways, there was a similarity in how we recover. I needed someone to teach me to trust my fellow alcoholics and Michael needed someone to help him trust his fellow vets. I figured both Dr. Goldman and Dr. Najari knew that and they didn't need me to tell them. But at least now I understood what we were up against in getting Michael to open up.

That's what I had been thinking about when, as if on cue, my pigeon Peter called. You remember Peter, the Wall Street lawyer who constantly bitches about his bosses? Truthfully, Peter is a good guy, just a pain in the ass sometimes, but this wasn't one of those times. Peter always wanted to drink because his boss was always ignoring him and he felt he wasn't getting a fair shot at making partner in the firm. But this time it was different, Peter had just been made a partner in the firm, and now he wanted to drink to celebrate.

Sounds crazy, doesn't it? Well, it is crazy because alcoholism is crazy. Do you really think sane people behave that way? In truth, we're mostly sane, we're just alcoholics. I forget that sometimes, especially when I'm talking with Peter.

According to Peter, the big problem would be that evening when he was going to a cocktail party thrown in honor of the new partners. He had been in AA long enough to know a lot of recovering alcoholics drink when things start going well. God knows that was what I had done. Of course, alcoholics also drink when things aren't going well. Alcoholics drink and will use any excuse to do so, that's what makes us alcoholics.

I congratulated Peter on his success and told him to meet me for lunch at the Worth Street Coffee Shop. We needed to sit down face-to-face and maybe go to a meeting, but I'd take it one step at a time.

Peter knew if he got drunk at the cocktail party, it would probably be overlooked under the circumstances. But he was smart enough to know the problem wasn't the cocktail party the problem was the next day, and the day after that and the day after that. The party would give him an easy excuse to have that "one" drink, but he knew in his heart he couldn't have just one drink. One is too many, and a hundred aren't enough when you're an alcoholic.

We had a good lunch and Peter decided to go to a meeting before going back to the office. I was pretty sure he'd be okay, but I told him to call me before the party and if things got too bad, during the party. If need be, I'd go to the party and yank his ass out of there, but I didn't tell him that. I just said to call me.

That night was my regular group meeting, and also the night I was going to meet Doug for our monthly dinner. When I told him about Peter and what was going on, he started to laugh. He reminded me of my own slip, which is AA slang for screw up, and how I had tried to rationalize what I had done. I'm good at rationalizing, especially when it comes to my own conduct, but it also works out well for my clients.

Doug thought Peter was in a tough situation, a lot tougher than the situation I was in when I slipped. But I wasn't really worried about Peter because I was convinced he'd be okay. When Doug asked me how I could be so sure, I couldn't resist saying because Peter had a better sponsor than I did. Luckily Doug has a good sense of humor and a high tolerance for my sometimes out of line humor.

In case you're wondering, Peter was okay that night. He got through the party just fine drinking club soda, and it wasn't because of anything I said to him. It was his working the AA program that gave him what he needed. All I did was remind him of that.

CHAPTER 24

I was on the phone talking with Peter about his big
night and his new position when Tommy wandered into
my office. I could tell by the look on his face he had
something good to tell me. so I rushed Peter off the phone.
Actually, I just told him I had to go, and then I hung up
on him. If you're taking notes on how to be an AA sponsor,
don't write that last part down.

I will say in my own defense that Peter didn't have
a problem. He was just babbling on and on about how
great the party was and how great it was to be a partner
in the firm, so I had no regrets about hanging up on him. I
had explained to him on more than one occasion there
was a difference between being his sponsor and being his
mother. If he had a problem with booze, he should call me,
but if he just wanted to brag or he wanted sympathy, he
should call his mother.

Anyway, once I had gotten Peter out of the way I
turned to Tommy who just smiled, sat down and
announced he had found Michael's sister, Claire.

A MURDER UNDER THE BRIDGE

I don't know how he does it, but Tommy is very good at tracking down people. Once he learned Costanza had a younger sister named Claire he started to search for her. All he knew was that she was about 58 years old, married to a man named Arthur Molinari, and was last known to be living in California, possibly Los Angles. But with that little bit of information, he had come up with an address and a phone number. He hadn't tried to contact her; he was leaving it up to me.

The whole day I toyed with the idea of calling Claire Costanza-Molinari, but I wasn't sure what to say to her if she even agreed to talk to me. I mean how do you approach a conversation like that? *I'm your brother's lawyer, he bashed in some guy's head with a hammer, and he won't talk, and I thought maybe you can help me out.* I had bounced the idea around with Gracie at dinner that evening, and she thought I needed a subtler approach, which was probably true.

After dinner, Gracie had one of those "girls' night out" things. I thought she was getting a little old for that sort of thing but, of course, I could never say that out loud.

I worry as I get older that I'm going to be one of those people who say out loud what they're thinking. If that happens, I'm not going to have a very pleasant, or for that matter a very long, senior life. Cause of death, he said out loud what he was thinking one time too often.

With Gracie off doing her thing, I didn't have much to do. I was sitting in my apartment, and I started thinking about Michael's sister. It was just after nine o'clock and I figured with the three-hour time difference in California, it might be a good time to call her. Six o'clock in Los Angeles, dinner time, she'd probably be home by then, if she was working. I dialed the number, it rang four times, then a woman answered. It was Claire Costanza-Molinari, and she didn't hang up on me when I told her who I was and why I was calling.

It was clear Claire loved her brother and was concerned for him, but she was also frustrated and a little bit angry. We spoke for over an hour, and I learned a lot about Michael in that hour.

Claire had nothing but good memories of her childhood and growing up with Michael, and she was happy to share the details with me. Their father was an electrician who had served in the Navy during World War II. He made a decent living and shortly after Claire was born, the family moved into a nice house in Flushing. Their mother stayed at home until Claire and Michael were in high school, then she took a job, not because the family needed the money but because she wanted something to do.

Michael had been a happy kid; he played sports and had lots of friends. Nothing in his childhood suggested any mental or emotional problems. He had never been in any serious trouble and but for a couple of neighborhood pranks, he was rarely punished by his parents.

He attended Holy Cross High School, where he was an excellent athlete but not a brilliant student. Michael's parents had wanted him to go to college, but Michael wasn't interested in continuing his education, so after graduating from high school he enlisted in the Marines. It was 1967, and the Vietnam War was raging, so the family was naturally concerned for Michael's safety.

Of course, everyone was very proud of Michael when he was awarded the Silver Star and relieved when he returned in one piece from Vietnam. But their relief was short-lived. Within a few months of returning home after his discharge from the Marine Corps, it became apparent Michael had changed. He showed no interest in getting a job, and he stayed out late coming home drunk most nights. His moods swung wildly from depressed to violent. He wouldn't eat with the family and frequently argued with his parents.

Finally, Michael got a job doing construction work, but he was fired after a couple of months because he'd show up late and drunk. He got another job doing more construction work, and this time the job lasted for about a year before he was fired. By early 1975 the family had all it could take, and Michael's father gave him an ultimatum, get help or leave the house.

Michael reluctantly went to the VA Hospital in the Bronx where he was diagnosed with PTSD. At the time, no one really understood what PTSD was or how devastating it could be. As a result, the family was probably less sympathetic to Michael's situation than they should have been. Everybody was busy preparing for Claire's upcoming wedding, and Michael who was seemingly doing better was mostly ignored.

After getting married, Claire and her husband moved to New Jersey and Claire's contacts with her family became less frequent. She'd call her mother once a week, and she and her husband would visit her parents once a month or so. During that period Michael's behavior was erratic. At times, he'd seem fine, and her mother would say Michael was working and doing okay. But at other times when Claire would visit Michael would stay in his room and not even come down to say hello.

In less than a year after Claire got married, Michael left home. From what Claire had been told by her mother, Michael, and his father got into a heated argument, and Michael hit him. An hour later Michael left the house and no one in the family saw him or heard from him for nine years. When their father died in 1980, Michael never showed up or called. Claire thought he might be dead, but she had no way of finding out for sure.

In 1981 Claire's husband, an aerospace engineer, was offered a good paying job at Hughes Aircraft in Los Angeles California, and the family, now consisting of Arthur, Claire, and their two children, moved west. Claire had tried to convince her mother to move with them, but she refused, saying she needed to remain in the house in Flushing because she was sure Michael would be coming home.

Then in 1985 Michael showed up at Claire's door. How he found her she didn't know, but there he was looking like a tramp. Her husband, Arthur, is a kind man and he agreed to let Michael live with them, but only on the condition that he get help. Michael agreed and went to the VA Hospital in Los Angeles. His treatment went well and Michael's mental status improved. He got a job and within six months he had moved into his own apartment.

As the months passed Claire saw less and less of Michael, but he did stay in touch, and she thought things were going well. There were periods when she wouldn't hear from him for a couple of months, but then he'd call and say he had been on an out of town job and he was fine. Michael would show up for family events, said he was still in treatment and seemed to be okay.

Then in March 1983 Claire got word their mother had suffered a heart attack and died. She called Michael right away and said she was making arrangements to fly back east and did he want to go with her? He said he'd call her back in a few minutes. That was the last she heard from him for seventeen years.

Michael never showed up for his mother's funeral and when Claire returned to California, she couldn't find a trace of him. His apartment was vacant, and the landlord said he hadn't seen Michael in weeks. His boss said Michael hadn't shown up for work in almost a month. Michael had just vanished once again.

The last contact Claire had with her brother was in 2000 when out of the blue he called on Christmas Day. Michael was mostly incoherent, at times crying and at other times yelling. The call lasted maybe five to ten minutes and ended when Michael abruptly hung up. Claire had tried to find out where the call originated, but had been unable to do so.

When I sensed our conversation was ending, I asked Claire if she'd be willing to help Michael. I knew it was a tough question to ask, but I had to ask it. She didn't answer right away. Then she said she loved her brother, but she wasn't sure how much more heartbreak she could take. I understood, so I wasn't going to push her, but then she added she'd at least talk to him if I thought it would help. I had to admit I didn't know if it would help, but I appreciated her offer and told her I would get back to her.

I thought at that point the conversation was over, but then Claire added that one way or another all of this

had to end for Michael. After that we said good-bye.
I had a tough time getting to sleep that night.

CHAPTER 25

The next morning, I had a sentencing hearing on an 18B case. The client, Benicio Olivera, was a twenty-year-old kid who had gotten himself mixed up in a big-time drug deal that had gone bad. The sad part was he was neither a user nor a dealer, just a local neighborhood kid looking to make a couple of fast bucks the easy way. He was the lookout, but apparently, he wasn't a very good one because the cops raided the place in the middle of the deal.

In the melee that followed, shots were fired and although only a couple of the bad guys and none of the cops were injured lots of guns were recovered. That meant everybody at the scene, including Beni, was charged with possession of a weapon.

All you had to do was look at Beni to know he wasn't the criminal type. If it hadn't been for the gunplay, I could have negotiated a very good plea deal for him. But when guns are involved the situation gets a lot more complicated. In New York gun possession is a big deal and if you get caught actually carrying an illegal gun you go to jail, and that's all she wrote. There's no way around it. In Beni's case, there was a slim chance he wouldn't do time because he hadn't been in actual possession of a gun; he was just charged with the group.

Beni had no prior record, had a job and was helping to support his sick mother. Just so we're clear, I'm not making up the part about him supporting his sick mother; he was really supporting her. After I explained it all to the ADA at Beni's arraignment and pointed out Beni's limited role in the deal, the ADA agreed to ask for a minimal bail amount.

Beni had managed to raise the bail money and had been free since the arraignment. That was good because Beni was better off the longer we stretched out the proceedings. In Beni's case, the idea that justice delayed is justice denied just wasn't true. When you represent a small fish in a big case, you want to hide in the weeds for as long as possible and let the DA concentrate his attention on the big fish. The longer your client is ignored, the better off he or she is when it comes to getting a plea deal.

As usually happens in cases like this, the big players didn't make bail, so they started cutting deals right away. While that was happening, I kept continuing Beni's case for over a year. Then after the DA had sent away the rest of the defendants, we negotiated a plea deal.

At that point, the DA wasn't going to try the case against a single defendant who had played only a minor role, so the DA agreed to reduce the charges against Beni to criminal possession of a weapon in the fourth degree, a

Class A misdemeanor. The sentence for a Class A misdemeanor is a conditional discharge or up to a year in jail. Since Beni had no prior record and after the Probation Department had confirmed the situation with his mother's health, the DA was agreeable to a conditional discharge.

That morning, Beni and I sat in court waiting for his case to be called. Regrettably, the calendar clerk working was unaware that my cases go to the top of the list. So Beni and I sat and waited while the sentencing judge, new to the bench, spent an inordinate amount of time lecturing defendants before shipping them off to prison.

Normally most sentencing judges get right to the point and just sentence the defendant, and that's it. In some of the more heinous cases, the judge will say something to the defendant. The judge that morning sounded more like a high school guidance counselor than a judge. It didn't seem to matter to him that his counseling after five sentencings had been met with a sneer, a "drop dead," and a "fuck you." The fifth defendant just stood there shifting from foot to foot waiting for the lecture to be over.

When Beni's case was finally called, the ADA requested conditional discharge as we had agreed. The judge gave Beni the conditional discharge along with a lecture I was beginning to think was going to last longer than the jail term Beni had faced.

When the lecture finally ended, Beni thanked me, and we both bolted from the courtroom. Beni was rushing to get as far away from the halls of justice as he could, and I was rushing to get to the Kirby Forensic Psychiatric

Center on time.

I was late, so instead of taking the subway and bus I hailed a taxi. The driver was a Pakistani man named Vikesh who insisted on talking on his cell phone while weaving at high speeds through the traffic on the FDR Drive. Whenever I get into a taxi, I look at the driver's license and note his name. I do it because I like to talk to the drivers and I think it's nicer if you call them by name.

Anyway, after we came within inches of colliding with a stretch limo, for the second time I suggested Vikesh get off the phone and concentrate on his driving. It wasn't a suggestion; it was more of an order or maybe a plea for my life.

In any case, he did get off the phone, and after that, he weaved at high speeds through traffic telling me about his fourteen-year-old daughter and the marriage he was arranging for her. He was very proud of the fact that his daughter was born here and was attending high school. Not because of what she was doing, but because it increased her value and reduced the amount of dowry he had to pay to her prospective husband. It wasn't clear from our conversation if the daughter knew about the marriage arrangements her father was making for her, but I was willing to bet the ranch either way she wasn't happy about them.

AA teaches you to be grateful about something every day. When I got out of the taxi at the Kirby Center, I was grateful to be alive. I paid Vikesh the fare, gave him a nice tip, and wished him and his daughter well, silently vowing never to set foot in his taxi again.

As Vikesh drove away, I thought about asking Gracie what sort of dowry I could expect to receive if I asked her to marry me. Then I thought about how she'd react, and in the interest of keeping all my body parts intact, I decided not to ask.

Thanks to Vikesh I was fifteen minutes early for my meeting with Dr. Najari and Dr. Goldman.

CHAPTER 26

When I got to Dr. Najari's office, Dr. Goldman was already there, and the two men were discussing Michael's case. This was the first time we had all met since learning Michael's identity, so the doctors wanted to catch me up on what they had been doing.

Even though knowing Michael's identity had given the doctors new ways to reach him, they hadn't made much progress. Calling Michael by name had produced some response, and talking about his military record had caused a slight emotional reaction. But nothing so far had made Michael respond verbally.

Unable to communicate with Michael verbally, the doctors had used an alternate means to formulate a personality profile. By showing Michael various visual images and measuring his bodily responses to those images, they had hoped to approximate the results of a standard personality test.

They had also spent a good deal of time changing and adjusting Michael's medications trying to balance between keeping him lucid yet calm. They were giving Michael low doses of antipsychotic drugs hoping to control any symptoms of psychosis.

Much of what the doctors were saying was going over my head, and I had to ask a lot of questions to understand what they were talking about. But there was one thing they said that struck me immediately and gave me hope my theory of Michael's case was on the right track. The doctors found when Michael was shown pictures of people in danger, his bodily response suggested empathy which was usually absent in patients suffering from PTSD.

According to Dr. Najari, PTSD usually impaired empathetic ability and caused difficulty in emotional and cognitive skills. But in Michael's case, there was no evidence his empathetic ability had been impaired. I asked both doctors if based upon that finding they could reasonably conclude Michael would have attacked Johnson if he believed Johnson was harming someone. I knew it was a tough question for the doctors to answer but at that point, I needed to know if my theory of the case had any chance of success or if I was just spinning my wheels.

The doctors thought it was a good question, but they couldn't come to an agreement on an answer. Dr. Goldman replied first and said Michael's attacking Johnson could have been motivated by his empathy for someone being attacked by Johnson, but he couldn't say that medically Michael's empathy was sufficient to be the motivation.

Dr. Najari spoke next and said he believed since Michael's conduct in attacking Johnson was out of character with his behavioral history, something had triggered his violence and his empathy for someone in trouble was likely the trigger. As Dr. Najari explained it, Michael having seen so many of his buddies die, often from horrific wounds, he would have been angry, and he would have wanted to avenge their deaths. While the desire for revenge may have been acceptable while he was a soldier, it was not acceptable when he became a civilian, and that created a conflict which drove Michael into his present mental state.

Dr. Najari believed Michael's empathy was so strong that if he saw someone being attacked, he would break through his emotional conflict and come to the aid of that person. Of course, he couldn't say for sure that was what had actually happened, but it was certainly possible. Dr. Najari said his conclusion was well supported by Michael's history and particularly his actions during the war resulting in his being awarded the Silver Star Medal.

According to the memo in Michael's file, during the battle of Hue while engaged in a fierce firefight he left his protected position, ran across an open square under enemy fire to help civilian medical personnel escape from a burning hospital hit by enemy mortar fire. Dr. Najari said Michael's willingness to put himself at risk under those conditions for total strangers evidenced how strong Michael's empathy was. Finally, Dr. Najari pointed out there was nothing in Michael's recent history to suggest he was violent and he certainly wasn't stupid, yet after the attack, he made no effort to hide or elude detection and capture.

After listening to Dr. Najari, Dr. Goldman said he could agree with Dr. Najari insofar as it was possible, but not certain Michael had acted to protect someone else from a perceived danger. That was enough for me, at least at that point. At a minimum the doctors could counter the profile of a killer the DA was likely to produce.

What the doctors had said fit nicely into my theory was that Johnson was engaged in a sexual assault when Michael killed him, but I still had no evidence to prove any of it. Johnson's pants halfway down, the scratch marks on his face, and his reputation were all circumstantial evidence, but not very strong evidence. The doctors' new analysis helped counter the typical profile of a PTSD sufferer, but I still needed a hell of a lot more for a successful defense, and most of what I needed had to come from Michael.

We talked briefly about my conversation with Claire, and the doctors were interested in what she had to say about Michael's childhood. They didn't think there was anything to be gained by her talking with Michael at this point, so it was decided to put that idea on the back burner for the time being.

Dr. Najari sensed Michael was a little hostile to the Center's medical personnel. He wasn't violent or aggressive toward them, but he had no tolerance for any of them. Dr. Najari believed this attitude may have been the result of his experience when he was wounded in Vietnam or his experiences at the VA Hospitals. Dr. Goldman had reached the same conclusion, so both doctors thought I might be in a better position than they were to reach Michael. They were both convinced Michael's war experiences had driven him into his present state and the only way out was to find a path to his inner self. They said there was no magic way to do it, and they were in no better position to reach Michael than I was.

I couldn't understand why the doctors thought I'd be better able to get to Michael than they could. Frankly, it scared me. During my career as a lawyer, I've had to talk to all kinds of people from scared-stiff kids to stone-cold killers. I was comfortable talking to them because I knew what the hell I was doing. Besides, I knew I couldn't do them any harm. But this situation was different. I had no idea what to say or what to do, and the doctors weren't giving me very much help. I was worried I'd do or say something that would drive Michael deeper into himself and that he'd never come out of it.

Dr. Goldman and Dr. Najari tried to assure me the risk of Michael going into a deep state of isolation was minimal, but they couldn't discount the possibility. Finally, I agreed to talk with Michael, but I wanted the doctors to give me as much advice as they could.

I spent an hour with both doctors preparing to talk with Michael. Some of what we discussed was familiar because the approach mirrored in many ways AA's approach with alcoholics. But, despite the doctors' assurances, I was still worried I might do more harm than good. In the end, I just figured the risk was worth it because if Michael didn't start talking he was either going to jail, or he was going to be locked up in a mental institution for maybe the rest of his life.

CHAPTER 27

The three of us went to the conference room where Michael was waiting, but I went in alone. Dr. Najari and Dr. Goldman went into an adjoining room where they could observe everything through a two-way mirror and listen to the conversation.

I hadn't seen Michael in over a week, and nothing much had changed. He looked the same, sitting in the same position just staring into space. It was almost as though he hadn't moved at all since I was last there.

I sat down in a chair across from Michael, pulling it up so we were just a couple of feet apart. As I moved closer, nothing in Michael's demeanor changed. But when I spoke his name and once again told him who I was and I needed his help, I thought I saw something in his eyes change. The hardness that seemed to always be there softened a bit. Not a lot, but enough to be noticeable. Or maybe it was just wishful thinking on my part.

I told Michael I knew he was a good man, a man who had done many brave things in his life, but now I needed his help to prove he wasn't a murderer. When I said the word "murderer," his jaw tensed and I thought that I might be losing whatever ground I may have gained. I quickly added that I didn't believe he was a murderer, but he had to help me understand what happened under the bridge. His jaw slackened.

I decided it was time to take a chance and test out my theory. I looked directly into Michael's eyes and said I knew he had saved somebody's life under that bridge. I didn't know who and I didn't know how, but I knew he did. Michael closed his eyes for a minute, and when he opened them, they seemed to have lost some more of their hardness. I was starting to feel a little bit more confident.

I told Michael I was a recovering alcoholic and had battled my own demons, none nearly as terrifying as his, but demons that nearly destroyed my life. I had seen lives lost to the demons, but I had also seen lives saved. Lives of people who under the hold of those demons had done terrible things, who had hurt others in so many ways but who, like me, had escaped from the demons. I told Michael I wanted to help him to escape those demons.

Michael looked away, then he looked back at me, and there were tears in his eyes. My heart started to beat like a drum, and I held my breath. I had no idea what to do or say next, but I knew I had to continue and I couldn't stop and consult with the doctors.

I slowly put my hand on Michael's shoulder and simply said that I knew and understood. Michael made no effort to move away or push my hand aside. Tears began flowing down his cheeks, and he began to sob.

I was frightened, not out of fear of what Michael might do to me, but what I might have done to him.

Following my instincts, I moved closer and put my arms around him and let him cry on my shoulder. You know I'm not a touchy-feely guy, so this hugging was a little foreign to me, but something told me it was the right thing to do.

Michael held on to me for a while, then he lifted his head and moved back in his chair. He didn't say anything, but the look in his eyes was softer than it had been.

I asked him if he would help me understand what had happened under the bridge, but he didn't respond. I asked him a couple of other questions, but he wouldn't answer me. He was just staring off into space. I tried a number of ways to reach Michael, all to no avail.

That's how the session ended. One step forward, one step backward. Still, the doctors were excited and pleased. They felt I had made at least a partial breakthrough, and it was something to build on. But we were at a critical junction legally, and we needed to make a decision.

In four days, we were due back in court, and I had to decide whether to enter a plea or request a hearing to determine if Michael was capable of helping in his own defense. If I entered a plea, Michael would be transferred from Kirby to Rikers Island Jail unless bail was granted and that wasn't likely. On the other hand, if I asked for the hearing, Michael would remain at Kirby for at least another thirty days, but after that he might wind up not getting a trial and be sent to a psychiatric institution for a long time.

After conferring with Dr. Najari and Dr. Goldman, I decided I had no choice but to request the hearing and hope we'd be able to get Michael to work with us in the thirty days we'd have before the next decision needed to be made. Dr. Najari agreed to appear in court, along with Dr. Goldman, to support my request for a further mental evaluation. I was confident that with Dr. Najari supporting the motion, the DA's Office wouldn't object.

CHAPTER 28

When I got back to my office it was late, but I did reach Joe Benjamin and gave him the news. When I was done, he started talking about what we were going to do next. The "we" part was something new because Joe never got involved in the actual handling of any case he assigned to me.

To be honest, I wouldn't have put up with the interference because my ego is too big and I never liked people trying to tell me what to do. Some of that attitude changed when I got sober, but I still have some attitudes that need adjustment. At least according to Gracie and Doug. Personally, I think I'm fine the way I am.

Anyway, given Joe's personal interest in Michael's case, I was okay with him butting in. To be honest, I appreciated his help because a lot of what was happening was new to me.

It was late, and I hadn't spoken to Gracie all day, so I gave her a quick call to find out if she wanted to eat out or meet at her place for some takeout food. Gracie opted for the little Italian trattoria we frequented on Mulberry Street, and we agreed to meet at my office in an hour. That gave me time to start working on the motion papers for Michael's case, which is what I was doing when I got a call from Doug.

I could tell right away something was wrong because Doug wasn't himself. Then he told me his wife, Laurie, had been diagnosed with stage two breast cancer and was in the hospital awaiting surgery. The news hit me like a ton of bricks, so I could only imagine what it was like for Doug. I asked him where he was and he said at home alone in his den. When I said I was coming right over he offered no objection.

I called Gracie and told her what was going on, then I hopped into a taxi and headed uptown to Doug's apartment on the Upper West Side. Doug had been sober for over twenty years. As my sponsor, he had gotten me through some tough spots in my life, but I never faced anything like Doug was facing now. As scared as I had been that day in trying to reach Michael, I was more scared that night of failing Doug when he really needed me.

One thing I had learned early in AA was how to pray. Not the way I had prayed as a kid, not the let's make a deal type of prayer, but real prayer. Prayer where you ask God not for a favor, but simply for the strength to handle whatever He throws your way. That prayer has yet to fail me, and I was sure it wouldn't fail me then. So in the taxi going to Doug's I asked God to give me the strength to help my friend Doug.

Doug met me at the door; he was alone in the apartment. Laurie was in the hospital, and his kids were at his sister's house. I didn't know what to say, so I just hugged him. Doug started to cry and for the first time in as far back as I could remember, I started to cry. We just stood there holding onto each other and crying. I told Doug whatever it took he had the strength to get through it for Laurie's sake and for the sake of his kids. Then we went into his den and talked for the rest of the night.

Doug had been in his office that morning when Laurie called and told him she had just had a mammogram, and he needed to meet her at the hospital. He went right away, knowing it was serious. At the hospital, he got the news the mammogram had revealed certain abnormalities and the doctors were doing a biopsy. Realizing at that point he and Laurie would probably be at the hospital all day, he had called his sister and had her pick up his kids.

The remainder of the day had been a nightmare, but Doug being Doug had held up well for Laurie's sake. Then he got home and broke down. He said he thought about going out and buying a bottle of vodka, and that's when he called me instead.

To me, Doug had always been a tower of strength, the one person I could never imagine going back to the bottle. I needed to think of him that way because I relied on his strength. But I was forced to face the truth; Doug was human, and he was an alcoholic, and he needed me. It was a reversal of roles, and it frightened me. Maybe if it had come about more slowly, I would have been better prepared for it. But it hadn't, and I had to rise to the occasion for my friend.

I can't say my prayers were answered, but it seemed like I knew what to say to help Doug that night. I guess that I knew from the start I couldn't make his pain go away. Nobody could and neither could the booze.

As an alcoholic, I had tried again and again to make the pain go away by drowning it with booze, but the pain always came back. Most times it came back even worse than it had been. The best, and maybe the only, thing I could do to help Doug was to remind him of what he had taught me. That he could and would survive the pain and eventually it would go away. I would share the pain with him as best I could, and I'd be there for him for as long as he needed me.

We sat together, talking at times, and sometimes in silence, until dawn. Then Doug said he needed to shower and get to the hospital, and I needed to get to work. I offered to go to the hospital with him, but Doug said he was fine and he'd call me later. He gave me a hug and a kiss on the cheek and said he loved me.

I'm telling you this story because it made me realize something very important, something I had never realized before then. Being sober was important to everyone around me in ways I had never considered. If Doug hadn't been sober, he never could have given Laurie the support and love she needed to get through this crisis. He would have done what alcoholics do and gotten drunk and felt sorry for himself. If I hadn't been sober, I would never have been there for Doug because I would have been out drinking.

You may be thinking, how could I not have known that? It seems pretty obvious, but not to an alcoholic. An alcoholic has one focus, himself and his booze. That's all that matters.

It took Doug's crisis for me to see how my conduct

was like a ripple in a stream going out in wider and wider circles. The ripples got smaller and less noticeable as they spread further and further away, but they kept spreading.

The same thing was happening in Michael's life. The trauma he had suffered in Vietnam caused him pain, and his reaction to the pain spread like ripples through his family, through his sister's family and through everyone around him. But unlike ripples in a stream, these ripples weren't dissipating, they were continuing to grow and spread and would do so until Michael came to grips with his demons.

CHAPTER 29

The next couple of days were hell. I spent most of those days at the hospital with Doug and then went to my office to work on Michael's case. I was able to get the DA's Office to support my motion to keep Michael at Kirby for another thirty days to determine if he was capable of assisting in his own defense.

Laurie's surgery went very well. When the final lab results came in a few days later, the doctors were confident that with chemotherapy and radiation treatment her chances of a full cure were good. Doug, of course, was ecstatic and no longer wanted me at the hospital. I protested, saying I'd be there as long as he was there, but he insisted it wasn't necessary. I would have argued more, but to be honest, I was exhausted, and I hadn't seen Gracie in a while. Besides, I had the hearing in Michael's case the next day, and I needed to see him again soon after that.

After leaving Doug, I decided to hit a quick AA

meeting before heading back to the office. I always carry a meeting schedule with me and in New York City you can find a meeting just about any time of the day or night, any day of the week. Luckily, there was a mid-day meeting only two blocks from the hospital, and I had plenty of time to get there.

Back in my office after the meeting, the first thing I did was call Gracie and let her know about Laurie, then we set up a date for that evening. It had been a while since we had been together and I admit I was horny. I hadn't thought much about sex the last few days, what with being at the hospital and working my ass off at night. But now with Doug's crisis just about over and the motion papers finished, my mind was free to wander back to familiar territory, and it wasted no time getting there. I'm not going to tell you what I was thinking, but it was definitely X-rated.

The hearing was scheduled for the next day, and I had some phone calls to make. So as much as I wanted to dwell on my X-rated thoughts, I couldn't. Instead, I asked Connie to order me a tuna salad sandwich on a roll and Diet Coke, then I called Dr. Najari. I reminded him that I needed him in court and asked if there had been any developments with Michael. Dr. Najari said Michael was about the same. He was communicating verbally with members of the staff, but he was still refusing to talk with the therapists about anything meaningful. Dr. Najari continued to believe I had the best chance of getting Michael to talk about his feelings, and I should meet with him as soon as possible. I explained that after the hearing that I had another case to deal with, but I'd come see Michael the following day.

By the time Dr. Najari and I were done talking, my sandwich had arrived, and between bites, I spoke with Dr. Goldman. He had nothing new to report, but confirmed he'd be in court for the hearing the next day. He also said he thought I would be the best one to get Michael to open up about what had happened under the bridge. Both doctors had a lot more confidence in me than I had in myself.

With the phone calls out of the way, I finished my sandwich and soda, then began outlining what I needed to do for Michael's case. When I had filed the motion papers, I had the case name changed from John Doe to Michael Costanza. In one sense, it didn't matter because until Michael was arraigned, there wouldn't be an actual pending case, and there wouldn't be an arraignment for at least thirty more days.

If the judge decided after the thirty days that the case could go forward, then Michael would be arraigned, and things would progress in the normal fashion from that point on. In the meantime, we were in a sort of limbo.

I had a lot of questions about the forensic evidence, all of which would be answered in the Forensic Reports. But I couldn't demand the reports yet because technically there was no pending case. The little information I had so far came from Richie Simone, but he wouldn't yet have the full Forensic Reports. Even if he did, he wasn't likely to give them to me.

Someone in the DA's Office had the reports, but I didn't know who was handling the case. ADA Washington who had handled the original arraignment hearing was still on the case, but only for the upcoming hearing.

The situation was unusual and required a little

"out of the box" thinking. My inclination was to ask Gracie to get me copies of the Forensic Reports. I had never asked Gracie to do anything like that before, and I wasn't sure how she'd react, so I decided to wait until we had sex before asking. I mean, it wasn't really a big deal; I was entitled to the reports. It was simply a matter of when, but why take a chance on her reaction?

I called the little Italian trattoria on Mulberry Street and made a reservation, then I called Gracie again and told her I was taking her out to dinner. She liked the idea of me making a date, and I figured I was scoring points. But then I started feeling a little badly because I was kind of manipulating the situation. Fortunately, my mind wandered quickly back into X-rated thoughts, and I got over my guilty feelings.

I was reviewing the Probation Department Report on Felix Arroyo, my client who was being sentenced the next day, when Tommy showed up. Tommy was working overtime looking for Latanya, but having no luck. Carlos, Latanya's boyfriend from school, still hadn't heard from her and had no idea where she was.

Latanya's mother was still refusing to talk to Tommy. He was getting frustrated, but there wasn't much I could do about it. I told Tommy to keep trying and while he was at it to see if there was anyone willing to testify about Lover Boy's propensity to sexually force himself on unwilling partners. Tommy left, promising to report again when he had something good to tell me.

I had about an hour before Gracie showed up, so I returned to the Probation Department Report on Felix Arroyo. The report was long due mostly to Felix's extensive criminal record.

Felix was one of those scumbag clients I hate. He was a gangbanger who sold drugs to kids, had a record as long as my arm, and had already spent twelve of his thirty-five years behind bars. Hardly a model citizen, this time Felix was charged with armed robbery, attempted murder, assault in the first degree, and resisting arrest. All the crimes occurred while Felix was attempting to rob a jewelry store on Canal Street, and it was all captured in living color on surveillance cameras. Felix's defense was that he said it wasn't him, just somebody who looked like him. Of course, the fingerprint evidence said otherwise.

If convicted, or should I say when convicted, Felix faced over fifty years in prison. That was if the judge imposed the sentences to run consecutively, which was what the DA's Office was asking him to do. Having the sentences run consecutively, meaning one after the other, is rare. But with Felix's record, it was a real possibility.

I managed to work out a plea deal under which the most Felix had to serve was twenty-five years. When I told him that by taking the deal he cut his possible jail time in half, he jumped at it. The deal was the best he was going to get, and he was smart to take it. Of course, the deal needed to be approved by the judge, but I didn't see any problem there.

I had just finished reviewing Felix's papers when Gracie showed up ready for our date. The restaurant wasn't far from my office, so we walked there. Walking through the streets of Chinatown is challenging, but also exciting. The streets are always crowded with people hurrying in all directions. I don't know where they're going in such a hurry, but no one except the tourists walks casually in Chinatown. Then there are the sounds and smells. The sing-song trait of the Chinese language and the aromas of the foods cooking in the many restaurants.

Gracie and I walked side-by-side with her arm hooked around mine. We twisted and turned our way through the crowd, but never lost contact. It's kind of like our life together. We're attached, but we're flexible. We may bend and we may twist, but we don't separate.

But I'm getting too philosophical, and that's not me so much. So let me get back to the important things. The meal that night was great, and since Gracie and I hadn't seen each other in nearly a week, we had a lot to talk about. After dinner, we dropped by Ferrara's Bakery on Grand Street for cannoli and espresso. Then we headed back to Gracie's apartment and topped the evening off with a great roll in the sack.

Afterward, while we were laying there contentedly in each other's arms, I brought up the topic of the Forensic Reports. Gracie thought about my request for a minute, then said it wasn't a big deal and she'd do what she could to get me the reports.

After a couple of really bad days, things were ending well.

CHAPTER 30

The next morning Gracie and I had coffee together, then she headed off to her office, and I headed back to my apartment to shower, shave and get ready for the hearing in Michael's case. The hearing was scheduled for ten o'clock, and I had arranged to meet Dr. Najari and Dr. Goldman at the Worth Street Coffee Shop at nine-fifteen, so I was a little pressed for time. I did manage to squeeze in a call to Doug who was doing fine and was expecting to take Laurie home that afternoon. I reminded him to attend a meeting and told him to call later in the day.

Dr. Najari and Dr. Goldman showed up at the coffee shop on time, and it didn't take long to prepare them for their role at the hearing. If things went as I hoped, neither would have to take the stand. Both had prepared short written reports which I had given to the court and to the DA's Office. Since the DA's Office wasn't opposing our position, it was all basically a formality, but I wasn't taking any chances. No matter what happened at the hearing, I was ready.

Before the hearing started, I caught up with ADA Washington who confirmed receiving the doctors' reports, and her office had no objection to our motion.

The motion was being heard by Judge Cooperman, a reasonable man I had appeared before a number of times. Cooperman was also prompt, so the hearing started right on time.

The first thing the Judge Cooperman said was he had read the papers, including the doctors' reports, so he was fully familiar with the facts of the matter. Since the DA's Office apparently had no objection to my request, he was prepared to grant my motion and issue an order. The proposed order called for Michael Costanza to be held for another thirty days at Kirby while he was evaluated by two psychiatrists from the Department of Mental Health to determine if he was fit to assist in his own defense.

If neither side had anything to add to the record, Judge Cooperman would issue the order. ADA Washington responded she had nothing to add, and I asked only that Dr. Najari be named as one of the examining psychiatrists.

Judge Cooperman noted my request and issued the order including Dr. Najari as one of the psychiatrists. The other examining psychiatrist, Dr. Mitchell, was selected by the judge from a list provided by the Department of Mental Health. In less than fifteen minutes we were done.

Now the clock was really ticking on Michael's case, and I needed to build his defense. I told Dr. Najari I'd be at Kirby the next day to meet with Michael and every day after that until I got him to tell me what had happened under the bridge.

I asked Dr. Najari if he thought bringing Michael's

sister into the picture could help. He wasn't sure, but he didn't think it would hurt, and he asked if she was willing to help. I didn't know, but so long as Dr. Najari didn't think it would be a problem, I was going to give her a call.

I had time before Arroyo's sentencing hearing to call Claire, but it was still too early in California. Besides, I needed some time to consider how I'd approach Claire. The difficult part was figuring out what I expected her to do.

When I got back to the office, Connie told me Gracie had called and wanted me to call her back right away. It was unusual for Gracie to call during the day, so I called her back quickly, hoping nothing was wrong. And nothing was wrong; the news was good.

Copies of the Forensic Reports in the Costanza case would be delivered to her office that afternoon, and if I wanted, I could pick them up at my convenience. I blew Gracie a big kiss and said I'd be by later to pick up the reports and if she wanted, we'd go out to the sushi restaurant for dinner. I asked her what more love can a man show for a woman than to eat raw fish. Gracie had a one-word answer, diamonds. I told you she was sharp and smart.

The Arroyo sentencing hearing was scheduled for one-thirty, and I decided I should at least go see Felix before the hearing. I went down to the holding cells and had him moved into a meeting room. After I had explained to him what would happen during the hearing and the sentence he could expect, he asked me if there was any way he could get out of jail sooner. I said only with a presidential pardon, but I presumed he wasn't a heavyweight political contributor. Not being deterred by my pessimism, Felix asked how he could get one, presumably meaning a presidential pardon. I asked him if he knew who the president was, but he didn't. I wrote down the president's name, along with the address 1600 Pennsylvania Avenue, Washington DC, gave it to Felix, told him to write a letter to the president, and ask for a pardon. Then I went upstairs to the courtroom and waited for the hearing to begin.

The hearing went as expected and Felix was sentenced to twenty-five years in prison. When the sentence was imposed, Felix leaned over to me and asked if the judge was the one he needed to talk to about a pardon. I told him no; he had to write to the president at the address I'd given him, then he had to wait. He asked how long he'd have to wait and as the court officers were taking him away, I told him probably twenty-five years. I thought it was funny, but I don't Felix thought so.

After the hearing, I dropped by Gracie's office to pick up the Forensic Reports. As she handed them to me, she smiled and asked if I had any diamonds for her. I said sheepishly I didn't, and she said, in that case, we would be having sushi for dinner.

CHAPTER 31

Gracie and I had dinner at the new sushi restaurant and even though I was the one who suggested eating there, I wasn't happy. Since the place opened a couple of weeks earlier, we had eaten there at least four or five times, and as far as I was concerned, that was too many times. I probably felt that way because I actually don't like sushi. But under the circumstances, I couldn't complain, so I sat there glumly eating my raw tuna and California roll.

Gracie often said my face is like a mood ring and she could tell just by looking at me what I was thinking. That night she had no problem figuring out what I was thinking, and she said if I intended on getting laid anytime soon I had better improve my attitude.

What was truthfully bothering me wasn't the raw fish; it was the fact that I was anxious to read the Forensic Reports and hadn't been able to do so yet. After I had picked them up at Gracie's office, I went back to my office intending to read them, but I got a call from Doug who asked me to go to a meeting with him. Naturally, I couldn't say no, so I wound up spending the next two hours with Doug at an AA meeting. After that, it was time to hook up with Gracie, and then there I was sitting in the sushi restaurant eating raw fish, feeling sorry for myself and building up this enormous resentment.

It was basically alcoholic thinking at its best, or I should say its worst. In AA, we use the acronym HALT, as a reminder not to get **H**ungry, **A**ngry, **L**onely or **T**ired. But there I was, tired, and hungry, and I was letting myself get angry, and those feelings took over my thinking.

Being an alcoholic, I always wanted instant gratification. Whether it was sex, or a drink or anything else, if I wanted something, I wanted it right then and there. I wanted to read the Forensic Reports, and I was giving in to my alcoholic thinking that I should be allowed to read them when I wanted to read them, and nothing else mattered. It was me, me, me.

By the time I finished my California roll, I had figured out what was happening, and I apologized to Gracie for my attitude. Gracie being the good soul she is, forgave me, adding simply, "If not diamonds, then gold."

We were just finishing dinner when Gracie got a call from her office. It seemed the riding ADA from her unit assigned to cover the Manhattan South Precinct had been rushed to the hospital with a case of appendicitis, and the Detectives from the Special Victims Division had just apprehended a serial rapist they had been after for a couple of months.

The riding ADA is assigned to a precinct house and shows up when the Detectives are interrogating a suspect in a felony case. The Manhattan South Detectives needed an ADA to witness the interrogation of their suspect. Unluckily for Gracie, no one from her unit was on duty that night, so Gracie said she'd handle the matter herself. The Detectives arranged to have a sector car pick her up at the restaurant and take her to the precinct.

Gracie apologized for having to run and said I could go back to her place and wait for her there, but she didn't know how long she'd be. I thought about it, but decided I'd be better off going to my place. I wanted to read the Forensic Reports, and I figured I'd be more comfortable doing so in my apartment. Besides, by the time Gracie got back, it would probably be too late to do anything anyway. We kissed good-bye, I wished Gracie luck and as she went off in the sector car, I hailed a taxi and headed home.

CHAPTER 32

I made myself a cup of coffee and finally took my first look at the Forensic Reports. Collecting evidence at a crime scene is usually the job of the Police Department's Evidence Collection Teams, except in homicide and sexual assault cases. In those cases, the Detective Bureau's Crime Scene Unit collects the evidence. As usual, the Unit had done a good job of processing the crime scene and documenting their findings.

I checked the report for any findings of bodily fluids, hoping there may have been semen found on the mattress or on Lover Boy's clothing. But none was reported. The blood on Lover Boy's clothes and the blood splatter around the body were from the victim. No other blood was found at the crime scene.

Laboratory examinations of Lover Boy's clothes produced no obvious trace evidence from contact with the perpetrator. Scrapings from under Lover Boy's fingernails produced skin cells of unknown origin. DNA analysis revealed the cells were from a female, but there was no identity match in the DNA database. Still, that little nugget of information might be helpful to Michael's defense.

Michael's clothes had been collected from the Tombs where he had changed into a prisoner's jumpsuit after his arrest. A full forensic examination of the clothing had produced no usable evidence, which meant there were no blood stains on Michael's clothing. That was a big plus.

I also found it interesting that there was no mention of any forensic examination of material taken from under Michael's fingernails. When I had first seen Michael, he was a filthy mess except for the tips of his fingers and his fingernails. The tips of his fingers had probably been cleaned during the fingerprinting process at his booking, but I couldn't figure out why they would have cleaned under his nails.

If the cops had cleaned under Michael's nails and if the DA tried to use anything they collected as evidence against him, we would have had a claim of an illegal search and seizure. But it seemed from the Forensic Reports that no material taken from under Michael's fingernails had been delivered for examination and analysis. At least that was one conclusion.

I'm a suspicious guy, and there are times when I question if the cops and the DA are playing fair. This was one of those times. If they had taken the material from under Michael's fingernails and had it analyzed, I'd have a right to see the results. If the material contained DNA matching Lover Boy's DNA, then that would be conclusive proof Michael had physical contact with Lover Boy. A big plus for the DA, so I was sure the DA would risk an illegal search and seizure hearing and try like hell to get the test results into evidence.

On the other hand, if the test results were negative for Lover Boy's DNA, it would be a big plus for the defense. But what if the test results were negative and weren't disclosed? I'd keep that thought in the back of my mind, and if we had to go to trial, it might be an issue I'd raise on cross-examination of the forensic witness.

The hammer which Michael was holding in his hand when arrested had been extensively documented and tested. Laboratory analysis of material on the head of the hammer confirmed it was Lover Boy's blood and brain matter. A full set of fingerprints lifted from the hammer's handle were a 100% match with Michael's fingerprints taken at his booking. The match was with the fingerprints of Michael's right hand which was consistent with Michael being right-handed.

There were no latent fingerprints on the hammer which I found to be interesting. Even if Michael was the only one who handled the hammer, unless the hammer had been wiped clean before he picked it up the last time, it should have some trace fingerprints on it. It was an interesting point, but probably not relevant.

The blood splatter analysis was also interesting. Based on the splatter pattern, the analyst had concluded Lover Boy was vertical to the mattress, that is, standing and not laying on the mattress when the blows to his skull were struck. Had he been horizontal, the blood splatter would have carried to the top of the mattress and beyond, but there was no blood at those locations. Also, there was significant blood accumulation on Lover Boy's neck and the back of his shirt, suggesting he was still standing after the first blows were struck. There was blood splatter on the ground behind where Lover Boy was standing when he was hit, but the photographs of the splatter pattern showed an uneven dispersion. That meant the splatter had either hit an intermediary object, such as the assailant, or something on the ground which was removed before the photographs were taken. The most likely of those choices was the assailant. So why was there no blood splatter on Michael's clothes?

The Forensic Reports were raising some issues about Michael's guilt, and I was starting to think I might have more of a defense than I thought. Most of it was conjecture and circumstantial which might be enough to raise doubts and give me leverage in plea bargaining. But if I hoped to get Michael acquitted, I'd need hard evidence.

It was funny, but I had gone from thinking we didn't have a shot at getting John Doe a day in court or anything less than twenty-five years in prison if we did, to thinking about an acquittal. That's the way it goes sometimes. Not very often, but sometimes.

I was going to look over the Autopsy Report next when I decided to give Claire Molinari a call. It was just past nine-thirty, which would be six-thirty her time, so I hoped she'd be in and I wouldn't be interrupting her dinner.

Claire answered the phone and, of course, she remembered who I was. After assuring me I wasn't bothering her or interrupting her dinner, she asked how Michael was doing. I told her we had finally gotten him to speak, but he wasn't fully communicative and it was going to be a problem. We needed him to talk about what happened under the bridge so I could prepare a defense, but so far he wouldn't talk about it. Claire wanted to know how she could help and I had to admit I didn't know. At some point I wanted her to talk to Michael, but I needed to bounce the idea off the doctors first. What I was looking for was some insight into Michael's past that might help me to better connect with him.

I asked Claire to tell me stories about Michael, stories from their childhood. Anything that could help me understand who Michael was and what kind of man he was or had been, before the war. Claire thought for a moment and then laughed and said she had a good story about Michael.

When Michael was ten years old and she was seven, he had found a pigeon with a broken wing in their backyard. Michael took the pigeon to his room and after bandaging the broken wing, kept the bird there for four weeks while it healed, all along keeping it secret from his parents. Claire wasn't sure if her mother knew about the pigeon being in Michael's room, but if she did she never let on. After four weeks, Michael set the bird free and it flew off, but Claire was pretty sure it kept returning to the yard and the window sill outside Michael's window.

When one of Michael's classmates at St. Kevin's came down with a serious illness and was bedridden for a couple of months, Michael spent four afternoons a week with the boy even though it meant missing the touch football games he loved playing. In high school Michael volunteered to tutor students who were having a tough time with physics, the one subject Michael did good in. He was also very active in the charity drives at the church.

I asked Claire if Michael was ever violent growing up. Had he been in many fights at school or in the streets?

Claire said as far as she knew, and she knew a lot about Michael, he wasn't at all violent growing up. She recalled only one time that Michael got into a fist fight, and it was on the school playground when some older kid was picking on Michael's best friend, Eddie. According to Claire, the other boy was bigger than Michael, but Michael held his own in the fight and eventually it ended in a draw.

When Claire mentioned Michael's best friend Eddie, I asked if she knew where Eddie was now, thinking maybe he could help, but she said Eddie had been killed in a car accident years ago. Besides Eddie, Michael had a lot of friends in the neighborhood, but Claire didn't know where any of them might be.

Then we talked again about Michael's behavior after he returned from Vietnam. The last time we had spoken, Claire had given me a good history of Michael's conduct after his return from the war, at least as far as she knew it. This time I was trying to see if Claire could give me a little insight into Michael's state of mind, so I asked her if Michael ever talked to her about his war experiences.

She said when he got back from Vietnam he wouldn't talk about what happened there, but some nights she'd hear him scream out in his sleep. When she'd ask him about it the next day, he would dismiss the incident as just a nightmare. However, one time when Michael was living with her family in California, he told her he had seen some very bad things happen in Vietnam and not all of it had been done by the enemy. Then he started to cry, and Claire held him in her arms trying to comfort him. Not knowing what to do, she asked him if he had done anything bad hoping if he had, talking about it might help him. He said he hadn't done anything bad himself, but he hadn't stopped the guy who did.

I was on the phone with Claire for the better part of an hour, and at the end of our conversation, I told her I'd stay in touch and would let her know if the doctors thought it was a good idea for her to talk with Michael. I could tell all of it was very hard on Claire, and I felt bad I was putting her through it. But I had to do everything I could to help Michael.

When I got off the phone with Claire, I was physically and emotionally beat. It had been a long day, starting with the hearing that morning, so I put away the Forensic Reports and the Autopsy Report and went to bed. There was no sense trying to get through the Autopsy Report when I was so tired.

CHAPTER 33

The next day I went to Kirby to meet with Michael for the third time since we had our breakthrough a week and a half earlier. At each meeting Michael progressed a bit and although we had some setbacks, at last meeting he was talking in full sentences and responding verbally to my questions. Sadly, the setbacks came when I started asking Michael what had happened under the bridge.

Dr. Najari held regular therapy sessions with Michael trying to free Michael's mind from the memories holding it hostage. Between sessions, he adjusted Michael's medications until he reached a reasonable balance that kept Michael awake and lucid, while at the same time in control of his paralyzing fears.

That morning when I met with Dr. Najari, I told him what Claire had said the night before about Michael's apparent guilt over not having intervened in some incidents he witnessed in Vietnam. Dr. Najari thought that was interesting. He reminded me the first time Michael spoke, he said that he was sorry for what he had done. Although he didn't say specifically what he was sorry for doing, we assumed he was talking about killing Lover Boy. But now with this new wrinkle, maybe he was talking about something that had happened in Vietnam.

Dr. Najari suggested when I sat down with Michael, I should approach the subject of his Vietnam experience cautiously. If I sensed any resistance on his part to talk about it, I should drop it. Dr. Najari feared if I pushed the issue it might jeopardize the progress Michael had made so far. I understood where he was coming from, but I reminded him we now had a deadline, and Michael was going back into the criminal justice system in thirty days. I needed some answers, and I needed them soon.

When I sat down with Michael, he had a smile on his face and I got the impression he was happy to see me. I explained to him I had been to court, and in a little while, he would be going back to court. We needed to prepare for a trial. I asked him if he understood what I was telling him and he nodded.

I asked him how he was feeling and he said he was feeling fine. Then I asked him if he remembered what had happened under the bridge and he nodded his head. I didn't push him for details, I simply said I'd be happy to listen if he wanted to talk about it. He said nothing for a while, then he whispered that he was afraid. I asked him what he was afraid of, but he didn't answer right away. I waited, and after a while, he said he kept dreaming he was back in Vietnam, and everybody around him was dying. He didn't want me to die, but if he talked to me, I might die with the others.

I asked him why he thought that and he said because bad things happened in Vietnam. I asked him to tell me about the bad things. Michael looked away, and for a moment I thought he might be going back into one of his withdrawn states. But then he said: "He shouldn't have done that."

I asked him who he was talking about and what he shouldn't have done. Michael looked back at me, and his eyes started to get a hard look. Then he started to sob, crying out "Why didn't I stop him? Why didn't I stop him?" He was breathing heavily and sobbing.

I didn't know what to do, but my gut told me I had to do something because we were at a critical point, so I moved closer to Michael and put my arms around him as I had done the last time. Then I followed my gut and told Michael whatever happened it wasn't his fault.

Even though I had no idea what Michael was talking about, I told him there was nothing he could have done to stop it. That seemed to calm him, so I continued. I said sometimes things happen we can't control; sometimes bad things happen and we can't stop them from happening. But that doesn't make us bad.

Michael stayed with his head resting against my chest and I could feel his breathing returning to normal. When I thought Michael had quieted down enough, I asked him what happened that he couldn't stop. Again, he didn't answer right away. He took a deep breath, sat up and then looking me straight in the eye he said "Logan killed that girl after he raped her."

I wanted to call a time out and consult with Dr. Najari, but I knew I shouldn't risk breaking the moment. I had to figure out on my own what to do next.

I took a chance and said, "Michael, you didn't rape that girl, did you?" He shook his head. Then I asked what he saw Logan do. He went quiet again for a few moments, then he said it had happened in a small village where the squad was bivouacked. He hadn't seen how it started, but he saw Logan getting off a naked girl's body, pulling up his pants, and laughing. The girl was crying. When I asked if he saw Logan kill the girl, he again shook his head. He said right after Logan got up, the squad was sent to a firefight outside the village. During the fight, the squad got separated, and his group was the last one to get back to the village. That was when he saw the girl laying there dead, a bullet hole in her forehead. He later learned Logan's group was the first to get back to the village.

I held my breath and asked Michael if the guy under the bridge was trying to rape a girl. He nodded affirmatively. But when I asked him for details he clammed up again. He gently pushed me away, and he got a distant look in his eyes and seemed to drift off. That's when Dr. Najari, who had been watching the session through the two-way mirror, came into the room. He said it was time for a break. Michael needed his medications, and he and I needed to talk. I gave Michael a pat on the shoulder and told him I'd be back, then went with Dr. Najari to his office.

Dr. Najari was very excited. He believed we had hit another breakthrough which could be the key to a successful treatment for Michael. He wanted to work with the new information, and he was afraid bringing up the recent incident under the bridge might cause Michael to regress and withdraw. It put me in a tough position. I wanted to help Michael get better, but in less than thirty days we were going to court, and if I didn't have the information I needed from Michael, he was going to prison for a long time, cured or not.

When I put it that way, Dr. Najari understood the problem and agreed I should continue trying to get Michael to talk about what happened under the bridge. But he asked if he could be present when we spoke. I had no problem with that as he would become part of the defense team, and anything Michael said would be protected by both the doctor-patient privilege and the attorney-client privilege.

When Dr. Najari and I went back into the room with Michael, he seemed to be more alert, and he smiled at us. I reminded Michael why I was there and told him we needed to talk about what had happened under the bridge so I could prepare his case. He nodded, and I took it as a go-ahead. I asked if he remembered what happened that day. He nodded again, but offered no details.

When I asked him to tell me what happened, he started talking about Logan again. I was about to interrupt him, but Dr. Najari grabbed me by the arm and shook his head. I kept my mouth shut.

Michael went on talking about Logan for a bit, then he slammed his fist down on the table and went quiet again, dropping his head to his chest. Dr. Najari interceded at that point and told Michael there was nothing he could have done at the time, and there was nothing he could do now that would undo what Logan had done. Michael looked up at Dr. Najari who continued. He reminded Michael the rape was over before he saw what Logan was doing, and he never saw Logan kill the girl. It wasn't his fault, and he had to stop blaming himself for what Logan had done.

Michael sat quietly, but he was keeping his head

up, which I took as a good sign. Dr. Najari may have thought so, too, because he suggested I continue my conversation with Michael. Over the next hour and a half, I questioned Michael about what happened under the bridge.

Progress was slow because, while Michael was answering most of my direct questions with a yes or no, he wouldn't elaborate at all. Even some of my direct questions, like did he hit Lover Boy with the hammer more than once, he wouldn't answer. By the end of our session, I had established there was a girl present at the scene, and Lover Boy was trying to force himself on her. Michael didn't deny hitting Lover Boy with the hammer, but neither would he confirm it or give any details.

At the end of the session with Michael, I met again with Dr. Najari and together we called Dr. Goldman. After discussing what had happened during the session, both doctors agreed Dr. Najari should work with Michael during the next couple of days dealing strictly with Michael's Vietnam issues, and I should stay away during that time.

Dr. Goldman believed if Dr. Najari could help Michael resolve the conflict from his Vietnam experience, Michael would be in a better position to talk about the recent incident. I needed Michael's cooperation desperately and if not talking to him for a couple of days was going to help, then I was okay with the plan. I did remind the doctors time was running out, and we needed to move quickly.

I left the Kirby Forensic Psychiatric Center that afternoon knowing only two things for sure. One, Michael's case was going forward and two, I had a lot of work to do to establish Michael's defense.

CHAPTER 34

After I left Kirby, I found a taxi nearby and headed back downtown. I now knew my theory that Michael was protecting a girl from being raped was right, but I still needed to find that girl. I called Tommy and told him what had happened with Michael and asked if he had made any progress in locating Latanya Jefferson. He said "No," but he was working on it, and he'd go back to the housing project and check around again.

I didn't like the idea because the TB Gangsters were a vicious group and they didn't take kindly to outsiders on their turf. Tommy said not to worry, and even though I knew he had his gun and was a black belt in that Taekwondo thing, I still worried about him. He just laughed and said he'd check in soon.

Next, I called Joe Benjamin and filled him in on developments. Joe asked if I was comfortable holding off seeing Michael while the doctors tried to work out his Vietnam problems. I told him I wasn't happy about it, but I didn't see that I had much choice in the matter. He agreed and said if I needed any help from his office to give him a call.

I called Doug to see how things were going. I had spoken to him earlier and knew Laurie was being discharged from the hospital, and I wanted to make sure everything had gone okay. He confirmed all had gone well and Laurie was resting comfortably. He and the kids were happy to have her home.

I asked him if he needed me to do anything and when he said no, I suggested we go to a meeting together. At first Doug was reluctant, but with a little pushing he relented and agreed to meet me at the eight o'clock meeting in the church around the corner from his apartment. It was a bit of a haul for me coming from Lower Manhattan to the Upper West Side, but it wasn't anything Doug hadn't done for me a million times.

When I was drinking, I wouldn't go out of my way for anyone or for anything. I was a selfish son of a bitch who cared about one thing and only one thing, and that was drinking. But that changed when I got sober. It didn't change all at once, and I can't even tell you when it changed, but it changed. I started caring about people besides myself, and I started feeling better about myself.

That's a big thing in getting sober, rebuilding your sense of self-worth. Convincing yourself you're a worthwhile person. After a long time of not caring, of hurting people, and of being totally and completely self-absorbed, you can't help but feel worthless. You try to ignore it and pretend you're not that bad, but there are times when the booze can't keep the truth from bubbling up into your consciousness. In those moments you know. You know what you've become and you hate yourself for it. But you won't change, so you drink more hoping to make the feelings go away.

I go to meetings so I won't forget what it was like, and I sponsor pigeons so I can help them get back their sense of self-worth.

Speaking of pigeons, I decided to call Peter and see how he was doing. Peter had been in the program for over six months and was doing well, so we didn't speak every day. But as I rode in the taxi heading back downtown, I realized it had been nearly a week since we last spoke and that worried me.

I called Peter's cell phone and got his voice mail which wasn't unusual because Peter didn't always answer his cell phone when he was in his office. I left him a curt message telling him if he didn't call back soon, I would fire him as my pigeon. Of course, I wouldn't do that, and Peter knew it, but I have a reputation to protect.

I had just hung up when my cell phone rang, and it was Gracie. She was checking in to see what we were doing that evening. She hadn't gotten home from the Manhattan South Precinct Station House until nearly two o'clock in the morning. So she was tired, and she was leaving her office early. If it was okay with me, she wanted to spend the night at home and have takeout for dinner.

That was fine with me, but I played the situation a little to get Gracie to go along with having pizza. Normally Gracie likes to eat what she calls "healthy," and I call "boring." So when we eat in, if it's not Chinese food, she usually wants a salad with tofu or something else like that.

Frankly, I don't know what tofu is, and I truly don't

want to know because I'm never going to eat it. Anyway, Gracie was too tired to argue with me, so I told her I'd be at her place by five-thirty with a nice Neapolitan pizza. The last thing she said was not to get a big one, so I felt kind of guilty when I ordered a large pie. But when you think about it, there isn't a lot of difference between the large and small sizes. Besides, I always have them cut the pie into eight pieces so what's the difference? Gracie would eat two and I'd eat the rest. Gracie would say it wasn't healthy for me, and I'd smile and belch. What can I tell you? It was a tradition.

I had no sooner hung up with Gracie than my phone rang and it was Peter. He said things were good, he was still sober, and I didn't need to worry about him so much. I told him so long as I was his sponsor, I'd decide when I should worry. I was tempted to hang up at that point, but I didn't. I was getting soft.

CHAPTER 35

Gracie didn't break my chops too much over the large pizza. I think she was too tired. When we were done eating, I had to run off to the AA meeting uptown with Doug, and Gracie said she was heading to bed, so I told her I'd go to my place after the meeting and call her in the morning.

I took the subway uptown and met Doug outside of the Redeemer Presbyterian Church on West 83rd Street. We chatted, and I could tell he was okay. As a matter of fact, he was better than okay and was anxious to take back the role of sponsor. Truthfully, I was glad to give it up. For the last couple of days, I felt like the student trying to teach the professor, or the son taking over his father's business. I figured I had done a good enough job because Doug was fine, but I was glad to be his pigeon again.

The meeting was okay, not great, but okay. That's just the way it is. Sometimes meetings are great and sometimes they're not. Two things you can always find at an AA meeting are coffee and nuts. But sometimes there's no coffee. I think you get what I mean by that.

That night it wasn't so much about the meeting as it was about me. So much about alcoholism is in your head that it's scary. I mean, when you forget that and you let your attitudes take control, you're in as much trouble as when you sit with a bottle of scotch in front of you. But I must say no matter how bad I think a meeting is, I always feel better when I leave a meeting than I did going in. That night was no exception, so I was feeling good when I left Doug on the corner of West 83rd Street and Amsterdam Avenue after the meeting.

I went home hoping to catch the end of the Yankees game. They were playing the Red Sox, and that's usually a good game. But on the way home I kept thinking about Michael's case, and I remembered I hadn't read the Autopsy Report. So when I got home, I pulled it out of my briefcase and read it carefully. I should have watched the Yankees game.

The report came from the Office of the Chief Medical Examiner of the City of New York. It was thorough and detailed as usual, but not very helpful. In the first section of the report, the Medical Examiner concluded the cause of death was "blunt force trauma to the back-left side of the decedent's cranium." As for the mechanism of death, the Medical Examiner reported: "two (2) splintering fractures of the parietal bone and one (1) splintering fracture of the occipital bone accompanied by lethal damage to the parietal and occipital lobes of the decedent's brain." The manner of death was "Homicide."

The time of death was estimated to be between ten to twelve hours before the body was discovered or, in other words, between six and eight PM the prior day.

In simple terms, William, Lover Boy, Johnson was beaten to death with a hammer. He was hit three times on the back of his head with sufficient force to splinter his skull and damage his brain. All of that I already knew and it wasn't particularly troubling seeing it in the Autopsy Report. The timeline matched up with Carlos' statement of when he saw Latanya running into her apartment crying. I wondered why Michael was still holding the hammer in his hand twelve hours after the murder. But that wasn't the most troubling part of the report.

What followed in the report was the troubling part. According to the Medical Examiner, the pattern of the fatal hammer wounds on Johnson's skull indicated the assailant was probably left-handed and probably six to eight inches shorter than Johnson who was six-two. I quickly checked Michael's medical records. He was right-handed and five-eleven.

In most cases that would be a good thing because it could be used to raise reasonable doubt. But in this case, it was a complication that might very well sink the justification defense. If there was someone besides Michael at the crime scene trying to stop Johnson from raping Latanya, they could have done so without killing him. Besides, even if someone else had been the one who had wielded the hammer, Michael was the one holding it when the cops arrived, and by not talking to the police he could possibly have made himself a co-conspirator to the homicide. A co-conspirator without a justification defense. At a minimum, the DA might try to charge him with hindering the investigation.

Assuming there were two other people at the crime scene besides the victim and Michael, I needed to know who they were. The only person who could tell me that was Michael, and he wasn't telling me. Sometimes the practice of law sucked, and this was one of those times.

The best I could think of doing with this new information was to talk to Richie Simone and see if I could interest him in reopening his investigation into the murder. If he thought it was worthwhile, I'd ask him to join me at the DA's Office to officially get the investigation reopened.

If I couldn't get the DA and cops to re-investigate the case, it would all fall on Tommy.

CHAPTER 36

They say if you practice law long enough you'll eventually get a case which surprises you. It was during the chaos with Michael's case, actually the day after I read the Autopsy Report, that I met Dr. Tai. I use the term doctor advisedly because that was an issue. One of several issues.

It had started out simply enough. Tommy had called and told me his grandfather had a friend, who had a friend, who needed a lawyer, and the old man had recommended me. The referral wasn't anything unusual; old man Shoo sent me a number of clients over the years. It was a criminal case which was right in my wheelhouse. But what made the case unusual was that the man, Kuan-Yin Tai, wasn't charged with violating the New York State Penal Law. He was charged with violating the New York State Education Law.

Dr. Tai had allegedly engaged in the unauthorized practice of medicine, a Class E felony punishable by up to four years in prison. If you happen to injure one of your "patients," then the charges increase to reckless endangerment or even felony assault. Since both are Class D felonies, the possible jail time increases to seven years. Who would have thought playing doctor could land you in prison?

Dr. Tai had already been booked and was free on $100,000 cash bail. As part of the bail arrangement, he had to surrender his Chinese passport to ensure he wouldn't flee the country. Upset with the bail terms, Dr. Tai had complained about his lawyer to old man Shoo who suggested he call me.

I usually won't take over a case from another lawyer, especially when I don't think the lawyer has done anything wrong because the problem most times is the client, not the lawyer. That's one reason I liked the 18B cases; the clients don't have the option of firing you. But this was an unusual case, and the lawyer Dr. Tai had been using was a local hack with a questionable reputation for legal ability, so I agreed to meet with Dr. Tai.

After talking with Dr. Tai, it was clear either his lawyer had no idea what he was doing in this case, or Dr. Tai hadn't been paying very much attention. Knowing the lawyer, I figured it was the former and I agreed to take over the case. I asked Connie to draw up a retainer agreement with a healthy fee arrangement and a large part of it up front.

Practicing medicine without a license isn't as rare as you might think. There are a lot of fake doctors practicing, especially in immigrant communities, and Chinatown has had more than its share of these jokers. Every so often the New York State Attorney General sends out a team of investigators to look for the quacks, and usually the arrests make big news.

Most times the cases are a clear-cut matter. But things get a little more complicated when you start talking about the field of Chinese medicine, some of which cannot be legally practiced without a license in New York. In Dr. Tai's case, it turned out to be a combination of issues. But to fully understand what it was all about, you need to know about Traditional Chinese Medicine, or TCM as it's known.

TCM dates back some 2500 years and involves a combination of herbal medicines, acupuncture, exercise, and massage. TCM is recognized as a legitimate medical science and, in fact, there's a New York College of Traditional Chinese Medicine offering a Master of Science in Health Science degree. While the practice of herbology does not require a license in New York state, the practice of acupuncture does.

Acupuncture licensing was one of the issues in Dr. Tai's case, the simple issue. Dr. Tai had a degree in TCM from Shanghai University and after legally immigrating to the United States ten years ago, he opened an office on Doyers Street in Chinatown. Regrettably, Dr. Tai failed to acquire an acupuncture license. The other issue, the more serious issue, involved Dr. Tai's other area of practice. It seemed after a couple of years practicing TCM strictly, Dr. Tai had branched out a bit and wandered into the field of traditional western medicine. Specifically, he began performing abortions, mostly on Chinese women in the country illegally.

Dr. Tai said it began as a favor for a friend which escalated into an occasional thing, done as an accommodation for friends or friends of friends. But then he became addicted to the tax-free cash, and it became a regular part of his practice. Eventually, it became the major part of his practice and it led to his downfall.

Word of mouth is a powerful thing in Chinatown, and it didn't take long for word of Dr. Tai's special practice to get around. Once word spread outside of Chinatown, Dr. Tai found he had more clients than he could handle on a part-time basis. Soon his backroom abortion practice was taking up more space in his office than his TCM practice, so he opened a new larger clinic on East Broadway with enough room to accommodate both practices.

Dr. Tai was pulling in lots of money, most of it in cash, and he was investing heavily in real estate not only in the United States, but overseas as well. He was also acting as a front man for friends in China investing in real estate in California. All that activity had put him on the Internal Revenue Service's radar, and they were auditing five years of his income tax returns. Dr. Tai wasn't worried because he and his accountant had covered his tracks well, so he gave little thought to the audits or the IRS.

They say it's the little things that trip you up and that was the case with Dr. Tai. He was right in believing his financial tracks were covered well, and the IRS was having a difficult time putting a case together against him. But a bright young IRS Agent of Chinese descent auditing Dr. Tai's business expenses found something he thought unusual. He was reviewing invoices for medical equipment purchased by Dr. Tai for his new clinic on East Broadway when he came across invoices for surgical-related equipment and supplies. Knowing that TCM did not involve any surgical or invasive procedures beyond acupuncture, he called the situation to the attention of his bosses.

The information was turned over to the New York DA's Office which, after a preliminary investigation, turned the matter over to the New York State Department of Education. And that was how it came to be that Dr. Tai was seated in my office telling me his tale of woe. His clinic had been closed, and he was facing possible jail time.

I take no public position on the issue of abortion because it's not anybody's business how I feel about it. I'm not running for public office. God knows what a disaster that would be. And I'm not in a position to prevent anyone from having an abortion, so what I think about abortion doesn't matter to anyone but me. And maybe God, but I'm not sure about that. At any rate, I don't let my personal feelings get in the way of my professional practice, except when it comes to rapists and child molesters.

I told Dr. Tai I would get in touch with the DA's Office which was prosecuting the case and see what kind of deal I could work out. I warned him he could face jail time and whatever we did in this case could have an impact on the charges the IRS brought against him. I also reminded him I only represented him in the state felony case and not in the IRS matter.

I've worked in Chinatown long enough to know if I couldn't work out a deal with no jail time, Dr. Tai would take off back to China. The $100,000 cash bail he had posted was meaningless to him and surrendering his passport was a joke. In Chinatown, if you had the right connections you could change your identity and passport as easily and as quickly as you changed your underwear.

If Tai skipped out, the DA would be upset and want to prosecute the case with the defendant in absentia, meaning absent, but who cared? It was, after all, only a violation of the New York State Education Law. Dr. Tai wasn't likely to make the FBI's top ten most wanted list nor would Interpol be interested in his case. In the end, in the interest of economics, the case would be dismissed.

I now had two reasons to go to the DA's Office. One, to try and work something out for Dr. Tai and two, to see if I could get the DA to reopen the investigation into Lover Boy's death. I called Gracie and asked her if she could find out who I should talk to in each case. I told her Shayna Washington had handled the original arraignment hearing in Michael's case, but I was pretty sure somebody else had the case by now. Gracie promised to check it out and get back to me.

In the meantime, Tommy had shown up, and I needed to talk with him.

CHAPTER 37

I told Tommy about the Autopsy Report on Lover Boy and the problems it created for our defense. We had to find out if there was indeed a third person at the scene of the crime at the time of the murder and if so, who and why. Short of that, we had figured out another way to make the facts fit our scenario.

It's hard to argue with the facts, especially when they're coming from the Medical Examiner. But you can argue with the conclusions, and that's what I was looking to do.

The facts were simple; Lover Boy had been hit three times on the back left side of his skull with blows that came in an upward pattern from a hammer identified as the one in Michael's hand when the police arrived. The Medical Examiner had concluded the perpetrator was left-handed, so the first question was could the blows have been struck by someone who was right-handed? As for the height of the assailant, which the Medical Examiner had concluded was six to eight inches shorter than Lover Boy, the question was, did the physical evidence rule out the possibility the assailant was taller? I couldn't answer these questions, but I knew someone who could.

Among the experts on the 18B Panel list are trained Medical Examiners, any one of whom could answer my questions, but one of whom was particularly good at it. He was Dr. James Garland who I had used as an expert in a couple of cases, and I liked him. He was smart, made a good appearance, had great credentials and most importantly he had a way with judges and juries. The only problem was that he only did one or two 18B cases a year, and I wasn't sure he'd take the case.

I needed Joe Benjamin's approval to hire any expert witness and while I knew he'd approve my request, I was hoping he had a relationship with Garland, and could convince him to take on Michael's case. I called Joe, told him about the Autopsy Report and said I wanted Garland on the case, but I was afraid he'd turn me down. Joe said he didn't know Garland personally, but he knew someone who was Garland's friend, and he'd reach out to him. He promised to do it right away, and I should wait to hear from him before I did anything else about engaging an expert.

Tommy had nothing new to report on his investigation. He was keeping in touch with Carlos and making regular trips to the housing project trying to find Latanya, but so far he had nothing. I was getting desperate and told Tommy I wanted to talk to Latanya's mother myself. He didn't think that was a good idea. It seemed Latanya's mother was staying put these days and as far as Tommy knew she hadn't left the project at all. If I were going to see her, I'd have to go into the project, and Tommy said that was too dangerous. I reminded him he had gone to see Latanya's mother, and he said he did it with a gun in his pocket. Good point. So what if he came along and brought his gun?

We argued about it, but Tommy gave in when I said I was going to see the woman with or without him. He said he'd take me, but we had to go during daylight hours, and while inside the project I had to do whatever he said.

I don't like taking orders from anybody, but I didn't have much of a choice but to agree. I wanted to see Latanya's mother, but to be honest, I wasn't going into the project without Tommy and his gun. I'd like to think in my younger days it wouldn't have been a problem, but that's not true. I've always been smart enough to know when I'm outgunned and when to avoid a fight. Even during my worst drinking days when I thought I was bulletproof, I knew enough to avoid fights I couldn't win, which were most of them. So occasionally I'd get knocked on my ass, but that was the worst of it.

Did you ever watch two drunks square off against each other? It's comical, sad in so many ways, but comical nonetheless. There's always a lot of yelling and a lot of "Oh yeahs," but rarely are punches thrown. Usually, because both guys are too drunk to stand up straight and throw a punch without knocking themselves off balance. Soon people get bored with the whole thing and either walk away, or some kind soul in the audience will break it up, much to the relief of the combatants.

Anyway, Tommy and I were planning our visit to Mrs. Jefferson when Joe Benjamin called back with good news. Dr. Garland had agreed to take on the case and was awaiting my call.

CHAPTER 38

I sent Tommy away and called Dr. Garland. He said he remembered me from a case a couple of years back and he looked forward to working on this case. I asked him what made him decide to take the case and he said two things. One, he owed a friend a favor and two, he had a soft place in his heart for Vietnam War veterans.

I believe there are a lot of people who have a soft place in their hearts for Vietnam vets and they should. I met a lot of Vietnam vets in AA and heard their stories, and I think those guys got a raw deal. They fought in an unpopular war and came home to a public that was not only ungrateful, but at times hostile. They were treated like they started the war when in truth all they did was what this country asked them to do and at great expense. I don't know if fighting the Vietnam War was the right or wrong thing to do, but I do know we owe something to those young kids whom we'd sent off to fight for us. I was glad people like Dr. Garland felt the same way, and they were willing to do something to help the veterans.

I gave Dr. Garland all the information I could over the phone, and promised to fax a retainer letter and a full copy of the forensic and Autopsy Reports to him right away. I told him the deadline we were under, and he promised to get back to me as quickly as he could.

When I got off the phone with Dr. Garland, Connie told me Gracie had called and left a message. Dr. Tai's case was being handled by Joe Fuller, and Michael's case was being handled by Marion Marshall. I knew Joe Fuller from my days in the DA's Office which could be a good or bad thing depending on how I had treated him. I couldn't remember doing anything bad to Joe, but frankly there was a lot I didn't remember from those days, and what I did remember was hazy at best.

I called Joe, figuring I'd find out soon enough what Joe thought about me. Apparently, I hadn't done anything obnoxious to him because when I introduced myself, he acted like we were old buddies or at least acquaintances. When I told him I was representing Dr. Tai and wanted to set up an appointment to talk about the case, he said that was a good idea, and we should do it as soon as possible. It sounded a little strange, so I asked him why the rush. He said the feds would be bringing multiple income tax evasion charges against the good doctor very soon, and he'd like his case against Dr. Tai resolved before that happened.

Joe knew as well as I did if Tai was convicted of any crime that involved him going to jail, he was going to skip the country. I don't know a great deal about income tax law, but I know if you're convicted of income tax fraud and evasion, you're going away for at least five years. The feds don't hand out very favorable plea deals and even the favorable ones they hand out require some jail time. The only way to avoid jail time with the feds is to turn in a bigger fish. In Dr. Tai's case, there were no bigger fishes to sacrifice, so the probability of him not going to jail on the federal charges was about the same as the Cubs winning the World Series.

As I said before, when a defendant skips out it causes problems for the Prosecutor, and that was what Joe was hoping to avoid. He figured if we reached a plea deal, he could close out his case before the feds brought their case, and then when Tai skipped, it would be the feds' problem and not his. It was good thinking, and it put me in a good negotiating position. We agreed to meet the next morning at Joe's office. I said I'd bring the coffee.

I was about to call Marion Marshall about Michael's case when Dr. Najari called. It had been a week since I had last seen Michael and agreed to stay away while Dr. Najari and his staff worked with him. The news was good. After learning about this Logan character and the rape, Dr. Najari had been able to reach Michael on a new level, and he was starting to make progress. After consulting with Dr. Goldman who had also visited with Michael, Dr. Najari felt Michael was at a point where I could meet with him and discuss what had happened under the bridge. I told Dr. Najari I'd be there in an hour.

CHAPTER 39

Remembering my last taxi ride to Kirby, I wasn't anxious to do it again, but I wanted to get there as quickly as I could, so I had no choice in the matter. Getting into a New York City taxi is like playing Russian roulette. It's a chance affair, and you have no way of knowing if you're going to survive. I know I exaggerate, but until you've ridden in as many taxis as I have don't discount what I'm saying. Remember that you stand an equal chance of dying in the taxi from a heart attack as you do from dying in a crash.

But I thought I was lucky that day. Why? The driver was a Jamaican named Lamont who happened to be a Catholic. The fact he was a Catholic was amazing because only two percent of Jamaicans are Catholic. I knew he was a Catholic because he had a St. Christopher statue on the dashboard of the taxi. For any of you who are not familiar with the finer points of Catholicism, St. Christopher is the patron saint of travelers and having a St. Christopher medal on your person or in your car assures you of a safe journey. At least that's what you believe if you're Irish or Italian Catholic. Having a whole statue of St. Christopher on your dashboard is the gold standard, so I had to feel safe, right?

Well it all turned out to be wrong. The moment Lamont hit the FDR Drive, he had me wishing Vikesh was behind the wheel. Lamont had excellent hand and foot coordination as evidenced by the fact that every time he hit the brakes, which was every five seconds, he'd hit the horn. So there we went up the FDR Drive, barreling down on slower moving vehicles until we came within inches of their bumpers and then Lamont would hit the brakes and the horn. I must say the maneuver did get the attention of most drivers in the slower moving vehicles and they made concerted efforts to get out of Lamont's way as quickly as possible.

Of course, being in New York City, there were some drivers who refused to move out of Lamont's way and instead gave him the middle finger salute. Undeterred by these drivers' failure to cooperate, Lamont went around them, not bothering to worry about traffic in the other lanes. Of course, the fact that both side view mirrors on Lamont's taxi were dangling from the doors didn't help. The result was most often a hit trick, with the other drivers slamming on their brakes while simultaneously hitting their horn and giving Lamont the middle finger salute.

Lamont seemed unable to hear my pleas and cries for mercy over the reggae music blaring from the radio, so I was left with two choices. Close my eyes and pray or leap from the moving vehicle. I closed my eyes and prayed. What I estimated to be ten minutes and dozens of middle finger salutes later, we arrived at Kirby, and I climbed shakily out of the death mobile.

Once again, thanks to a taxi driver I was grateful and surprised, to be alive. As I paid Lamont, I vowed never to get into his taxi again. That added up to about four hundred, the total number of taxis I vowed never to get into again. Okay, so maybe I'm a little over-dramatic, but I think you can understand where it comes from. If you can't understand it, just come to New York City and take a taxi ride.

I met Dr. Najari in his office, and he was surprised I had gotten there so quickly. I was afraid if I told him the story I just told you, he'd put me on his couch and start treatment, so instead I just said traffic was light.

Dr. Najari was very pleased with the progress Michael had made in the last few days and thought I'd be happy as well. He said Michael now communicated entirely in full sentences and rarely regressed into his silent mode.

Earlier that morning Dr. Najari told Michael I was coming to see him to talk about his legal case. Michael had understood what Dr. Najari was saying and agreed to the meeting. It was after that conversation Dr. Najari had called me. I hoped we were finally going to get to the truth.

Dr. Najari gave me some advice as to how I should approach Michael about the events, suggesting I work my way up to the details, beginning with casual matters. I asked if I should mention Michael's sister, Claire, and that I had spoken with her. Dr. Najari said he didn't think it would hurt, so he left it up to me to decide what to do about it.

The moment I went into the conference room and saw Michael I could tell things had changed. He looked much more relaxed, the tension was gone from his face, and his eyes were soft and calm. He stood, smiled at me, said "Good morning," and stuck his hand out for me to shake. I shook his hand and told him I was glad to see him doing so well. We took our seats, and I began.

Heeding the advice from Dr. Najari, I asked Michael how he came to be living under the bridge and what he recalled about his time there. He said as far as he could recall after he left Phoenix a couple of years ago, he had walked east with no destination in mind. He had spent some time in St. Louis and Atlanta, then headed north. He stayed mostly in bigger cities because it was easier to get lost. In smaller towns, people tried to help him, but he didn't want their help. In the big cities he could get food and clothes from the shelters, and he would be left alone.

About a year ago he got to New York City and had been moving about the city ever since. For a while, he lived in the tunnels of Grand Central Station, a popular area for the homeless, but the police had begun a crackdown in the area, so he moved south. Another place he found a lot of homeless people was under the Williamsburg Bridge, and he had stayed there for a while. But it was too crowded for him and too many people hassled him, so he moved a little further south to under the Manhattan Bridge. He found the old construction storage site and enough material to build a little hut and that's where he had been living.

So far Michael had remained relaxed and was talking calmly, and I wanted him to stay that way, but I needed to get into some details. I looked over to Dr. Najari who suggested Michael tell us a little bit about what it was like living under the bridge.

Michael said it wasn't bad. He had his places where he got food from dumpsters behind restaurants or behind food stores. Sometimes he'd go to shelters for a hot meal, and occasionally if the temperature dropped really low he'd go there to sleep. But mostly he stayed in his little hut because he felt safe there. He didn't have as many nightmares when he stayed under the bridge by himself. Sometimes he'd get lonely, and that's when he'd start hearing the voices, and then the nightmares would come back.

I felt we had built a rapport between us and I decided to talk to Michael about Claire, hoping it might strengthen whatever tie we had built. I told him I had spoken with Claire and she was worried about him. When Michael heard that, he looked a little sad, and I was afraid I had overstepped in bringing up Claire. But then he smiled and said he hadn't spoken with Claire in years and he felt guilty for all the pain he had caused her. He asked how she and her family were doing, and I said they were doing well and Claire wanted to talk with him. I was pushing the truth a little because Claire never actually said she wanted to talk to him, only that she would.

Michael wanted to talk with Claire, but he didn't want to burden her with his legal problems. When he said that, it gave me an opening to talk about his defense. I glanced over to Dr. Najari who apparently understood why I was looking his way and he gave me a nod of approval.

I told Michael it was a good reason to get his legal

problems squared away, but to do that I needed some information. Then I asked Michael to tell me what happened under the bridge the day of the incident. He hesitated, but only for a moment. Then he told me the story.

He had gone to one of the dumpsters behind an Italian restaurant and collected some half-eaten pasta meals dumped there after the luncheon crowd had left. He took the food back to his hut and was eating when about eight o'clock this guy showed up. A short time later three girls came by. He had seen the guy hanging out around the park across the highway, but he'd never seen him inside the storage area.

Two of the girls were laughing and joking with the guy, but the third girl looked like she didn't want to be there. I assumed at that point that the third girl was Latanya Jefferson.

Then the guy grabbed the third girl and told the other two to get lost. The two girls left while the third girl was struggling to get out of the guy's grip. Michael said he didn't know what was going on, but he wasn't going to get involved because he didn't want any trouble with the cops. He was afraid if the cops came they'd make him leave his hut. But then the guy began trying to take off the girl's clothes, and that's when he came up behind him and hit him with the hammer.

It was a good story, but I knew it wasn't entirely true. I asked Michael where he'd hit the guy, and he said he'd hit him in the head. I asked where in the head and Michael said it was in the back of his head, while moving his right hand and arm up and down to show me how. I asked him how many times he hit him and Michael said he didn't remember exactly, but it was more than once. When I asked him if he was standing up when he hit the guy, I think Michael realized there was a problem with his story, so he said that he thought so. It was a strange answer, but a good dodge that gave him time to think things out.

I decided not to press matters at that point and asked what happened to the girl. Michael said she ran off and he never saw her again. He didn't know her name or where she lived.

I thanked Michael for talking with me and said we had done enough for the time being, and I'd be back soon to talk some more. Michael smiled and said "Okay," then asked if he could speak with Claire. I promised to check with her and get back to Dr. Najari, so he could make the arrangements.

When we got back to Dr. Najari's office, I explained to him what was in the Autopsy Report, and how it was at odds with what Michael had just told us. I said I had an expert who would try to fit it all together, but I was sure there was a third person who had committed the actual murder, and Michael was protecting that person. Dr. Najari was at a loss to explain why that might be, but he felt strongly that we needed to explore the matter carefully.

I said I'd call Claire that evening and if she were agreeable to speaking with Michael, I'd give her Dr. Najari's phone number. In any event, I'd be back very soon to talk with Michael again.

It was after five o'clock when I left Kirby, and as much as I wanted to get back downtown as quickly as possible I still wasn't quite over my taxi ride there, so I ignored the line of taxis and took the bus and train back. All the way back downtown I thought about Michael, and wondered if he could have used his left hand to kill Johnson. Why were Michael's fingerprints the only fingerprints on the hammer? Who else was at the crime scene and why?

I had a lot of questions and no answers. If I couldn't get the answers from Michael, I needed to get them from someone else and so far, Latanya Jefferson was the star candidate. Only I couldn't find her. I needed to talk with Latanya's mother and soon.

CHAPTER 40

On the way back downtown I called Doug to check on how things were going with him. Everything was good, Laurie was feeling much better and had insisted he go back to work, so he was in his office. The last of the lab reports and biopsy results had come back, and everything was looking good. Laurie's radiation treatments would begin in a couple of days, and the doctors were confident if there were any cancer cells left after the surgery, the radiation treatments would destroy them.

Laurie had been through a lot, and so had Doug and the kids. It would have been easy for a recovering alcoholic to fall into an ocean of self-pity and use the situation as an excuse to drink. But God bless Doug; he had risen above his own pain and gave strength and hope to Laurie and the kids. I only hoped if I faced a similar situation with Gracie, I'd have the same strength and courage Doug had shown.

When you're forced to think about things like that, you realize how much you love someone. Not that you don't know it anyway, it's just you become more conscious of it. So I called Gracie to make plans for dinner, and I told her I loved her. I knew she knew, but I don't say it enough, and I fear the day when I wouldn't be able to tell her that I love her.

I still hadn't called Marion Marshall, the DA handling Michael's case, but at that point, I didn't know what I could say. I had too many questions and not enough answers, and until I had some answers, there wasn't much I could say to the DA. So instead of calling Ms. Marshall, I called Tommy and told him we were going to see Latanya's mother the following day.

I had an appointment to meet with Joe Fuller to work out a deal on Dr. Tai's case in the morning. After that, I planned on going to my noontime AA meeting over on Houston Street. But then I was free and Tommy and I would pay a visit to Mrs. Jefferson.

When Tommy and I finished planning our meeting with Mrs. Jefferson, it was time to go to the sushi restaurant for dinner with Gracie. How did I get roped into eating at the sushi restaurant again so soon? The explanation falls under the heading "no good deed goes unpunished." Having professed my love for Gracie, I couldn't very well turn down her request for dinner at the sushi restaurant. I think she knew it and that she'd scammed me, but what the hell? It wouldn't kill me. At least I hoped not, but that's always a concern of mine when I eat raw fish or ride in a taxi. For a supposedly tough guy, I guess I'm not that tough, am I?

CHAPTER 41

I was sitting at my desk reading the New York Post waiting for Tommy to show up when Connie announced Pablo Blanco was on the line and wanted to talk to me. Pablo was an old 18B Panel client I had represented some years ago on a drug rap. At the time he was a young street dealer working the streets in Queens, but he got arrested in Manhattan carrying a felony load of cocaine. Actually, he wasn't carrying the drugs on his person and therein lay the rub.

The drugs were hidden in the trunk of the parked car in which Pablo was sitting. Apparently, a couple of patrol cops suspected Pablo of being a drug dealer, so when Pablo spit out the car window, the cops issued him a summons for violation of the Health Code and another summons for a parking violation. Neither offense rose to the level that warranted an arrest.

Pablo, being a hot-headed and dumb bastard, tore up the summonses and threw them in the cop's face. That was his first mistake. Then when he was ordered out of the car, he refused. Mistake number two. Mistake number three was wrestling with the cop when the cop pulled him out of the car because that amounted to assault which did warrant a lawful arrest.

When a police officer makes a lawful arrest, he can search the suspect and the suspect's car for weapons or evidence of a crime. The cops had searched, but found nothing because the drugs were well hidden. That's when the cops made their mistake. They had Pablo's car towed and impounded, which they could do as long as it wasn't for the sole purpose of searching it.

Of course, when the NYPD technicians searched the car, they discovered the cocaine in a compartment welded to the top of the wheel well. After talking with Pablo, I made a motion to exclude the cocaine from evidence claiming it was the product of an illegal search and seizure.

I argued the cops had provoked Pablo into the assault situation by harassing him with the two summonses, strictly for the purpose of searching him and his car for drugs or a weapon. I knew that alone probably wasn't a winning argument, but it wasn't my main point.

When the cops searched Pablo and his car at the scene, their conduct was questionable, but probably not sufficient to warrant excluding evidence if they'd found drugs when they searched the car. But they didn't find drugs when they searched it. It was what happened afterward that made the search illegal.

At the evidence suppression hearing, I established that any time a driver is arrested, the standard procedure is to leave the vehicle at the scene. That was the procedure even if the vehicle was illegally parked, so long as it wasn't interfering with the flow of traffic.

The vehicle remains at the scene until towed by the NYPD Transportation Bureau to one of the city's tow pounds, and held there pending release. A car at a tow pound is not searched again unless a warrant has been issued.

In Pablo's case, the cops, for some unstated reason, stayed with the car until the tow truck arrived. Then, according to the tow pound's records, the car was searched by the NYPD Tech Squad within an hour of arriving at the tow pound.

Put that way, it sure looked like the cops had Pablo's car towed and impounded for the sole purpose of searching the vehicle, and that's a violation of the Fourth Amendment to the United States Constitution.

The judge agreed and tossed the cocaine and with it went the drug charges. Under the circumstances, the two cops weren't anxious to take the stand and testify in the assault case, so we negotiated the charges down to a couple of violations. Pablo paid some fines, promised not to spit on the sidewalk again, and he walked out a free man.

Was I happy with the result? No. I think drug dealers are scum, but somebody must represent them. I just wish the cops wouldn't make my job so easy sometimes.

But now Pablo was calling me some five years later, and I wondered why. I picked up the phone, but quickly found out why he was calling. Pablo Blanco was no longer a poor small-time street dealer, he had moved up to a mid-level distributor position, and was doing well. At least he was doing well until he was arrested and charged with a violation of New York Penal Law § 220.77, operating as a major drug trafficker. To make matters worse, he was also charged with half a dozen weapons violations.

This wasn't an 18B Panel case because Pablo had plenty of money to pay for a lawyer and in fact already had. At his initial court appearance, he had been represented by his usual "abogado," as Pablo referred to him using the Spanish word for lawyer. But for reasons Pablo said he would explain when we met, he no longer wished to employ him. His abogado had apparently done well for Pablo because Pablo was out on bail. It was $500,000 cash bail, but he was walking around free.

I told Pablo that I wasn't sure I wanted to take his case because I was very busy, which I wasn't. I was busy with Michael's case, but since Joe hadn't sent me any new 18B Panel cases in a while, I had some free time. My reluctance had more to do with conscience than with free time. I've represented drug dealers whenever Joe sends one of them my way, but I do that because it's part of the job of an 18B lawyer. But the only reason for me to take Pablo's case was for the money, so I had to think about it.

It turned out I'm a very shallow person because I didn't have to think about it very long. In fact, it was less than a minute before I was negotiating a fee with Pablo and setting up an appointment date. I did warn Pablo that based on what he had told me and the charge he was facing not to expect any miracles.

CHAPTER 42

I had spent the night at Gracie's place, and it was from there that I called Claire Molinari. It wasn't a long conversation; I just told her Michael was improving and he wanted to talk with her. She asked me if he was really getting better, and all I could say was she'd have to ask Dr. Najari about him. I gave her Dr. Najari's telephone number and told her he would be expecting her call. There was a hesitancy in her voice, and I suspected she might not call. I hoped she would call because I believed Michael could use her support, but I couldn't blame her if she didn't.

It was all a question of how much pain someone could take, and it seemed Claire had taken more than her share. I was starting to feel guilty for calling her in the first place. After all, it had been over ten years since she had heard from or even about Michael, so I had to believe she had come to grips with the situation. Then along I came and probably stirred up a whole hornets' nest of old emotions, and now Claire had to face the problem all over again.

I asked Gracie what she thought about all of this and, as usual, she had a good take on it. She said if she were in Claire's position, she'd want to know about Michael's condition because leaving it uncertain didn't resolve it. As much as Claire may have thought she had resolved things with Michael, he was still her brother, and it was only natural for her to always wonder whether he was dead or alive. Gracie thought maybe Claire could keep Michael out of her mind most of the time, but she didn't think she could do it all the time. It made sense to me, and I believed Claire would call and talk to Michael. I'd just have to wait and see.

I keep some clothes and stuff at Gracie's place, so the next morning we had time for a leisurely breakfast of coffee and bagels before heading off to work. Most of the time Gracie has a stock of bagels in the freezer. But that morning there were no bagels in the freezer. Normally when we want bagels and there are none in the freezer, we go out for breakfast. But that morning Gracie said to show my love for her, I should run out and pick some up.

This love thing was getting old fast. I reminded Gracie I'm a very shallow person, and if she kept pushing me, our affair could be over. Of course, that wasn't true. The affair being over part wasn't true; the other part about me being a shallow person was true.

Gracie said she understood, but she didn't say what she understood. I wasn't sure where that left me. I didn't have time to find out because I had a busy day coming up, and I still had to go get bagels.

The first thing on my schedule was the meeting with Fuller on Dr. Tai's case. It was an interesting meeting, to say the least. Joe acted like he had an open-and-shut case against Dr. Tai, which he did, and I acted like I had a complete defense to charges, which I didn't. The posturing was normal for those kinds of negotiations. What was unusual was how quickly we gave in to each other.

Of course, our purpose was to arrive at a quick plea deal which didn't involve jail time. Dr. Tai would take the deal, and the case could be closed before the feds brought their charges and Dr. Tai fled to China. That way Dr. Tai's fleeing the jurisdiction wouldn't affect Joe Fuller or me.

Our mutual goal was clear. We just had to make sure we achieved it in a way which wouldn't be criticized by Joe's bosses. So we argued back and forth, then after nearly an hour of this nonsense, we arrived at a plea deal. Dr. Tai would plead guilty to a misdemeanor charge of practicing acupuncture without a license, pay a minimal fine, and that would be it.

I called Dr. Tai right from Joe's desk, got his approval for the deal, along with a lot of compliments on my legal ability. Just like that we were done. Of course, we still needed to go to court to finalize the deal, but Joe assured me we could do it the next day. As Joe put it,, "There was no sense taking any chances."

I went to a noon AA meeting on Houston Street because I like going to meetings, and that's a meeting Peter goes to twice a week, so it gives me an opportunity to see him face-to-face.

Peter was there looking good and sounding good. His new status as partner had gone to his head, and he was wearing an Armani suit which probably cost more than all the clothes in my closet. But if that's what turned his crank I didn't care so long as he didn't drink and kept coming to meetings. After the meeting, we grabbed a quick sandwich and a cup of coffee at a nearby coffee shop. After that, I went back to the office and waited for Tommy so we could go see Mrs. Jefferson.

CHAPTER 43

Tommy wasn't happy that I planned to go see Mrs. Jefferson. But he was resigned to the fact that I wasn't going to change my mind, no matter what he said. However, he insisted when we were on the housing project grounds or in the building that I do whatever he told me to do. That included leaving the housing project if he thought there was a problem. I didn't feel like arguing with Tommy. Besides, I didn't have much of a choice but to agree, so I agreed and we walked to Two Bridges.

There are at least four ways to get into the center of the four buildings that make up the housing project. The main alleyway that runs through the project offers two ways in, one from the east side and one from the west. The alleyway on the west side was where the TB Gangsters sold their drugs, so Tommy thought it best to avoid that way in. He said the gangbangers would be suspicious, and we didn't need a confrontation if we could avoid one.

Following Tommy's advice, we entered the project

grounds through the walkway on the south side. The walkway runs between two of the buildings and because it's not very wide, it's generally deserted. That day was no exception.

The walkway empties into the main square in the middle of the four buildings. Running through the middle of the square, west to east, is a roadway connecting the two alleyways between the north and south buildings. There's a playground surrounded by grassy areas with trees and benches on each side of the roadway. The roadway is supposed to be used by only emergency vehicles and no other traffic. But the kids driving into the alley on the west side to buy drugs don't usually bother to make a U-turn. Instead they drive through the middle of the project and out the alley on the east side.

We were going into the southeast building, so we didn't have to cross the center of the square. But we did have to walk along the perimeter of the square for about fifty yards to reach the building entrance. There were some gangbangers sitting on the benches across the square on the north side, but the playground and benches on the south side obscured us from their view, such that they didn't take any interest in us.

Inside the building we took the elevator to the fourth floor. Although the walls were all tagged with graffiti, the hallways looked clean.

Tommy led the way to Apartment 4G and rang the bell. No one answered, so Tommy rang it again. After a minute, someone inside wanted to know who we were. It was a female voice, but it sounded like a mature voice, not the voice of a child, so I figured it was Mrs. Jefferson and not Latanya.

Tommy identified himself as a private investigator and me as a lawyer, saying we needed to speak with her about a serious matter. She said "Go away." Tommy banged on the door, said we wouldn't go away until we had spoken to her, and she'd need to call the cops if she wanted us to leave.

Tommy knew she didn't want the cops to come. In the first place, the TB Gangsters didn't like it when residents talked to the cops, and they made their feelings known once the cops had left. In the second place, Mrs. Jefferson knew why we were there, and she had no interest in sharing that knowledge with the cops.

It was a standoff with Tommy banging on the door asking Mrs. Jefferson to let us in. Finally, after about ten minutes, the door opened and she let us in.

Mrs. Jefferson was a beautiful woman, but her face was lined with pain. She was tall, maybe five-foot-ten and thin, with mocha-colored skin. She looked as though she might have been crying because her eyes were red, but they were also hard and penetrating, and her jaw was set tightly. Something about her look told me she wasn't going to cooperate with us.

I explained to Mrs. Jefferson why we were there and asked her if we could speak to Latanya. She said Latanya wasn't there, and she wouldn't let us speak to her if she were there.

She refused to say where Latanya was. I kept badgering her but she wouldn't relent. She was obviously an intelligent woman. After a while I think she figured out what was going on. I say that because she told us without too much prompting that Lover Boy had been bothering Latanya and may have attempted to rape her.

At the time, I thought she was protecting Latanya; it wasn't until later that I learned the truth.

Mrs. Jefferson was playing us and playing us well, I might add. She wouldn't say when or where the incident had happened. Her explanation, or should I say excuse, for not telling us more was that the TB Gangsters controlled the project, and she feared for her life and the lives of her children. I'm sure that was partially true, but we both knew that wasn't all of it.

I pushed her, promising we'd arrange protection, but that didn't change anything. She still refused to cooperate. Then she said we had to leave and if we didn't, she'd call the police. She'd had enough and I could tell she was serious, so we left.

Tommy and I were now both certain Latanya Jefferson was the girl Lover Boy was trying to rape when he was killed under the bridge. But unless we found her, that knowledge wasn't going to do us any good. I had too many unanswered questions, and a client who wasn't telling me the truth.

CHAPTER 44

Once we were out of the housing project and safely back on the nearby streets, I told Tommy he was free to go. I was going to walk over to the 7th Precinct and talk with Richie Simone.

I found Richie at his desk and said it looked like he had nothing to do all day but sit there and read the newspaper. That probably wasn't the best way to start a conversation when I'm going to ask for a favor, but sometimes, or should I say most times, I can't help myself. Richie, no slouch himself when it comes to retorts, said maybe he could get somebody to shoot me, then he'd have something to investigate. With the smartass comments out of the way, I got down to business.

I explained that the conclusions in the Medical Examiner's Report didn't match up with the facts of the case as I could prove them. Richie listened, nodding occasionally, but otherwise without making a comment. When I was done laying out the discrepancies, I asked Richie what he thought and whether he'd be willing to reopen his investigation. Richie found my points interesting, but he didn't think there was enough to warrant reopening the investigation. Besides, it wasn't his decision to make. The order to reopen the investigation had to come from either his boss, the Chief of Detectives, or from the DA's Office.

If I had thought about it more, I probably would have figured it out on my own. But even with that being the case, I figured if the request came from Richie, it would carry more weight than if it came from me. I made my pitch to Richie who said he couldn't do it because he didn't believe there weren't any inconsistencies between the Medical Examiner's findings and the charges against Costanza, and if there were, I could argue them at trial.

I told Richie he was beginning to sound like a judge and asked how he came to his conclusion. He explained, and I had to admit his answers made sense. There was no reason to rule out the possibility that Michael held the hammer in his left hand when he attacked Johnson. Besides, unless Michael held the hammer in his hand for the whole twelve hours from the time of the assault until the police arrived, it had to have been wiped down or there would have been additional trace prints. As for the height of the assailant, if Johnson were leaning forward or bent down, the angle of the blow would have been consistent with a taller assailant. There was no evidence of a fourth person at the scene, or for that matter, even a third person. My theory of rape, while possible, was just a possibility supported only by weak circumstantial evidence.

When Richie put it that way, I knew he was right. Everything I was arguing might raise reasonable doubt at trial, but it didn't warrant reopening the investigation. Maybe when Dr. Garland completed his analysis, I might have more to work with, but until then the NYPD investigation was going to remain closed. It would be up to Tommy and me to come up with new evidence.

I thanked Richie for his time, and he wished me well. I left the 7th Precinct feeling low and decided to walk back to my office. It was a long walk back to Mott Street, but I needed time for my mood to improve.

I walked down to Grand Street, then over to Mott Street. As I walked into the confines of Chinatown, I was once again taken by its mystique. Even though I've been working in Chinatown a lot of years, occasionally when I walk down its streets, for some unexplainable reason I get ridiculously sentimental.

I first rented an office in Chinatown in the back room of Shoo's Restaurant because the rent was cheap. I should tell you when I say office, I mean a desk because that was all I actually rented. An old wooden desk in a storage room that I shared with Shoo's grandson, Tommy. Eventually I got a filing cabinet, but that was about it.

At the time, I knew very little about Chinatown and was only there because of the cheap rent. I had been fired from the DA's Office because of my drinking and with no law firm willing to take a chance on me, I first opened a nice office of my own on Broadway. But it didn't last long because of my drinking. So with no money and no clients, I rented the desk in the back of the restaurant and took on 18B cases.

It didn't take me long to like Chinatown. In the beginning, I liked it for the wrong reason, but eventually I came to like it for the right reason. What was the wrong reason? I liked it because I was isolated there. When you're a drunk you want to be isolated. You don't want people around you because they might tell you that you're a drunk, you might have to agree, and do something about it. No, you'd rather stay in your little isolated alcohol-created cocoon and pretend everything is okay.

You might have your booze buddies who drank with you in the bars, but they were just acquaintances. No one really, just people like you who drank too much. The worse they were, the better you could feel about yourself.

So living in a broken-down tenement in a slum neighborhood on the Lower East Side and working in Chinatown, I had managed to isolate myself completely. Actually, not completely because fortunately for me, Joe Benjamin had wedged his way into my sorry world and forced me into AA. The rest, as they say, is history.

Why do I still like Chinatown? Because I have come to appreciate it's a special place. A world of its own, almost totally separate from the rest of the city that surrounds it. You walk a block and a half from the courthouses on Foley Square, and suddenly you find yourself in another world. The sounds are different; the smells are different; the whole atmosphere is different. It's a closed world, a private world only partially open to outsiders. You are welcome to shop and eat in Chinatown, but unless you're Chinese you're not privileged to come inside that world. A world governed by a two-thousand-year-old culture.

Despite efforts to modernize the community, many of the old buildings dating back to the mid-1880s to the early 1900s remain standing. They're brick buildings no wider than four bays, and three to seven stories high. The

Shoo's building is one of those old buildings. My office, on the other hand, is now in one of the new buildings on Mott Street.

While Manhattan's Chinatown remains the largest Chinese community in the Western Hemisphere with an estimated population of over 100,000 people, it is now only one of many Chinese communities in New York City. Still, Manhattan's Chinatown is unique in its history. For instance, many people don't know it, but there was a Chinese Opera House built in 1892 that staged Chinese Operas until 1905.

When I got sober I came to appreciate the uniqueness of Chinatown and thanks to my relationship with the Shoo family, I was granted at least partial access into the private world that is Chinatown. Even as the boundaries of Chinatown grew outward from the original historic seven-block area to an area of more than fifty-five blocks, I remained one of the few Caucasian lawyers with an office in Chinatown and Chinese clients.

CHAPTER 45

By the time I got back to the office, it was getting close to six o'clock, and I found a message Connie had left on my desk to call Dr. Najari. Hoping he hadn't already left his office, I dialed his number and was relieved when he answered the phone. He said Michael was still doing fine and had spoken with his sister, Claire, earlier that afternoon.

Dr. Najari, with Claire's permission, had listened in on the call that he described as a bit strained. That was expected, but it did end on a high note. Michael apologized to Claire for all the trouble he had caused her and everyone else, and promised to stay in therapy and take his drugs for as long as necessary. Claire, who was a bit cold when the conversation started, warmed and told Michael she loved him and always would, but she couldn't take the pain of watching him destroy himself. She was giving him one last chance to get himself straightened out and if he was trying, she would do everything she could for him. Michael said he understood and if he didn't keep his word, he wouldn't expect to hear from her again. At the end of the conversation, they each sent their love to the other, and Claire promised to call again soon.

I asked Dr. Najari if he thought the conversation had any impact on Michael's state of mind. He said Claire's reassurance that she loved Michael was probably helpful. Michael's PTSD was complex and complicated by his psychotic depression. Dr. Najari believed it was caused not only by the simple trauma of war and what is known as survivor's guilt suffered by most PTSD patients, but also by overwhelming misplaced guilt from the Logan incident. Rebuilding Michael's self-image and freeing him from his paralyzing guilt that drove him into his non-responsive state would take time. But it didn't mean Michael couldn't function normally, or nearly normally, during the recovery process. Between the therapy and the drug regimen, he was progressing and that was the reason for his original call to me.

With the final court date coming up, Dr. Najari and Dr. Goldman had met that afternoon and discussed Michael's case. They both agreed he had progressed sufficiently to be able to assist in his own defense, and that was the conclusion they would give to Judge Cooperman when we all appeared in court. I had known for a while it was the most likely outcome and, in truth, I was happy about it. I felt we had good defenses, and rather than have Michael locked up in a mental institution for God knows how long, he'd be better off going to trial.

Now the burden was on me to establish his defense. Either the defense was justification because he was the only one there and he was protecting someone from being raped, or I raised reasonable doubt based on someone else having done the killing. Either way, I needed evidence and witnesses to testify. At that point, I had very little evidence and no witnesses. On top of that, I had a client who wouldn't tell me the truth.

Fortunately, we had some time before we faced the actual trial, and I was hoping the judge would order Michael held at Kirby. There was no way the judge would grant bail, so he would order Michael held in custody pending trial. Normally, that would mean Michael would be sent to Rikers Island, but I was hoping with Dr. Najari's and Dr. Goldman's help, we could convince the judge to keep him at Kirby so he could continue his therapy.

I still hadn't given up hope that the DA would reopen the case, but it was looking more and more like a long shot, and I wasn't counting on it happening. I planned on visiting Michael again the next day and trying to convince him to tell me what happened.

Then I had another idea. Maybe Claire could get Michael to tell her exactly what happened under the bridge. I needed somebody to tell me what happened, and I was running out of people to look to for answers.

I wasn't in a particularly good mood when I met up with Gracie for dinner. Fortunately, we were going to my favorite little Italian restaurant on Mulberry Street where the chef, fresh from a small town in Sicily, makes the best Pasta alla Norma in the city. The place is great, so I'm not going to tell you its name because I don't want it getting too popular. I'm guided in this instance by what Yogi Berra, the longtime catcher for the New York Yankees, famous for his turn of a phrase once said,

"Nobody goes there anymore. It's too crowded." So if you want go there, you'll have to find the place on your own. And don't expect any help from Gracie because she's with me on this.

The place also has a fabulous dessert. An Italian grain pie that's better than any cheesecake you ever tasted. I'd tell you more but I'm afraid if I did, it would only encourage you to find the place. So that's all I'm going to say on that front.

By the time dessert arrived I was feeling much better, but a little guilty over my moodiness, so I took Gracie's hand and told her again how much I loved her. I thought it was a nice touch.

After dinner, we were walking back to Gracie's place when out of the blue she asked if I thought we should move in together. The question took me by surprise because it was so out of character for Gracie to even think about something like that. Gracie is the most independent woman I've ever met, and she guards her independence like a mother bear guards her cubs. Besides, I value my freedom as much as Gracie values hers, so the thought of moving in with her scared the crap out of me.

I stopped dead in my tracks and looked at Gracie with what must have been an open-mouthed stare. She started to laugh so hard I thought she'd fall over. That's when I realized she was putting me on. When she finally caught her breath, she told me to knock it off with my professions of love because it was scaring her. At that moment, I wanted to tell her I loved her, but I knew better.

CHAPTER 46

The following morning, I met with Pablo Blanco who showed up with two punk bodyguards that I made wait in the reception area with Connie. I wasn't worried about them being out there with Connie because she's a tough woman. As I closed the door to my office, I heard her tell one of the two punks to get his goddamned feet off the furniture.

Once we were alone in the office, Pablo recited his tale of woe. Since he'd last seen me, he had moved up in the Columbian drug cartel, and he was now a distributor running a couple dozen street dealers in Upper Manhattan and the Lower Bronx. He was one of ten distributors working Manhattan and the Bronx under a boss named Ramon Sanchez aka "El Principe," the Prince.

Sanchez fancied himself to be another Machiavelli, hence his street name. Whenever the territorial lines in his little kingdom got blurred as they had in Pablo's situation, the Prince mediated the dispute. Most times the Prince turned out to be more like Al Capone than Nicolo

Machiavelli and people wound up dead. But that didn't seem to be the case with Pablo.

Pablo and a distributor from the Bronx, Amando Guzman, were having a territorial dispute and neither wanted the Prince to mediate. Pablo knew that Guzman was having a tough time, mostly because he was a user as well as a dealer, and that always meant trouble. Guzman was in the hole to the cartel and owed his street dealers money, so Pablo figured he was ripe for the taking. But apparently Guzman had clout with the Prince, and Pablo believed he had been set up by the Prince.

Normally Pablo sent two of his trusted crew to do the pickup from the cartel's distribution point in Queens. But this one night the Prince tells Pablo he needs to speak to him, so he should come personally for the pickup. Pablo being a suspicious guy, which you must be in the drug business to stay alive, loads himself and his two bodyguards into his SUV with enough weapons to fight a war. But when he gets to the pickup, there's no trouble. He delivers his $100,000, has a little chat with the Prince, and leaves with bricks of cocaine worth a street value of over $750,000.

While they're still in Queens, one of his bodyguards says he needs to take a piss, so the other bodyguard pulls into a gas station on Northern Boulevard. The two bodyguards get out and a minute later five cop cars, with lights flashing and sirens blaring, pull into the gas station and surround Pablo's SUV. Pablo is arrested, but the bodyguards who were apparently forewarned and part of the plot are in the wind.

I looked over the Arrest Report Pablo had brought with him, and I told him it looked bad for him. The Prince did a great job setting him up, and I didn't see any way out.

There was no way Pablo wasn't looking at doing a long stretch in state prison. Of course, it didn't come as a big surprise to Pablo who said he already knew that, which is why he had come to see me. His lawyer, or abogado as he kept calling him, was a cartel lawyer, and Pablo had a plan the cartel wouldn't like. Pablo would roll on the Prince and other bosses in the cartel for a pass and protection until he testified. After that, he had his own plans to disappear.

I told Pablo what he was doing was dangerous. If the cartel had even a hint of what he was up to, they'd hunt him down and kill him. The cartel had a long reach, and I wasn't sure how far it might go into the local precincts or even the DA's Office.

This was going to take some doing, and I wasn't exactly sure where to start. I had Pablo sign a retainer agreement and asked him if he brought the fee we had agreed on. He had indeed, and he opened his briefcase and dumped out twenty banded packs of twenty-dollar bills and a small cell phone. In all, $40,000 in cash.

I gave Pablo my best "really?" look, but he assured me the money was clean. At least the bills were bundled in Bank of America bands. As far as I could tell, none of them were wrinkled up like they had been used in a secretive drug transaction.

You might think I like being paid in cash, but I don't. Not because I'm so straight-laced, but because I know where it can lead. Let's be honest, when you're paid in cash there's always the temptation to pocket the money and not report it to the IRS. You figure, what hell, this one time I won't report it, so who am I hurting? But what happens when you do makes it easier the next time . Then pretty soon you're like my TCM client, Dr. Tai, and you're doing it all the time. That's when you're in big trouble.

It's like my drinking. I didn't start out drinking alcoholically. I started out like everybody else, drinking for fun, drinking socially. But then I went further and I started to use alcohol to make me feel better, and I drank more and more. Then I crossed the line into alcoholism, and there was no going back.

Soon I lost all sense of truth. It started when I lied to myself and said I didn't have a drinking problem. Then I lied to everyone else. I lied about everything, even things I didn't have to lie about. I lied because if I allowed myself to think about the truth, I'd have to admit I was an alcoholic, and there was no way I was ever going to do that.

I know what it is to slide down a slippery slope, so I don't like being tempted by cash. If I go down that slippery slope, I could end up losing my law license, or going to jail, or both. And I could wind up being an active drunk again.

I don't do well on slippery slopes and my life in sobriety is too good to risk over the income tax on $40,000. So the money was recorded on the books and went into the bank. I deposited the money a little at a time, so I didn't have to fill out any forms which might trigger an investigation as to where the money came from. If I'm paying the income tax on the money, I figure I've done my duty.

I gathered up the bundles of bills and stacked them neatly in one of my desk drawers. Now Pablo was officially my client, and I had to figure out what I could do for him.

The cell phone was for me to use to contact Pablo. He couldn't risk having me call him at a bad time or even have my number on his cell phone. So we'd communicate using burner phones. For now, I could use the phone he dumped on my desk. If things changed, he or one of his boys would bring me a new cell phone to use.

I wanted to ask him if now that I had a drug dealer burner phone, he could get me the sunglasses and gold chains to finish the outfit. But I thought better of it. Besides, I didn't want to risk losing the forty grand.

CHAPTER 47

Over the next few days, I struggled with trying to figure out how to best defend Michael when he wouldn't give me a straight answer that fit with the forensic evidence. I had visited Michael three times that week, and I was happy to see he seemed physically and mentally back to normal.

Even so, Dr. Najari cautioned me that Michael's condition was fragile and far from cured. His seemingly normal behavior was in no small part the result of the combination of antidepressants and antipsychotic drugs he was being given daily.

As much as I tried to get Michael to tell me what had really happened under the bridge, he kept insisting he was the one who hit Johnson with the hammer. Heeding Dr. Najari's advice, I hadn't pushed the issue very hard.

Then during my last visit, frustrated and against my better judgment, I had confronted Michael with the facts in the Autopsy Report starting with the blows seemingly coming from a left-handed assailant. Michael was no fool. He said it might seem that way because, as he recalled, Lover Boy had moved his body to the right just as he started hitting him. As for the height of the assailant, Michael had an answer for that too. He said he had approached Lover Boy in a low posture advance, just as he would have approached an enemy in combat.

I was almost positive Michael was protecting whoever committed the murder, but I wanted another opinion, so I asked Dr. Najari if he agreed. Dr. Najari said nothing came up in the therapy sessions that would confirm my suspicion, but his gut told him I was right. He laughed and warned me that his gut didn't qualify as an expert on the subject.

I wanted to know why Michael would lie and accept blame for a murder he didn't commit. Dr. Najari couldn't give me a positive answer, but he believed it was tied into Michael's guilt over the Logan rape incident. It was likely that Michael viewed whoever killed Lover Boy as a hero, a hero who did something Michael felt guilty for not having done in the Logan incident. Dr. Najari speculated that by protecting the person who had killed Lover Boy and taking the responsibility on himself, Michael was trying to rid himself of the guilt he felt over the Logan affair.

It made sense, but Dr. Najari didn't think the problem could be worked out in the short-term, and I didn't have the luxury of waiting for the long-term. Michael's best defense was that he hadn't committed the crime and since some of the forensic evidence supported that claim, I could probably raise reasonable doubt in a jury's mind. But I couldn't do it without Michael testifying as to exactly what happened by explaining why he was holding the murder weapon and why only his fingerprints were on it.

If I raised the possibility of a third individual doing the killing and Michael didn't testify, the DA could tie him to the crime as a co-conspirator. Holding the murder weapon in his hand and not telling the police about anyone else being at the crime scene was damning.

Of course, he didn't tell the police anything and he didn't have to, but if he were innocent, the jury would expect him to have said something. Besides, juries always like defendants to take the stand and tell their side of the story. The problem was if I put him on the stand he was going to say he did it by himself, so I couldn't do that.

If he was going to insist on saying he did it, we were left with the justification defense, but for that I needed witnesses, and I didn't have any. I needed Latanya to tell the jury that Lover Boy was in the process of raping her when Michael intervened and saved her. Very simple but for the fact that I didn't know where Latanya was and what she would say. She knew the truth about who was at the crime scene and depending on how she testified, Michael could be exonerated or implicated. If there was someone else there besides Michael, Lover Boy and Latanya, the justification defense was likely to take a big hit unless we could show there was no other way to stop the rape except by using deadly force.

It was all a criminal defense lawyer's nightmare, too many issues, too many questions, and not enough answers or evidence. The last thing you ever want to do as a lawyer is to go to trial not sure of the facts and not sure of what your defense is. You might as well sit on one of the spectator benches because nothing good was going to come from being at the counsel table under those circumstances.

We were just two days away from the hearing before Judge Cooperman would make a decision about whether Michael went on trial or to a mental facility for the criminally insane. I knew both Dr. Najari and Dr. Mitchell, the second psychiatrist from the New York State Department of Mental Health, were going to testify that Michael had regained lucidity and could assist in his own defense. Therefore, the judge would order the case to go forward.

I would ask the judge to set bail, which the DA's Office would naturally and rightly oppose. Then I would ask the judge to order Michael held at Kirby, so he could continue to receive treatment to make sure his mental state didn't deteriorate. Dr. Najari and Dr. Goldman were prepared to testify that putting Michael in Rikers Island and depriving him of therapy could cause him to slip back into his non-communicative state.

I was scheduled to meet with both doctors to prepare them for their possible testimony the next day, and was preparing my notes when the phone rang. It was Marion Marshall, the ADA who was now handling Michael's case. The case had reached the point where Ms. Marshall, the senior ADA, would replace the junior ADA, Shayna Washington.

Ms. Marshall asked if we were prepared to proceed on the matter, and I assured her we were. She said this type of case was new to her, and I admitted that despite my nearly thirty years in practice, the case was new to me as well.

We chatted a while and finding her to be a

seemingly decent sort, I asked her if she would oppose my motion to have Michael held at Kirby instead of Rikers. I explained our concerns and that I had the psychiatrists ready to testify. Ms. Marshall said she didn't think she'd oppose the motion, but she needed to clear it with her boss. I thought that was fair enough.

I figured since I had Ms. Marshall on the phone and we were getting along so well, I might bring up the topic of reopening the investigation. I pointed out the discrepancies in the Medical Examiner's Report and gave her my best reasoning. I thought it was going well, so I was disappointed when Ms. Marshal replied that there was no way in hell the investigation was going to be reopened.

Then she explained why it was never going to happen. She had also noticed what seemed to be discrepancies in the report. But after meeting with the Medical Examiner, she was confident they weren't actually discrepancies. But not to worry, the Medical Examiner would clear it all up when he testified.

I have been around long enough to know what that meant. Loosely translated, what Ms. Marshall said was, "The guy made a mistake writing it up that way but I met with him, explained the problem, and we worked it out, so don't expect the Medical Examiner to be much help at trial."

I still hadn't heard from Dr. Garland, but now I needed him more than ever. This case was totally crazy. I was beginning to think I had gone down the Alice in Wonderland rabbit hole, and maybe I had.

In the beginning, I thought I'd use Dr. Garland to confirm or refute the Medical Examiner's findings, depending on Michael's testimony. If we were going for reasonable doubt, I wanted him to support the report's findings. If we were going for justification, I wanted him to attack the report's findings.

You're probably asking yourself how I can ask a supposedly independent expert to testify a certain way? Especially when the two possible opinions I'm looking for are exact opposites. Good question. It's called wiggle room. I'm not saying most experts are whores, but the good ones, or at least those that lawyers think are good, can find wiggle room.

You may think that sounds corrupt, and maybe it is. But go on the Internet, and you'll find support from supposed "experts" on any position and its opposite. Why? Because, in most cases, nothing is ever black and white. It's all shades of gray, and that's where the experts make their money. Most of the time, it amounts to nothing more than saying the glass is half-full as opposed to the glass is half-empty. Get a couple of good expert witnesses together and ask them the question about the glass, and they'll argue over it for an hour citing scientific studies, and they'll make it all sound good.

If you don't believe me about this, ask any trial lawyer who's ever hired expert witnesses if he wants a written report right off the bat. The answer is no because the lawyer wants to know what the expert thinks before he gets a report that he's required by law to turn over to the other side. If the expert's opinion doesn't suit the lawyer's needs, the expert either uses wiggle room and changes his opinion, or he gets fired.

Don't get me wrong. If the issue in the case was whether the sky was blue, no legitimate expert would say the sky is green. But you could easily find one that would say it's not blue. Maybe it's cerulean, or maybe light blue, so whoever said it was blue is wrong. See how easy it is. All shades of gray, or in the example, shades of blue.

In Michael's case, the forensic evidence is subject to interpretation; therefore, it's not positive proof of any issue. I knew that all along, and that's why I wanted Dr. Garland on the case to either support or counter the findings. Just as the Medical Examiner was apparently changing his position; Dr. Garland would probably be comfortable challenging it if that's what I needed.

That was my state of mind when I called Dr. Garland to find out what he thought about the forensic evidence. As I suspected, he found nothing conclusive. The blows were delivered to the left side of the skull suggesting the assailant was left-handed, but the evidence was inconclusive.

Now here's where we get into it, and where the lawyers earn their fees. I asked him if he could say with a reasonable degree of medical certainty that the assailant was left-handed. Dr. Garland said "No," he couldn't say that. Then I asked him if he agreed that the physical evidence reasonably suggested the assailant was left-handed, and he said he could say yes.

As far as I was concerned, the next question was the critical question. Based on the evidence, would the Medical Examiner be able to testify with a reasonable degree of medical certainty that the assailant was or wasn't left-handed? Dr. Garland thought about it for a minute and then replied, "Not unless he's going to lie."

I know the Medical Examiner isn't going to lie on the witness stand so at best, he'll say the forensic evidence doesn't prove the assailant was left-handed. Then on cross-examination, I can get him to agree that he cannot say with a reasonable degree of medical certainty the assailant wasn't left-handed. That would leave us with the reasonable possibility that the assailant was left-handed, with no absolute evidence he wasn't.

I was sure the Medical Examiner would argue a bit, but in the end, he'd still have to say that his opinions lacked medical certainty. Then depending on the direction we needed to go I could leave it there or have Dr. Garland testify that in his opinion the evidence suggested the assailant was left-handed. Then we'd have a battle of the experts, and the jury would decide who they believed.

When I asked about the height of the assailant, Dr. Garland had a somewhat different opinion than I had hoped for. Yes, the blows could have been delivered by a taller man, but only if the assailant were stooped over when he delivered the blows. I asked if it was possible the victim was bent over, like trying to mount someone, when he was struck, and Dr. Garland said it was possible but very unlikely. Had the victim been bent over, there would have been blood splatter from the blows on the top end of the mattress or on the ground beyond the mattress, but there weren't. So much for that theory.

I told Dr. Garland not to prepare a written report yet, and I'd get back to him after the arraignment, once I was sure I had all the Forensic Reports. So far, I had only gotten the reports through Gracie's contacts and until Michael was arraigned, I couldn't officially ask for the reports. It was possible there were more reports, and I didn't want Dr. Garland preparing any report until we had seen the State's evidence.

A MURDER UNDER THE BRIDGE

I called Joe Benjamin as much to get some input from him as to fill him in on what was happening. Joe agreed this was the craziest case either of us had ever encountered, but unfortunately he had no good ideas for going forward. We'd be playing it by ear as we went along.

CHAPTER 48

It never rains but it pours, or so goes the proverbial phrase. I was working late when my cell phone rang and it was Doug. Laurie had a radiation treatment the next day and he needed to go with her, but he had a court appearance on one of his matrimonial cases he'd been unable to adjourn. Could I cover it for him? I know nothing about matrimonial law and have never even been married. Of course, I had taken a course in what at the time was called Domestic Relations way back when I went to law school, but not only did I not remember anything from the course, I was fairly certain the law had changed since then.

Doug said he hated to ask me to cover the appearance, but all his regular stand-ins were tied up and he was desperate. He assured me it was just a status conference to advise the court which items on the case's agenda list had been taken care of and which items remained open. It shouldn't take more than fifteen to twenty minutes. The clients would be at the conference, and although the divorce was contentious, Doug didn't expect any problems.

You know how I feel about Doug, so there was no way in the world I was going to turn him down. Doug faxed over the pertinent papers and said he'd notify the client I was standing in for him. The client was Marjorie Davenport whose name I recognized from page six of the New York Post. Marjorie's husband was Charles Davenport, a millionaire investment banker who, according to Doug's notes, was courting a famous fashion model. Apparently, Marjorie didn't approve of the courtship and had filed for divorce. The couple had been married for fifteen years and had two children, a boy thirteen and a girl eleven. They also had a Russian Wolfhound dog that seemed to be drawing more attention in the proceedings than the children.

The conference was scheduled in New York Supreme Court on Centre Street before Judge Hilda Moskowitz at three o'clock in the afternoon. I figured that gave me ample time to prepare.

That night when I got to Gracie's place and told her I would be appearing in divorce court, she found it very amusing. It was our regular movie night, the night we pick out an old movie and watch it for the umpteenth time. Gracie thought she was being funny and suggested we watch "Kramer vs. Kramer" never realizing how prescient she was.

The next morning, I went to the office and cleaned up some overdue correspondence and for the first time in weeks, I left the office without even thinking about Michael's case. I went to the law library at the Supreme Court and read the Domestic Relations Law. I always want to be prepared when I go to court, and I certainly didn't want to let Doug down.

By noon I was done and I wandered over to the DA's Office across the street to ask Gracie out to lunch at Shoo's. We hadn't been there in a while, and I missed seeing old man Shoo. I especially missed his lamb in garlic sauce. Gracie asked if I thought it was a good idea to have garlic sauce before going to a court conference, which was a good point, so I made a mental note to pick up breath mints before the conference.

After that, things starting going south. First off, I forgot to pick up the breath mints, but that was the least of it. At a quarter to three I met Mrs. Marjorie Davenport outside of Judge Moskowitz's courtroom and introduced myself. When Marjorie kept turning her head away as I spoke to her, I realized that I'd forgotten the breath mints. So that's when I started looking at the ceiling and walls as I spoke to her. That was bad, not too bad, but things got worse, a lot worse.

Marjorie and I went into Judge Moskowitz's courtroom, and I went up to the judge's clerk to report in, carefully keeping my distance and never looking directly at the clerk.

Finally, at a quarter after three Mr. Charles Davenport and his lawyer arrived, and amid apologies, explanations about traffic and hostile glares we wound up seated around a table in Judge Moskowitz's chambers. It was tight quarters, so whenever I spoke everyone got a fragrant sample of old man Shoo's lamb with garlic sauce.

Charles' lawyer seemed to be a decent guy and the judge who I had never appeared before seemed to have a good handle on the case, so I wasn't expecting any real problems. That was until I noticed the looks exchanged between Marjorie and Charles. I've seen less hostile looks on the faces of grizzly bears ready to attack. For the record, on the Discovery Channel I've actually seen the faces of grizzly bears ready to attack. Sometimes when I can't sleep, I watch the Discovery Channel or the Cooking Channel, anything that might put me to sleep. But I digress.

We got through the agenda list easily. The judge seemed satisfied, Charles' lawyer seemed satisfied, and I didn't know enough not to be satisfied. As for Marjorie and Charles, they just grunted. Then things took a nasty turn downward. The judge said the next issue to be addressed was custody and we, meaning the lawyers, should start preparing positions if the parties planned on contesting joint custody.

That's when Marjorie, without my prior knowledge or advice, offered her opinion on the subject stating, "There's no fucking way my children or my dog are going near that drunken, cheating bastard and his whore girlfriend." I thought Marjorie had stated her position very concisely, but I felt she was being a little harsh. I was doing my best to calm her down when Charles chimed in saying, "I'm no fucking drunk, you fucking bitch."

Judge Moskowitz was apparently used to such outbreaks and suggested that both parties be quiet and leave the talking to their lawyers. I thought it was a good idea, but I didn't know what to say. So I fell back on my AA training and said in my experience when someone protests over being called a drunk, they're usually a drunk. Mind you, I was just trying to be helpful, but apparently Charles didn't take well to my comments.

He leaned over the table and said "You don't know what you're talking about, you foul-mouthed, stinking son of a bitch." I was offended, not by the foul-mouth comment, but by the comment that I didn't know what I was talking about.

I'm not one to let a comment like that go unchallenged, so I said I did know what I was talking about, and I was damn good at spotting drunks and he fit the bill. That's when he hit me, and that's when Judge Moskowitz called for her court officer who escorted Charles out of the room.

He hadn't done me any harm because he was half-standing and half-sitting when he swung at me. His fist barely reached my mouth because I had pulled back when I saw the punch coming. The judge admonished Charles' lawyer over his client's conduct, then she apologized to me, which I thought was very nice of her. That was it; we were done.

Once outside the courtroom, Marjorie began laughing and turned to me, said thank you, and gave me a big kiss on the mouth, garlic breath and all. I asked why she was so happy. She said I had just shown the judge how violent her soon-to-be ex-husband could be, and she intended to ride that pony all the way to the promised land and a big settlement.

When I called Doug and told him what happened, he didn't share Marjorie's enthusiasm. At first he thought I was pulling his leg, but eventually he believed me and we had a good laugh over the whole thing. Of course, Doug suggested I stick to criminal law cases and avoid matrimonial cases which I agreed was a good idea.

Matrimonial cases were much too violent for me.

That night when I relayed the story to Gracie we had a good laugh, but later I couldn't help but think how much hatred there was between Charles and Marjorie. To be honest, I couldn't understand it, and I couldn't imagine how it could happen.

The only real relationship I've ever had with a woman is my relationship with Gracie, and it came in two parts. Part one started way back when I worked in the DA's Office and ended when I started drinking too heavily. I couldn't recall hating Gracie when she left me. Oh, I blamed her for everything going wrong in my life, and maybe I hated her a little bit for leaving me when I thought I needed her the most. But the feelings I had toward her were nothing compared to the hatred between the Davenports.

I had a client once who killed someone who posed a mortal threat to his family, and I couldn't understand how he could do that. Just like I couldn't understand how the Davenports could come to hate each other so much. Maybe I lack passion, or maybe I'm just too shallow to reach such emotional peaks. Whatever it is, I'm happy to be me.

CHAPTER 49

The day before Michael's hearing was a busy one. It started with a meeting with Tommy to see where we stood and what more we could do to find Latanya. Tommy had been keeping close tabs on Carlos who continued to claim he hadn't heard from Latanya, and he still didn't know where she was. Tommy believed Carlos was being straight with him and if Carlos heard anything about Latanya, he'd let him know.

As for any other leads, Tommy was coming up empty. He had developed a couple of contacts in the TB Gangsters, young kids who were minor players, and while they didn't have any hard information to give him, he could judge the mood of the gang by what these kids told him. The gang leaders were still hot for revenge and actively looking for Latanya and Tyrone. There was talk of upping the bounty, but so far it remained at ten-thousand dollars on each of them. As long as there was a bounty on the kids, there was no way their mother would bring them back home.

A MURDER UNDER THE BRIDGE

Tommy had tried to keep an eye on Latanya's mother, but he couldn't spend all day at the housing project. All he could manage was to watch for her coming and going to work, and he only saw her a couple of times. Each time he saw her, she was accompanied by a very large man who Tommy took to be some sort of bodyguard.

Tommy had followed her one morning, hoping to find out where she worked. He managed to keep her in his sight without being detected all the way to an office building on Pine Street, but he lost her in the crowded lobby. He hadn't seen her since that morning and suspected she either changed her schedule, or wasn't going to work.

Getting nowhere at the housing project, Tommy tried another approach. He had a contact at the Board of Education and was working to find out if Latanya's school records had been recently transferred anywhere. He was waiting to find out before he talked to any of Latanya's teachers. He had already talked to most of her classmates, so he knew she was a good student and he learned who her favorite teachers were. Maybe, just maybe, she had confided in one or more of her teachers as to where she was going. Tommy intended to find out.

It was clutching at straws, but we were running out of options. Assuming Judge Cooperman was going to order Michael's case to go forward, the arraignment could take place as early as the day after the hearing.

In a felony case, the defendant doesn't enter a plea at the first arraignment hearing. Bail is considered, but entering a formal plea is put off until after the case is presented to a grand jury and an indictment returned. Usually, the case goes to the grand jury within a couple of days of the original arraignment hearing, and the next hearing happens right after that.

The Constitution gives a defendant the right to a speedy trial, so the DA must move the case along or it can be dismissed. That doesn't mean all cases move fast because the defense can slow down the process if it chooses to do so. That's what I had done in Beni's case because it was to his advantage. In Michael's case, we might have to slow things down to get all our ducks in a row. But I wouldn't be able to do that unless Michael was being held at Kirby. If the judge sent him to Rikers, it would be a disaster, and I'd have to move the case along as quickly as I could.

I told Tommy to find out whatever he could and to do it fast. Then I called Richie Simone and asked for a big favor. I asked him to go to the Jefferson apartment and interrogate Mrs. Jefferson on her daughter's whereabouts. The request was way over the line and I knew it, but I was desperate, and Richie owed me. Naturally at first, Richie said there was no way he could do that. But after I explained why, and I threatened and bullied him, he agreed to do it. But he said it was all unofficial, and he'd go that evening when he was off duty. He'd do his best, but if she clammed up and wouldn't talk, he wasn't going to threaten her in any way. I thanked him and told him to call me on my cell after he spoke to her.

I was getting ready to leave for Kirby to meet with Michael, then with both Dr. Najari and Dr. Goldman to prepare for the hearing when Connie announced Mr. Benjamin was on the line. Joe wanted to know where things stood and what my plans were for the hearing. I explained what was happening. Thinking of my conversation with Richie, I asked if he had any pull in the DA's Office that he could use to get the investigation reopened.

We needed to find Latanya and all I had to work with was Tommy and Richie Simone in an unofficial capacity. If the DA reopened the investigation, he'd have all of NYPD's thirty-five thousand cops at his disposal to find her. I liked those odds better. Joe said he'd do what he could, but I shouldn't hold my breath. As the Administrator of the 18B Panel, he didn't have an exactly cozy relationship with the DA. Having criticized the DA's Office on numerous occasions, he didn't think he'd get very far asking for a favor, but he'd try. That was all I could ask for.

Between meeting with Tommy and the call with Joe, I was behind schedule, so instead of taking the subway and bus to Kirby as I had planned, I had to go by taxi. You remember what happened the last couple of times I went to Kirby by taxi, don't you? Well, this time it was different.

The driver was an elderly man of Eastern European descent who drove so cautiously I started to think I could have gotten to Kirby faster if I had walked all the way. But I couldn't complain because I got what I wished for, a cautious taxi driver who got me to my destination without once scaring the crap out of me. So when we finally got to Kirby, I thanked Karole and gave him a big tip.

The visit with Michael would be the last chance I'd have to convince him to come clean with all the facts before the hearing. It wouldn't impact or change whatever happened at the hearing, but I'd feel a lot better knowing

Michael and I were on the same page before we went back into the court system.

I dropped by Dr. Najari's office just to check in and see if there were any last-minute developments I should know about. Dr. Goldman was already there and conferring with Dr. Najari when I arrived. Both doctors had seen Michael earlier that morning and said his status was unchanged. Dr. Najari reported Claire had called two more times since I last saw Michael, and while the conversations seemed to put Michael more at ease, he still hadn't offered any new information about what happened under the bridge.

Talking with the doctors, I got an idea how I might try approaching Michael and I ran it by them. It was a bit different from the way I had approached him in the past and maybe even a little radical, so that's why I wanted the doctors' approval. They conferred and concluded my plan was unlikely to do any harm, but I needed to move slowly and cautiously, and if I noticed any change in Michael's demeanor I should stop. They'd both observe us through the two-way mirror and if they detected a problem, they'd intercede.

It was time for me to sit down with Michael.

CHAPTER 50

Michael smiled at me when I came into the conference room. He looked about as relaxed and at ease as I had ever seen him, and I took that to be a good sign. I reminded him we'd be going back to court the next day and that it was likely his case was going to go forward. He just nodded and didn't ask any questions. Dr. Najari had warned me Michael's condition was still fragile and any shock could cause him to regress. Not wanting him to be surprised by anything that happened at the hearing, I described each step in the proceedings. When I was done, I asked him if he had any questions. He didn't.

I moved a little closer to Michael, put down the legal pad I had been reading my notes from, and said, "Someone killed William Johnson under the bridge and I know it wasn't you." I kept looking into Michael's eyes, and he kept looking into mine.

Then I said, "William Johnson wasn't Logan, and you didn't kill Johnson or Logan. But I know you did save a girl from being raped under that bridge. I know you couldn't have saved the girl in Vietnam, but I know you helped save that girl under the bridge. I just don't know how and that's what I need you to tell me." I didn't say anything else, I just kept looking into Michael's eyes as they narrowed and then he looked away. He looked up at the ceiling for a minute, then he looked me square in the eyes again and said, "I can't."

I was getting very frustrated, but I wasn't about to give up. I asked Michael, "Are you saying you killed William Johnson?" When he said "Yes," I said "Bullshit!" I said it purposely loud and with an edge that made Michael draw back slightly, but he never flinched and never took his eyes off mine.

Once again, I went line-by-line through the items in the Medical Examiner's Report that contradicted Michael's claim. When I was done, I slammed the report down on the table and looked back at Michael. He looked straight at me and said, "I explained all of that."

I took a deep breath and looking Michael straight in the eye, I yelled, "Bullshit!"

Michael didn't respond; he just kept looking me in the eye, his facial expression unchanged. The ball was in my court. I kept my eyes locked on Michael's eyes and said, "I don't know who you're protecting or why, but if you keep lying to me, I can't help you, and you're going to jail for a long time."

That wasn't necessarily true, but it was possible, and I was hoping the realization he might end up in jail would make him cooperate. But it didn't work. He just kept insisting he had killed William Johnson.

I argued with Michael for an hour. I threatened to withdraw from the case, and I even lied to him and said I had a witness who would testify he hadn't killed Johnson. None of it worked; Michael refused to relent. What frightened me the most about Michael's behavior during all of this was his calmness. He wasn't at all nervous, or even agitated by my badgering.

By the end of our session, I knew Michael wasn't going to change his story. But I needed to find Latanya if I was going to keep Michael out of jail. It was ironic that I had two strong possible defenses–one, the defendant didn't do it; and two, justification. But my client was torpedoing both. Defenses without supporting evidence don't work, especially when your client doesn't support either one.

I was frustrated, but I didn't want to leave Michael on an angry note. So I softened up and made nice for a while until he was smiling at me again, and then I left.

I met with Dr. Najari and Dr. Goldman in Dr. Najari's office, and I prepped them for the next day's hearing. I generally explained how things would proceed, and I told them once again what I needed them to say if I called them as witnesses. Both doctors agreed they had no problem giving the testimony I needed, so I drew up a list of questions I would ask them.

When we finished with the prep session, Dr. Goldman and I were getting ready to leave when Dr. Najari asked if I could stay a moment because he wanted to talk to me about something unrelated to Michael's case. I said "Sure," and sat back down.

After Dr. Goldman had left and closed the door on his way out, Dr. Najari said he had told a little lie. What he wanted to talk about did relate to Michael's case.

During one of Michael's early therapy sessions,

before anyone even knew who he was, and while he was only semi-lucid, he kept repeating, "No, I did it. Say I did it." At the time Dr. Najari didn't know what it meant and thought it wasn't important, but now it seemed very relevant. He had heard everything I just told Michael, and he wanted to make sure I knew I was right so I wouldn't give up on Michael. I promised Dr. Najari I wouldn't.

I knew Dr. Najari had just violated doctor-patient confidentiality, and I could tell it hadn't been easy for him to do. I tried to ease his conscience by telling him it was important because it confirmed what I believed, and gave me hope that the truth would eventually come out.

Still, I was curious as to why he had done that so I asked him flat out why he told me. He said there were too many soldiers from the Vietnam War, from Desert Storm, from Afghanistan, and from Iraq, all suffering from PTSD and nobody was helping them. Too many were falling through the cracks, and too many were being ignored. Michael needed help, and whatever it took to help him, Dr. Najari was determined to do.

That said a lot about Dr. Najari. Doctor-patient confidentiality, like lawyer-client confidentiality, exists to protect the patient or client. But what happens when confidentiality hurts the patient or client? I'm not smart enough to figure out the answer to that question. I don't even know if I could tell you honestly what I'd do if I were faced with that situation. But I certainly can't and won't criticize Dr. Najari for having the courage to do what he believed was in the best interest of his patient. In fact, given the possible consequences he faced in doing so, I applaud him.

It's strange, but when I saw Gracie that night I didn't share that bit of information with her. Don't get me wrong; I just don't share everything with Gracie. I respect attorney-client privilege and never disclose anything a client tells me in confidence. But the other stuff I most always share with Gracie. I had no attorney-client relationship with Dr. Najari. So there was nothing preventing me from telling Gracie what Dr. Najari said, but in some strange way I felt protective of the man. I didn't want anyone, not even Gracie, possibly thinking less of him.

CHAPTER 51

I was very uptight when I left Kirby. I get that way when things aren't going well, or maybe I should say when things aren't going my way. Part of it has to do with my wanting to control everything, a common trait in alcoholics, and one we have to deal with all the time in sobriety. We have one of those silly sayings in AA that usually helps me. It's "Let go and let God." But that day, when I left Kirby I couldn't let go.

I called Doug but he was in court. So while I was on the bus leaving Randall's Island headed for the Upper East side of Manhattan, I looked for an AA meeting. I found there was a four o'clock meeting at St. Monica's Church on East 79th Street, and just knowing I was going to a meeting made me feel a little better.

Some people give me a hard time because I talk about AA a lot. Typically, the ones who like it the least are the drunks, but I don't want to be judgmental. In AA. it's called taking someone else's inventory, and I don't do that. At least not out loud. Let's face it; there's a lot of truth in the old saying "It takes one to know one."

So why am I telling you all of this now? Because when I got to St. Monica's, there were two guys standing outside the basement door arguing and blocking my way in. The one guy was saying he doesn't belong there, and the other guy was saying he did. All I was trying to do was mind my own business and get past them and through the door. But that wasn't to be.

The one guy who was saying he didn't belong there asked me if I was going to the AA meeting. When I said "Yes," he asked me if I thought he had to go. I gave him the standard AA answer, "I don't know, only you can decide that, but why not give it a try? It can't hurt."

The other guy started to agree with me, and the first guy decided to take a swing at him except I'm in the way, so he landed a shot on my shoulder. Suddenly I'd become a human punching bag. First there was Charles in divorce court, then this drunk on 79th Street throwing punches at me.

I told the guy to calm down and, of course, the other one started telling the first one he should listen to me because I'm probably an alcoholic and know what I'm talking about. I thanked the guy for his endorsement, then after smelling his breath, I told him he might want to consider going to the meeting himself. He, of course, took exception to my comment and told his friend I didn't know what I was talking about, and they both walked off happily, probably headed for the nearest bar.

When I left the meeting, I was in a much better mood until Connie called. She said Marion Marshall had called to say the DA was opposing my application to have Michael kept at Kirby pending trial. They wanted him sent to Rikers. I immediately called Dr. Najari, gave him the news, and said I was going to need his help the next day. I asked him to meet me at the Worth Street Coffee Shop at eight-thirty the next morning. Then I made the same call to Dr. Goldman.

I called Gracie and told her I'd be working late at the office, and I'd grab a bite to eat before I got there. But I wanted to see her, so I'd come by her place afterward. She said it was fine, but she could tell from my voice that something was wrong. I told her about the DA's position on Michael's detainment, and she was surprised the DA was taking such a hard-line. I knew she couldn't do anything about it, but I asked her if she could find out what was behind the decision.

I called Joe Benjamin and gave him the bad news. He was upset and said he'd try reaching out to friends who might have some pull in the DA's Office, but he wasn't confident it would do any good. He even offered to come to my office and help me with my argument. I appreciated the offer, but said that I worked better alone. Joe understood and wished me luck.

Just before going down into the subway and riding back downtown, I called Shoo's Restaurant and ordered an egg roll, some fried rice and spareribs to go. By the time I got off the subway and over to Mott Street, my order was waiting. I ate dinner at my desk getting ready for the next day's hearing.

Shoo had thrown in the traditional Chinese fortune cookie. When I broke it apart and read my fortune, I could only hope it was true. It read, *"You will have good luck very soon."* Of course, I never saw one that said you were going to have bad luck, or you were going to die soon.

A MURDER UNDER THE BRIDGE

I had just finished off the last of the spareribs when Richie Simone called. He had visited Mrs. Jefferson, but she refused to cooperate. He tried his best, but she wouldn't tell him anything, so he had no choice but to leave. I thanked Richie for trying, then I called Tommy, told him all the bad news, and asked if he had anything good to report. Unfortunately he didn't.

By the time I finished up in the office and got to Gracie's place, she was sound asleep, so there wasn't even going to be any sex. It had turned out to be an officially shitty day, but I hoped that the next day would be better. Not wanting to leave fate to chance I set the clock alarm back half an hour. That way I had something to look forward to in the morning which made going to sleep easier.

CHAPTER 52

Setting the alarm clock back half an hour did the trick, and we started the day off very happily. At least I sure did, and from the sounds of things Gracie did also. I hoped it would continue that way.

Shortly before 8:30 I arrived at the Worth Street Coffee Shop. Dr. Najari was already seated at my reserved table in the rear, but Dr. Goldman had not yet arrived. Dr. Najari and I ordered coffee and bagels, and before they reached the table Dr. Goldman showed up.

One more time, I explained to both doctors that the DA was going to oppose my application to keep Michael at Kirby rather than being sent to Rikers Island Jail. I needed them to convince Judge Cooperman it was imperative to keep Michael at Kirby. That was why we were going to go over their testimony again. We only had one shot at this, and I was determined to give it the best we had, and so were Dr. Najari and Dr. Goldman

When we were done, we walked over to the Supreme Court Building and made our way to Judge

Cooperman's courtroom. Inside the courtroom I took my seat at the counsel table while Dr. Najari, Dr. Goldman and Dr. Mitchell, the second Department of Mental Health psychiatrist, took seats in the gallery. Marion Marshall was seated at the other counsel table and we exchanged greetings. Once I was settled in with my papers all in order, Marion came over to talk.

She was sorry about opposing my application, but word had come from "upstairs," so her hands were tied. Sensing she was being sincere I told her I intended to call witnesses if the judge would allow me to do so, and I hoped she wouldn't ask for a continuance or a delay. She said since that issue never came up during the meeting with her boss, the decision was hers, and she had no intention of delaying the proceedings. That was the best news I had heard in a while, and I was grateful Marion was doing the stand-up thing.

A little after 10 o'clock Judge Cooperman took the bench and the hearing started. The judge asked if the two psychiatrists from the Department of Health were present, and Ms. Marshall and I both replied that they were. The judge then wanted to know if they had reached a conclusion as to whether the defendant was mentally fit to assist in his own defense, and again we both responded affirmatively.

The two psychiatrists had prepared their written reports which were marked as exhibits and entered into the record. The judge looked over both reports, noticeably flipping quickly to the conclusion pages.

After reviewing the reports and finding both doctors had arrived at the same conclusion, Judge Cooperman suggested we save some time by having only one of the doctors testify. Marion Marshall and I agreed, and at my suggestion Dr. Najari was called to the witness stand.

Judge Cooperman asked him several questions, the key question being whether Michael Costanza was mentally fit to understand the charges against him and to assist counsel in defending the charges. Dr. Najari answered simply yes. His final question was whether the report entered into evidence contained Dr. Najari's professional opinion and the basis for it. Again Dr. Najari responded affirmatively.

After his questioning, the judge offered Ms. Marshall the opportunity to question Dr. Najari. Ms. Marshall declined the offer and the judge asked if I had any questions for Dr. Najari. Knowing I'd be given that opportunity, I had prepared Dr. Najari, hoping we could squeeze in some testimony about Michael's fragile mental state.

I had to proceed carefully because if I made the point too obviously Marion Marshall would have to object. While she was sympathetic, she still had her marching orders, and I couldn't expect her to just lay down. So I inched along slowly, much to the agitation of Judge Cooperman.

Prodded by the judge to move it along, I got to the point and asked Dr. Najari if it was possible Michael's mental condition could revert leaving him uncommunicative again. Marion Marshall started to stand to object, but apparently thought better of it and sat down without objecting. Dr. Najari replied that it was not only possible, but it would be probable under certain conditions. Judge Cooperman seemed interested in the line of questioning, so I decided to go forward.

The next question was a big one. I knew Marion would object to it, and I had no idea how Judge Cooperman would rule. If he allowed the answer we'd have gotten a bonus, but if he sustained the objection I'd be down to one chance of getting the answer into the record. I'd have to convince the judge to let the doctors testify on my application to keep Michael out of Rikers Island Jail.

I held my breath and asked Dr. Najari under what conditions was it probable Michael could revert to an uncommunicative state. As expected, Ms. Marshall objected, claiming the question called for speculation and was irrelevant to the issue of the defendant's present mental state.

I argued the issue was the defendant's ability to assist in his own defense not only now, but through the conclusion of the case. How could I properly cross-examine a prosecution witness if my client couldn't comment on the witness' testimony? In order for the defendant to receive a fair trial, he had to be able to assist in his own defense during the entire trial. Therefore, any testimony about the circumstances threatening the defendant's ability to do so was relevant.

Judge Cooperman thought about it for minute, then overruled the objection, and allowed Dr. Najari to answer. Dr. Najari replied if Michael wasn't provided with ongoing regular therapy, as well as his medications, or if he was placed in a hostile environment without proper counseling, it was probable he would revert to his prior mental state. I couldn't have asked for a better answer had I written it myself.

I decided to leave it at that, and wait for Judge Cooperman's decision before going any further. Once I said that I had no further questions for Dr. Najari, Judge Cooperman asked Marion Marshall if she now had any questions for Dr. Najari, and she again said "No." Dr. Najari was excused from the witness stand.

To save time, Judge Cooperman simply asked Dr. Mitchell, the second Department of Mental Health psychiatrist, if his professional opinion was contained in his written report, which had been entered into evidence. When the doctor replied affirmatively, Judge Cooperman thanked him, then he adjourned the hearing for an hour, said he would consider the matter, and give his ruling when we reconvened.

CHAPTER 53

It was a nice morning so rather than wait in the courtroom or in the hallway, we went outside and across Centre Street to Thomas Paine Park. We no longer needed Dr. Mitchell, so he left and headed back to his office at Kirby.

I admit that I was nervous. I'm always a little nervous whenever I go into a courtroom. It's part excitement, part adrenaline and part fear, all of which keep me doing it.

In Michael's case there was a lot of worry thrown into the mix. Worry because I wasn't sure exactly what I was doing. I hadn't handled a case like Michael's before, and it made me uneasy. I was comfortable enough in the courtroom, but it was the strategy that had me worried.

It was ironic. There I was sitting on a park bench between two psychiatrists and having this mental crisis, and instead of them helping me, I'm lecturing them. But at least I was smart enough to know I needed to talk to someone. So I excused myself and called Doug.

As I said before, I'm not a true believer in the benefits of psychiatry and besides Doug's advice is free. Five minutes on the phone with Doug, and I was back to being myself. I was still worried about the case, but I had regained my confidence. It wasn't because Doug gave me advice about the case or we even talked about the case. It was simply Doug knows me; he knows what makes me tick; and he knows how to reach me. And, of course, because I trust Doug, I listen to Doug. I don't just hear what Doug is saying; I listen to him and that's different. It took me a while to learn the difference, but once I did, my life got easier.

I can't describe my relationship with Doug any better than that. If you want to know more, you'll have to become an alcoholic, drink heavily for ten or fifteen years, then go into AA and get yourself a good sponsor. That's probably more trouble than it's worth, so I suggest you just take my word for it.

After I spoke with Doug, I called Joe Benjamin and let him know how the hearing had gone so far. He said he had tried to reach out to someone in the DA's Office through a friend, but apparently it hadn't worked out. That was okay because, as I told him, Marion Marshall was being more than fair with us. I promised I'd let him know where we stood as soon as the hearing was over.

It was well past mid-morning, and I was tempted to buy a couple of Sabrett hot dogs from my buddy Pete who worked the cart in the park. But I didn't want to take a chance on being late getting back to court. So instead, we went directly back to Judge Cooperman's courtroom and took our places while my stomach grumbled in protest.

Judge Cooperman took to the bench and announced

his decision. The defendant, Michael Costanza, had been found fit and able to participate in his own defense by two qualified psychiatrists from the Department of Mental Health, so the case against him would go forward. He then asked if there were any other matters to be decided, and I said there was one, the matter of detention.

I explained to the judge I did not expect the court to grant Michael bail, given his lack of community contact, his being homeless and the possible risk of him fleeing the jurisdiction. However, I asked Judge Cooperman to consider the real risk to Michael's fragile mental condition if he was removed from Kirby and deprived not only of his full-time therapy, but of the surroundings that had produced his recovery.

I reminded the judge of Dr. Najari's earlier testimony concerning the circumstances under which Michael would probably revert to his prior mental state. If that happened, the defendant would be unable to assist in his own defense, and the proceedings would have to be suspended. We'd be right back in the position we were in to begin with.

For that reason, I asked the judge to order Michael detained at Kirby rather than sent to the Rikers Island Jail. I mentioned that I could offer further testimony of Dr. Najari and additional testimony from Dr. Goldman to support our position.

Judge Cooperman asked Marion if the DA had any objection to the defendant being held at Kirby. Marion did indeed object, asking that the defendant be sent to Rikers Island Jail. She argued Michael could be given his medication and receive therapy at Rikers just as he could at Kirby, so there was no reason to afford him any special treatment.

I responded that keeping Michael at Kirby wasn't giving him special treatment. It was providing the environment needed to insure that his mental state remained stable so his case could proceed. If he was sent to Rikers and his mental state reverted, then his case could not go forward, and he'd have to be sent back to Kirby anyway. Given what Dr. Najari had said, if Michael was sent to Rikers, he was probably going to wind up back at Kirby with his case in limbo. So why take the risk, when all that needed to be done was to detain Michael at Kirby?

Judge Cooperman looked uncertain. He asked if I was prepared to offer the testimony from the psychiatrists right then and there, and I said I certainly was. The judge turned to Marion and asked if she wanted the hearing adjourned to allow her time to prepare a response. I held my breath hoping Marion would keep her word and she did. She said she was prepared to proceed.

Not knowing how much time Judge Cooperman was going to give us, I decided to call Dr. Goldman to testify first. A new witness always draws slightly more attention than a repeat witness, and I wanted the judge's attention focused.

As soon as I started asking Dr. Goldman questions, I could tell why he was favored by so many lawyers as an expert witness. He was smooth, engaging and very credible. As we moved along, the judge occasionally interrupted to ask a question of his own.

When I finished asking Dr. Goldman questions, it was Marion's turn to cross-examine him. I had never seen Marion in court, and I had no idea how good she was, but

I soon found out. She had a laser-like logical focus that got her right to the point, and she asked questions that left the witness with no wiggle room. As much as I worried she'd hurt us, I had to admire her style.

It eventually all came down to one question. Could Dr. Goldman state "with a reasonable degree of medical certainty that unless Michael Costanza was detained at Kirby, his mental state would revert, and he would become uncommunicative?" It was a good question, and Dr. Goldman was left with no choice but to answer honestly, and say no.

Marion was finished. She had done her job, and she couldn't be criticized by her bosses. However, she left a crack open for me, and I was about to exploit it. But to do so effectively, I needed to get the right answers from Dr. Goldman. I was counting on his skill as an expert witness to understand where we needed to go and help get us there.

I began by asking Dr. Goldman if he was familiar with the facilities at the Rikers Island Jail, which, of course, he was. Then I had him describe Michael's medication regimen and how, when and by whom it was reviewed and altered. As I had hoped, Dr. Goldman understood the importance of the question. He explained in detail how Michael's mental condition was evaluated every twelve hours to ensure his medications were working effectively and no changes or adjustments were needed. I asked him to describe the treatments Michael received at Kirby. Again Dr. Goldman, apparently knowing where I was going with all of this, answered with a lot of detail.

Finally, it was time to exploit the one small

opening Marion had left for me. I took the formal route, and asked Dr. Goldman the preliminary legal question. Did he have "an opinion which he could state with a reasonable degree of medical certainty, as to what would happen to Michael Costanza's mental state if he was detained at Rikers Island Jail." As Dr. Goldman knew from his long experiences testifying in court, it was a one word answer. He said yes.

Now it was time for my big question, "What is that opinion and what is the basis for your opinion?" That's all a good expert witness needs, and Dr. Goldman was a good expert witness. I sat back and listened during the next five minutes as Dr. Goldman explained how and why Michael could not possibly maintain his present mental state if detained at Rikers Island Jail.

I must say his testimony was a thing of beauty. He moved easily and logically from one point to the next, covering everything we had discussed in our prep sessions.

When he was done, and Marion was offered the opportunity to re-cross- examine Dr. Goldman, she wisely declined. She had done the best she could, and she was experienced enough to know any attempt to argue with Dr. Goldman would only hurt her position.

I offered to put Dr. Najari on the witness stand, but Judge Cooperman said he had heard enough. Based upon the testimony of Dr. Goldman, he was ordering that Michael be held at Kirby under a full detention order. He then instructed Marion to take the case to the Grand Jury as soon as possible. After that, the case would be put on the calendar for a formal arraignment and moved forward through normal channels.

Outside of the courtroom I thanked Marion and told her how much I appreciated her understanding. She said simply, it was the right thing to do, and with that answer I knew Marion was a good person. As opposing lawyers, we each have a job to do that often puts us at odds with each other.

There are times when I don't like my opposing counsel, like when they're assholes. But most times we get along and there's no reason we shouldn't. Then there are times, like then with Marion, where we work together for the greater good. You never sacrifice your client's interests for any reason, but sometimes you give an inch because as Marion said, it's the right thing to do.

After parting company with Dr. Najari and Dr. Goldman, both of whom were naturally very happy with the outcome of the hearing, I called Joe Benjamin. Then I called Gracie and invited her to lunch. I needed to talk to her about my problem with Pablo Blanco.

CHAPTER 54

Any time I want to have a quiet conversation with someone at lunchtime, I go to either the Worth Street Coffee Shop or Shoo's Restaurant. Gracie opted for Chinese food, so it was Shoo's.

Seated at a table away from the lunch crowd, I explained to Gracie I needed to speak to someone in the DA's Office who wasn't in the pocket of the Columbian drug cartel. Gracie naturally took exception to my suggestion. People in her office weren't corrupt, but she knew damn well somewhere in the organization there was someone who was on the take. It had always been that way and would always be that way. Corruption and graft were as much a part of government as inefficiency and pensions.

Someone, I don't remember who, once said if we didn't have graft in government, no one worth their salt would become a politician. That it's probably true tells you how sad the whole thing is.

So now you know I don't have a very high regard

for government. I don't mean the concept of government because I know we need governing. What I don't care for is how government typically operates, even without considering the graft. With the exception of the military, I can't think of a single government agency that operates efficiently and economically. And when I say the military, I'm talking about the Armed Services themselves and not the Department of Defense.

Just think of the National Debt. Can you name one single company or individual who could go so many decades operating at a deficit and not be out of business and in bankruptcy?

Did I know for certain someone in the DA's Office was on the Columbian drug cartel payroll? No, no more than I could say for certain old man Shoo used MSG in his food. But in both cases it was the odds-on bet.

The problem with not knowing exactly who's on the take is that you don't know how that person may be linked to other people. You may be dealing with a straight shooter, but the person's secretary could be the leak. Or maybe it's the person's associate, or girlfriend, or wife, or bartender. Are you getting an idea of why I was concerned about who I talked to regarding Pablo's deal?

Gracie suggested I talk with someone in the Violent Criminal Enterprises Unit, and offered to reach out to get me a contact I could trust. I accepted the offer, and promised her a night of bliss in return. She said dinner at the sushi restaurant would do just fine. Damn, how do I get myself into these situations?

If Pablo was actually ready to give up the Prince and the other Columbian drug bosses, it was a very big deal. Once word got out, there would be a very large contract on his life, and every hood in the city would be looking to kill him. Pablo had to hope I could cut him a deal and get him into a protected location before word got out. He said he didn't need witness protection after he testified, but he sure needed it beforehand.

I can't say I was overly thrilled with the situation myself. It wasn't unheard for gang members to work over lawyers when trying to locate witnesses. I imagined with a contract for maybe as high as a million dollars out on Pablo's life, some enterprising hitman might be at my door asking me where he was. But at that point it wasn't an issue, at least I didn't think so.

I parted company with Gracie on Mott Street, outside of Shoo's, promising to meet her later at the sushi restaurant. She headed south back to her office, and I headed north to my office and a meeting with Tommy.

CHAPTER 55

Things were quiet in the office. With no new 18B cases and my old cases all under control, there wasn't much for me to do. Connie said Peter had called which was unusual because he normally called me on my cell phone, not on the office phone. That worried me, so I called him right back. It turned out everything was fine. He had dropped his cell phone into a toilet bowl and it had all his numbers on it, so he had to look up my office number and call there. But now he had a new cell phone, so everything was okay. He started to explain how he had dropped the phone into the toilet, but I said "too much information" and hung up. With Peter, you must be direct sometimes.

Tommy arrived tired and depressed. He had been staking out the housing project hoping to find Latanya, but he had no luck. Nothing had come of his attempts to locate her through the Board of Education, and follow-up visits with her teachers and classmates turned up nothing. Tommy was convinced Latanya wasn't in the neighborhood.

So if she wasn't in the neighborhood, where could she be? Obviously, Mr. Jefferson wasn't living in the apartment with Mrs. Jefferson, so was he alive and, if so, where did he live? Maybe Latanya was with him. It was another long shot, but we had nothing else, so Tommy said he'd get right on it.

Shortly after Tommy left, Gracie called on my cell phone and suggested I call Rita Meyerberg in the Violent Criminal Enterprises Unit. She was a Deputy DA and someone Gracie assured me I could trust. Gracie had spoken briefly with Rita, saying only that a friend of hers had information on the drug cartel and wanted to speak with someone in the DA's Office. She had given Rita my name, so she'd be expecting my call.

I called Rita right away. I explained, hypothetically, that I had a client who had information on high-ranking members of the Columbian drug cartel, and he was willing to exchange that information for a price. Of course, Rita asked if my client was presently under indictment and if he was, why wasn't I talking with the ADA handling his case? I explained while my client was under indictment he feared if word got out about his attempted deal he'd be killed, and he didn't trust the ADA handling his case. In fact, officially I wasn't even handling his case for fear that alone would tip off the bosses. Rita understood the situation and assured me I had come to the right place.

Rita agreed to see me the next day, but she warned me that she was skeptical about me having anything worthwhile to offer. I promised to bring along enough information to convince her otherwise. Now I had to deliver, so I pulled the burner cell phone out of my desk drawer and called Pablo.

Pablo was delighted I was working on his case. Things were getting hot for him, and he wasn't sure how much longer he could stay on the street. That was good because it would probably make it easier for me to ask him for the information I needed to take to Rita.

I know how guys like Pablo think, so I wasn't surprised when he didn't want to give me any information until he had a deal. But Pablo isn't stupid, so he understood he had to give up something to start the negotiations.

We finally came to an agreement. No names, no addresses, only past delivery locations the cops could verify, and the current delivery locations for the South Bronx. Once the negotiations got serious, Pablo promised to give me names and addresses in both New York and in Columbia. I wasn't sure that I had enough to motivate Rita, so I convinced Pablo to give me one name and address. I promised I'd keep that information as a last resort bargaining chip and would only use it if I had to. Pablo trusted me, and I got the name and address.

I knew that I was about to get myself into the middle of a big and dangerous mess. I just didn't know how big a mess it was going to be.

That night I had to pay off my debt to FBI Agent Michael Chang for getting me Michael Costanza's files. I met Agent Chang at Ruth's Chris Steak House and we enjoyed a leisurely and very expensive dinner together. I think I mentioned the last time I took Agent Chang to dinner at Ruth's Chris he ate a lot, and I paid for it with my lungs. Well, Agent Chang's appetite hadn't diminished since then; in fact, it may have grown, so the dinner cost me my heart, kidneys, spleen and liver. Seriously, I enjoyed the evening with Michael; he's a good guy even if he's a glutton.

CHAPTER 56

The next morning Marion Marshall called. She was taking Michael's case to the Grand Jury that afternoon. She didn't expect Michael to testify, but she wanted to give me notice anyway. I confirmed that Michael had no intention of appearing, and thanked her for the notice.

Ninety-nine times out of a hundred there's nothing to be gained by a defendant appearing before the Grand Jury. Of course, most of my clients have been low-life gangbangers and assorted scumbags with bad attitudes. I'm sure if any of them appeared before a Grand Jury, the jurors would look for a way to give them the death penalty.

I only had one client who insisted on appearing before the Grand Jury. I called him Mr. Genius. He was charged with murdering his girlfriend, but swore he was innocent. Of course the facts said otherwise, but it didn't seem to bother Mr. Genius.

Mr. Genius was arrested when the police responded to a call from neighbors about a woman screaming, and they found him alone in the locked apartment with the dead woman. Mr. Genius admitted he had been in the apartment all night, but said he didn't kill the woman. He claimed someone must have broken into their apartment and murdered the woman while he was sleeping next to her. There was no sign of forced entry and as I mentioned, the police found the door locked when they arrived. None of that mattered to Mr. Genius, who believed he could convince a Grand Jury not to indict him.

Despite my vigorous objection, he appeared before the Grand Jury. The law allows me to appear with a client, but I'm not allowed to say or do anything. So I sat there silently while Mr. Genius told the jurors he and his girlfriend were sleeping when someone must have broken into the apartment and killed her. Then he said, "I swear it wasn't me and you can believe it because I don't lie. So are we good?" Apparently not. One of the jurors confronted him with the testimony of the neighbor that his girlfriend was screaming on the night she was murdered. That's when Mr. Genius offered his logical explanation saying, "That can't be. See, I told you I was sleeping. If she was screaming, I couldn't be sleeping, could I? Now are we good?"

I think you know the answer to his question. But just to finish the story, Mr. Genius currently resides at the Clinton Correctional Facility in Dannamora and will be living there for the next twenty-plus years.

But Mr. Genius wasn't on my mind that morning. Michael Costanza was, and there were two things I was sure of as I sat at my desk. One, Michael wasn't going to appear before the Grand Jury, and two, the Grand Jury was going to indict him.

Unless I slowed the proceedings down, the case would move quickly through the system to trial. It had been just over two months since the murder and Michael's arrest. While the case had been in limbo, it hadn't stopped the police and the DA's Office from preparing for trial. Now that the case was again officially on track, I had to prepare an updated discovery demand and put the DA on notice of any affirmative defenses I intended to use. That meant I had to notify the DA if I planned on claiming Michael was justified in killing Lover Boy.

The justification defense is an admission that the defendant committed the murder, but had an excusable reason for doing so. I wasn't sure I wanted to make that admission, but with Michael insisting he had killed Lover Boy, I didn't seem to have much of a choice.

The law allows a defendant to plead alternative and inconsistent defenses. Technically it's called pleading in the alternative, which doesn't sound bad. But it doesn't sound as good when you apply it to the facts. Simply put, it comes out this way, "I didn't do it. But if I did do it, I had a good reason for doing it." Trust me, juries are not ordinarily open to alternative defenses.

A lawyer friend of mine, who practices civil law, used a hypothetical dog bite case to illustrate the problem with alternative defenses. Defense one, I don't own the dog. Defense two, I own the dog, but it doesn't bite. Defense three, the dog I own bites, but it didn't bite the plaintiff. Defense four, the dog I own bites, and it bit the plaintiff, but it didn't hurt. I think that makes the point.

Unless Michael changed his story about killing Lover Boy, I had to use the justification defense. But unless we found Latanya or someone else to back up the justification claim, it wasn't going to work. I was getting very frustrated and running out of ideas. That's when I decided to call Claire to ask her to talk with Michael and convince him to tell us the truth about what had happened that night under the bridge. It was still much too early in the morning in California to make the call, but having a plan at least made me feel better.

It was time to go see Rita Meyerberg, and hopefully work out a deal for Pablo Blanco.

CHAPTER 57

Rita Meyerberg was a small, slightly overweight woman who appeared to be in her late fifties or early sixties. She had only been working in the New York DA's Office for five years which explained in part why I didn't know her.

Prior to coming to New York, she had been a Senior Deputy in the Philadelphia District Attorney's Office and headed up the Dangerous Drug Offenders Department of the Special Operations Division. It was a unique arrangement in which the ADAs were cross-designated as Special Assistant United States Attorneys able to prosecute cases in federal court, as well as state court. It was a clever way of moving drug and gun cases out of the state court and into federal court where the penalties were more severe.

Rita turned out to be a pleasant, but no-nonsense woman who knew her stuff when it came to drug crimes. After we exchanged some pleasantries and she told me about her background, she got right to the point. If I had something worthwhile to offer, I had to put it on the table. Otherwise, there was no sense of us wasting each other's time.

I said my client was a mid-level dealer who was being pushed out of the organization. He knew his arrest had been set up by his bosses, and once he got to prison he'd probably be killed. His only way out was to cut a deal that kept him from going to prison. He was smart enough to know he'd only get a deal like that if he had something big to offer, and he said he did.

As a show of good faith, I gave Rita the information on the past drug delivery locations, and suggested she check them with the police to verify my client knew what he was talking about. But Rita was tough and said that wasn't good enough. I said it was just a start to verify my client's knowledge. But Rita stuck to her guns. If I didn't have anything more to offer, the meeting was over. I was boxed in, so I gave her one of the current delivery locations in the Bronx. It was a location the cops didn't know about.

Rita was interested, so now I had a little bit of leverage. I needed her word that the cops wouldn't raid the location before we had a deal because it might expose my client. I knew the DA's Office has its own investigators, and I suggested she use one of them to confirm what my client was saying. If she couldn't give me her word they wouldn't raid the place, my client would have the delivery location changed.

I could tell we were close to a deal, so I shut up. The ball was in Rita's court. She thought things over for a minute and then said she'd have her people check out the information, and if it was good, she'd get back to me. I was getting ready to leave Rita's office when she asked why my client didn't want witness protection as part of the deal. I told her I didn't know, but I thought he was being dumb.

I was leaving the DA's Office when Tommy called on my cell. He was excited and wanted to see me right away. He had some good news, but he didn't want to tell me over the phone, so he asked me to meet him at Shoo's Restaurant.

CHAPTER 58

Seated at a table in the back of the restaurant, Tommy said he had heard from Carlos Ramirez. Latanya had called him. She was staying at an aunt's house in Longs, South Carolina, not far from Myrtle Beach. I had no idea where either Longs or Myrtle Beach was, and had only a faint recollection of South Carolina from my grade school geography class. But that didn't matter. What mattered was we now knew where to find Latanya, the one person I was counting on to tell me what happened under the bridge. She could either prove Michael hadn't killed Lover Boy, or if he had, he'd acted in her defense when he whacked him with the hammer.

Carlos had given Tommy the phone number Latanya had called from. Tommy ran a check on the number, and it turned out to be a private landline at a house in Longs, which he presumed belonged to Latanya's aunt. Tommy had considered calling the number, but he was afraid the call would spook Latanya or her aunt, and they might move her again.

Locating Latanya was good, and we were both excited, Tommy more so than me. He had already figured out he could fly to the Myrtle Beach Airport, rent a car, and be in Longs in less than an hour. All he needed was for me to give him the go-ahead. I was ready to do just that, but first I wanted to be sure we had a plan that would work.

If Tommy suddenly turned up at Latanya's aunt's house unannounced, was Latanya likely to talk to him, or was it more likely someone would shove a shotgun in his face and chase him off the property? Tommy's a persuasive guy in New York, but I wasn't sure how well he'd do in Longs, South Carolina. To be truthful, scenes from the movie, *Deliverance*, kept popping into my head.

I don't want to cast aspersions on Longs, even though God knows, I never intend to go there. But if you saw *Deliverance*, scenes from the movie automatically enter your head whenever small backwater southern towns are mentioned or banjos are played. Fortunately, Tommy hadn't seen the movie.

Tommy suggested having Carlos go with him, and that sounded like a good idea. I was sure Joe Benjamin would approve the trip, so that wasn't a problem. The problem was keeping the trip quiet, so none of the TB Gangsters found out about it. Tommy going by himself wasn't a problem, but involving Carlos was another story altogether.

Carlos liked to talk, so once Tommy brought up the subject of going to Longs to see Latanya, he had to get Carlos out of the neighborhood right away before he told anyone about the trip. Tommy assured me it wouldn't be a problem because Carlos was in love with Latanya, and would do anything to help her. I took Tommy at his word, and said I'd clear it with Benjamin, and he could go as soon as we figured out what the hell he was going to do when he got there.

I left Shoo's in a good mood. We had finally gotten a break and it was a big one. We still needed to get Latanya to cooperate and there was no guarantee she would, but at least we knew where she was. I wasn't putting all our eggs in that basket, so when I got back to the office I called Claire.

It was a little past nine o'clock in the morning, California time and Claire was home. I asked her if she'd spoken to Michael recently, and she said a couple of days ago. Things were improving between them and if he wasn't sent to jail, she was considering inviting him to live with her and her husband for a while. I said she was being very kind to her brother, but unless he started giving me some straight answers about the murder, his chances of avoiding a jail term were slim. As I expected, she asked if she could help in any way.

I explained to Claire the problem I was having in putting together Michael's defense, and asked if she was willing to ask him some questions I needed answered. It wasn't going to be easy. She might have to lie to him and maybe bully him a bit, but if we didn't get answers to those questions Michael was most likely going to jail. Claire didn't like the idea of having to lie to Michael, but she understood the seriousness of the situation and agreed to do it.

For the next half hour, I gave Claire a list of questions and some ideas on how to approach Michael with each question. I filled her in on the forensic findings, and explained how she could best use the findings to confront Michael if he lied to her.

When I was done prepping Claire, I set up a conference call with Claire, Dr. Najari and me. Actually, Connie set up the conference call; I just watched her do it. But I was the one on the call.

Dr. Najari suggested the best time for Claire to call was the next day after 2 o'clock (EST). It would be after Michael's noontime therapy session, and after he took his medications. Claire said she was available then and would call, but she was afraid if she pushed Michael it might do him harm. Dr. Najari didn't think that would happen, but he said he'd be listening in on the call. If he thought there was a problem, he'd warn Claire and she could back off.

I wouldn't be in on the conversation, but Dr. Najari said he would call and let me know how it went as soon as it ended. I thanked Claire for her help and we all hung up.

Now I had two irons in the fire and, for the first time in a while, I was starting to feel confident about Michael's chances. I didn't have anything definite, but I was feeling good.

I called Joe Benjamin and shared the good news, and got him to agree to send Tommy and Carlos down to Longs, South Carolina. I didn't know how much it was going to cost, but it seemed cost was no object when it came to defending Michael.

It was Thursday, the third Thursday of the month, which meant the lawyers' AA group was meeting that afternoon in the basement of the Supreme Court Building. I hadn't been paying attention to the time, so I had to run to get there before the meeting started. I didn't want to miss the meeting because it's always a great meeting, and it's also my chance to see my pigeon, Peter.

CHAPTER 59

The lawyers' AA group meeting is always good for a few laughs. You know, when I started going to AA meetings what impressed me right away was how happy most of the people there were. I had expected to find a bunch of miserable drunks sitting around bitching about one thing or another. But what I found were mostly happy men and women who were a lot more relaxed than I was. I soon learned what they had was called "serenity" and I wanted it.

Just so you understand, when I say the meeting is good for a few laughs, that doesn't mean it's frivolous. It only means recovery and fun aren't mutually exclusive. That's particularly true when it comes to lawyers, especially trial lawyers. Many trial lawyers are notorious drunks. I think it comes with the job.

Anyway, I ran into Peter and Doug at the meeting. After the meeting, Peter cornered me and told me he has a new girlfriend. She's not in the program and drinks, not a lot, but some. Did I think it was a problem either for her or for him? I said not if she had a great ass. Peter is used to my style of sponsoring, so he knows after I give him my smartass comments, I'll say something brilliant. Well, maybe not brilliant, but smart.

Peter's concerns aren't unique. All drunks in recovery have those same concerns in one form or another. How can I go out with friends who drink if I don't drink? What are people at the party going to think when I don't drink? Do I have to stay home to stay sober?

I reminded Peter he's living in a world where people drink. Since he was in AA, he'd gone to any number of functions where people were drinking. So what's the difference if it's a girlfriend, or the guy from the office next door?

As long as his girlfriend accepted the fact he was an alcoholic and didn't drink, it shouldn't be a problem. However, if he found her encouraging him to take a sip, or to try just one drink, then it was time to run, no matter how great her ass might be.

After the meeting, I hooked up with Gracie at her office, and we went out to dinner. I was still thinking about Peter when I asked Gracie if she ever felt uncomfortable being out with me because I didn't drink. She laughed and said not nearly as uncomfortable as she had been when she was out with me, and I had been drinking. I had to laugh, then I had to call Peter and tell him what Gracie had said.

It reminded me of the time early in my recovery when I told Doug I was worried about what my clients would think of me not drinking. First, he said if they didn't like me sober, they probably wouldn't like me drunk. Then he thought about it for a while and said,

"You keep telling me all of your clients are scumbags, and all of sudden you're worried about what they're going to think of you because you don't drink?" He had a point there.

Gracie surprised me by asking if her drinking made me uncomfortable. She had asked the same question years earlier when we had gone on our first date after I went into AA. I told her then that her drinking didn't bother me, and it didn't. Since then the question never came up until that night.

I asked Gracie what prompted the question, and she said she never thought to ask after our first date, but maybe she should ask occasionally. I assured her it wasn't necessary, and if her drinking ever bothered me, I'd be sure to let her know. I probably should have left it at that, but you know me. I had to add a smartass comment. I said if she ever stopped drinking she might not be such an easy lay. Did you know being hit in the head with a piece of Italian bread can leave a mark?

CHAPTER 60

When things start going badly, it usually happens in bunches, and that's what was happening with Michael's case. First, Dr. Garland called and asked if I wanted him to continue working on the case because, frankly, he didn't see how he could help me. As much as I didn't want to admit he was right, I knew he was. Since I didn't know the facts, I was clutching at straws, hoping I could get Garland to support some half-assed theory.

I needed fact witnesses and until I had at least one willing to testify, an expert witness wasn't going to do me any good. I could play around as I mentioned earlier, but without a supporting fact witness I'd just be kicking up a lot of dust and nothing else. I told Garland he could close his file and send me his bill. If things changed, I'd let him know, and he could reopen the file.

A little while later Dr. Najari called. Claire had spoken to Michael. Dr. Najari thought she had done an excellent job following the plan I laid out for her the night before, but it didn't work. Despite everything, Claire said

Michael continued to insist he killed Lover Boy.

Dr. Najari wasn't surprised because he didn't think Michael's insistence on taking responsibility for Lover Boy's murder was a conscious decision. Rather, it was the product of a subconscious conflict between reality and his guilt over the Logan incident. If that was true, there wasn't much any of us could do in the short term to change Michael's mind.

I had only one option for Michael's defense. It was getting Latanya to come back to New York and testify. The only problem was that I had no idea how I was going to do it.

I was thinking about Latanya when Connie came rushing into my office. She had been listening to her radio and just heard Pablo Blanco had been gunned down and killed in the Bronx. I don't know why, but the news hit me hard. I didn't particularly like Pablo; as matter of fact, I couldn't stand what he did. But for some reason I felt badly about him being killed. Maybe it was the way he died, being gunned down in the street. Laying there with people staring at him.

Maybe I'm getting soft in my old age. If I am, I probably don't belong in this business any longer. I mean, you've got to be tough to survive as a criminal defense lawyer. If you're not tough and cynical, you start believing all the hard luck stories your clients hand you. Then you suffer when you find out they were lying and they're sent off to prison.

Most young lawyers tend to believe their clients, and they want to fight for them against all odds. It's a nice thing, but it's stupid. You learn quickly that truth is whatever you can prove, and it certainly isn't what your client tells you.

I never had a client who didn't claim he was innocent. And not just in the case of street crimes. You've seen all the politicians and businessmen charged with fraud or bribery professing their innocence, claiming they can't wait for a trial to prove their innocence and clear their names. The next time you see them is leaving court in handcuffs after they've been convicted.

If you're not cynical, you can wind up hurting your client. You have to look at a client's position realistically to know what kind of deal to cut. If you believe your clients' cock-and-bull stories, and don't challenge them, you're going to turn down good deals. In the end, clients wind up doing more time.

Sooner or later you come to realize if you aren't cynical, you're going to pay a big price in this business. Fortunately for me, I started out on the other side of the criminal justice system. When you work in the DA's Office you get cynical right away. It's part of the job. When I moved over to the defense side, I was already hard-core cynical and nothing happened to change me. At least I don't think so. That's why I was puzzled over feeling badly about Pablo being killed.

News of Pablo's demise got around fast. Within an hour, I got a call from Rita Meyerberg asking if I had heard the news and telling me she was closing out her file on Blanco. What could I say? I figured it was over, but it wasn't over.

A week after Pablo was killed, I got a letter in the mail. It was from Pablo, but there was no return address on the envelope. There was a cover letter, handwritten by Pablo, instructing me to turn over to the authorities the enclosed information about the Columbian drug cartel in New York. Included with the note were a half-dozen pages of handwritten notes about the cartel's operations, including names, addresses, and drug locations. It was Pablo's revenge letter.

By the way, in the note Pablo said I should keep the fee. The sentiment was nice, but what else did he expect me to do with it? Send it back to him? I guess I could have sent him a check.

I decided rather than call Rita, I'd drop by her office and give her the letter in person. She was surprised to see me, and looked a little skeptical when I said our business wasn't quite finished. Then I dropped the letter and the other pages on her desk, and told her to go get the bad guys.

CHAPTER 61

I was sitting in my office with the door closed trying to figure out my next move in Michael's case when Tommy came bursting into the room with a young Latino boy in tow. The boy was Carlos Ramirez, Latanya's friend, and he seemed as puzzled as I was why he was in my office.

Tommy sat the confused boy in a chair and explained what he was doing there. It seemed word was getting around the housing project that Carlos knew something about Latanya's whereabouts, so Tommy had grabbed him off the street for his own protection. Now Tommy needed someplace to stow Carlos until they left for Longs to try and convince Latanya to come back to New York. Tommy thought maybe I could keep Carlos at my place until then.

There was no way I was going to babysit a 15-year-old kid, not to mention we could be facing a kidnapping charge. I asked Tommy if, by chance, he had mentioned any of this to Carlos' mother, so she wouldn't report the boy missing. He said he hadn't thought about it, but he'd take care of it. I suggested while he was doing that, he might want to figure out a way to get the kid some clothes and maybe a toothbrush. He might also consider how we were going to feed him. I assumed Tommy never had a pet when he was growing up, or if he did, it hadn't lived very long.

Once I got Tommy focused, we put together a workable plan. Carlos would stay with Tommy in one of the apartments upstairs from the restaurant. Tommy would let Carlos' mother know what was happening, and pick up some clothes for the kid. But he wouldn't tell the kid's mother exactly where Carlos was. Hopefully Tommy and Carlos would be going to South Carolina soon, so the kid wouldn't have to spend too long cooped up in the apartment.

Just to be safe, we convinced Carlos to turn off his cell phone and give it to Tommy. Carlos was concerned that Latanya might try calling him again, so Tommy was going to check the phone every couple of hours. If Latanya called Carlos, Tommy would have Carlos call her back, but only while Tommy was there listening in. Carlos didn't particularly like the plan, but he was a smart kid and realized he didn't have a say in it.

Things were getting very complicated, and I was worried if we weren't careful, the whole situation would explode on us. But since Claire's effort to get Michael to tell the truth about what had happened under the bridge had failed, the only chance we had to get to the truth was through Latanya.

I thought there was time to work out a plan, but with this new development our timeline had tightened. It wouldn't be long before the gangbangers realized Carlos was missing and went looking for him. Carlos was somewhat of a loose cannon and since we couldn't keep an eye on him 24/7, even if he was upstairs from the restaurant, he was a risk. Too many loose ends; too many risks. I wasn't a happy camper and for good reason.

CHAPTER 62

Usually good things don't follow when Tommy bursts into my office unannounced. For two days, Carlos had been staying in Tommy's apartment upstairs from the restaurant, and Tommy was going off the deep end. At the moment, Tommy had the kid parked in an apartment old man Shoo was having renovated. It had no furniture, no appliances and no phone, but it did have lock-down windows.

Tommy wanted the kid out, but he couldn't find a safe place to put him. He begged me to take Carlos to my place, but it wasn't going to happen and Tommy knew it.

I told Tommy to sit down and relax, and we'd figure it all out. Frankly, I had already decided to send Tommy and Carlos to South Carolina the next day. I had just gotten off the phone with Joe Benjamin and gotten formal approval for the trip. I still thought a part of the cost was coming out of Joe's pocket, but it didn't bother me as much now because I had paid for Agent Chang's dinner at Ruth's Chris.

As it turned out, I had to advance the money for the South Carolina trip, but I still had some of Pablo's fee in my desk drawer, so it wasn't a problem.

I told Tommy to sit with Connie and figure out how he and Carlos were going to get to South Carolina. After that, we'd talk about what he was going to do when he got there.

It didn't take Connie long to work out the logistics. Tommy and Carlos would fly to Myrtle Beach, South Carolina, on Spirit Airlines out of LaGuardia Airport. There were two flights a day, one in the morning and one in the evening. Tommy preferred the evening flight because he didn't want to get up early. I didn't care which flight they took. Connie booked the evening flight for the following day using my credit card.

Tommy would need a rental car which he'd book himself at the Myrtle Beach Airport. The only thing left was the motel or hotel room. But before we booked any rooms, I wanted to make sure Tommy and Carlos knew what to do when they got down there.

I still had no idea how we'd convince Latanya to come back to New York. But first things first, we had to make sure she was where we thought she was. So Tommy's first job was to confirm Latanya was in South Carolina living at her aunt's house.

Carlos was going along only because we couldn't figure out what else to do with him, and he sure as hell wasn't staying at my place. Tommy only agreed to take him along if they had separate rooms. I couldn't very well say no, especially if Tommy wouldn't agree to take him if I said no.

I didn't want Tommy or Carlos talking to Latanya

or her aunt until we knew what we were doing. I was worried if Tommy approached them, they'd get spooked and take off. If Latanya was there, I wanted her to stay there until I knew for certain we could bring her back to New York. Tommy agreed that was the way to go, and said he'd be careful not to let Latanya see Carlos.

Eventually we found a place for the dynamic duo to stay in South Carolina. Tommy wanted to stay in one of the ocean front resorts in North Myrtle Beach, and I wanted them to sleep in the rental car. We compromised and booked them into the Day's Inn in a place called Little River.

After the arrangements had been made, Tommy said he needed some cash for expenses, including a suitcase for Carlos. I had no problem advancing cash for living expenses because it was understandable, but not for a suitcase. I suggested Carlos put his stuff in Tommy's suitcase, but Tommy wanted no part of that. We almost agreed on a plastic bag for Carlos' stuff, but then I started feeling a little badly for the kid, and gave Tommy an extra $50 for a suitcase.

I would have lent Carlos my suitcase, but I don't own one. I've never been away long enough or far enough to need one. Gracie has tried a couple of times to get me to go away with her, but so far I've been able to resist. She's gone to some Caribbean islands or somewhere like that once or twice since we've been together, and I missed her while she was gone. But I have no desire to leave Manhattan. Gracie swears she's going to get me to Europe, but it'll be a cold day in hell before that happens.

Anyway, I'm rambling here, so let me get back to the story. Connie printed out a couple of things, which I think she said were the plane tickets and the hotel reservation. Tommy took the papers and the wad of cash I had given him from the Pablo money and left. Now it was just a matter of waiting for confirmation that Latanya was in South Carolina at her aunt's house. After that, I wasn't sure what we were going to do.

CHAPTER 63

The rest of that day and the next day while I waited for Tommy and Carlos to arrive in South Carolina and report back, I didn't have much to do. I made a new demand on the DA's Office for any additional Forensic Reports and spoke with both Dr. Najari and Dr. Goldman to make sure Michael was still okay. I was glad to hear he was doing well, and both doctors were very optimistic about a full recovery, provided, of course, he stayed in treatment.

With nothing else to keep me busy, I was restless and for me that's not a good thing. When I got restless back in the day, I drank, but I hadn't done that in years, and I wasn't about to start. But just to make sure, I went to a couple of meetings.

I called Doug a few times and went over to Gracie's office and pestered her a bit. She finally had enough, and told me to leave and find something constructive to do. So I went and bought myself a couple of Sabrett hot dogs and sat on a park bench and ate them.

It's amazing, but when you're waiting for something and you have nothing else to do, time stands still. But when you're busy, very busy, there's never enough time. I know I'm not telling you something you don't already know, but I'm trying to give you a sense of what I was feeling during those couple of days.

I think I was worried that I hadn't come up with an idea about what we were going to do next. That's something else that bothers me, uncertainty. I don't know if it's an alcoholic thing, but I know a lot of people in AA feel the same way. It probably comes from us wanting to be in control of everything, so when we realize we're not in control and everything is uncertain, we get nervous.

That first day I almost called Tommy and told him to change his flight to the early morning departure, but I didn't. So on the second day, the day Tommy and Carlos finally left for South Carolina, I spent most of the day looking at my watch.

They weren't leaving until 6:30 that night and not arriving until 8:30, but I still spent most of the day looking at my watch. That night at dinner it drove Gracie crazy, and at one point she threatened to leave the restaurant if I didn't stop looking at my watch. I don't know if she realized it or not, but after she said that I kept adjusting the napkin on my lap.

I hate to admit this, but even while we were making love that night I took a quick peek at the clock on the nightstand. I know I'm bad, but sometimes I just can't help myself.

CHAPTER 64

The next day about mid-morning Tommy called from Longs, South Carolina. The flight had gone well, and he and Carlos were all settled in at the hotel. At that moment, he was sitting in a car with Carlos outside of Latanya's aunt's house. So far they hadn't seen Latanya, but her brother, Tyrone was in the yard playing catch with a couple of other kids. So it was likely Latanya was around somewhere. Tommy, following my instructions, was making sure neither he nor Carlos could be seen from the aunt's house.

I was about to hang up on Tommy when something hit me. I didn't know very much about Latanya's brother, and I began to wonder why he was in Longs. I asked Tommy how old he was, and Tommy said he was thirteen. My mind started to race. He was playing catch, so I asked Tommy whether he was left-handed or right-handed. There was a pause that seemed like an eternity, but then Tommy said Tyrone was left-handed.

I don't know why I ignored Tyrone for so long.

Maybe it was because I was concentrating so much on reaching Michael, or maybe I was just getting old and slipping. But whatever it was, Tyrone was now front and center on my mind, and I had a new theory to work on.

If Tyrone had killed Johnson, then everything was starting to make sense, including Michael's mumbling "Tell them I did it." Latanya probably told her mother what had happened under the bridge and, of course, Mrs. Jefferson knowing what her son had done, wouldn't go to the police. But believing the TB Gangsters would probably find out what had happened and seek revenge, she sent both kids to hide out at her sister's place in South Carolina.

I needed to find out what Latanya and Tyrone had to say. But with Tyrone facing a possible murder charge, and both he and Latanya on the TB Gangsters' hit list it wasn't likely either one would be very cooperative. The only one who could get them to cooperate would be their mother, and I needed to talk with her right away.

I told Tommy to stay put and make sure neither Latanya nor Tyrone saw him or Carlos. Once they confirmed Latanya was in Long's, I wanted both of them back in the hotel, and staying there until they heard from me.

With Tommy in South Carolina, I'd have to go into the project alone to talk with Mrs. Jefferson. While I wasn't thrilled with the idea, I knew I had to do it. I thought about calling Richie Simone and asking him to come with me, but I figured given the circumstances, Mrs. Jefferson wouldn't want to talk in front of a cop. That left me with no choice but to go on my own.

CHAPTER 65

It was early evening and just starting to get dark when I got to the housing project, so it wasn't the best time to be going into the place. I had intended to enter through the walkway on the south side, the same way Tommy and I had gone in. But when I arrived, there were a couple of TB Gangsters hanging out about halfway down the path, so I walked on.

Now I had problem. I couldn't very well enter by way of the alley from the west because that's where the gang did its drug business, so the area was full of gangbangers. If I went around and entered by way of the north walkway, I'd have to walk across more of the open square, and there were likely to be some gangbangers sitting on the benches. That left only the alley entrance on the east side of the project.

The entrance to the building was close to the corners near the north-south walkways. That's why using the walkways as an access route was preferable to the alley entrance. If I used the alley, I'd have to walk almost the entire length of the southeast building on the wide roadway, which would make me plainly visible from any number of locations. I hated to think about the possible consequences, but I didn't have a lot of choices. It was either use the alley entrance or wait for the gangbangers to clear out of the south side pathway.

I'm not the bravest guy in the world, at least not since I got sober, but there comes a time when you must put away your fears and do what you must do. Someone once said bravery wasn't the lack of fear; it was acting despite your fears. I'm not saying what I did was brave, only that I was scared, but did it anyway.

I tried walking down the alley as casually as I could, keeping my head down and not trying not to shake too much. My heart was beating like one of Cozy Cole's drums during Topsy Part II, and I was trying to figure out what I'd do if the TB Gangsters confronted me. Unfortunately, I couldn't come up with a scenario that didn't end with me either dead or in the hospital.

Somehow I managed to get to the front door of the southeast building without being spotted. Once inside I had a decision to make. Should I take the elevator or the stairs to the fourth floor? When I was there with Tommy, it was during the early afternoon, and we hadn't seen anybody around, so we took the elevator. But since it was much later, there was a good chance someone would be using the elevator. Of course, the stairs could be a problem as well. My dilemma was solved when I heard the elevator motor start running, and I made a beeline for the stairway door.

Going up cautiously, stopping on each landing and listening for footsteps, but only hearing my beating heart,

I finally made it to the fourth floor. I took a minute or two to catch my breath and after checking to make sure there was no one in the hallway, I made my way down to Apartment 4G.

I banged on the door and called out for Mrs. Jefferson. She came to the door, but didn't open it. She apparently looked through the peephole, and I think she recognized me because she asked what I wanted and not who I was. I said I needed to talk to her, and asked her to let me in. She said we had nothing to talk about, and I should leave.

I decided I had to take my best shot, so I said I knew the truth about what happened under the bridge and where her children were. There was silence on the other side of the door, then I heard the locks turn and the door opened. I asked if I could come in, and she stepped aside to let me pass. She relocked the door, then led me into the living room and invited me to take a seat.

Once we were seated, Mrs. Jefferson begged me to forget what I knew and to leave her and her children alone. I said I couldn't do that, but I had no intention of hurting her or her children. I just needed Tyrone and Latanya to come back to New York, and explain everything that had happened under the bridge.

If they did that, everything would work out fine. But Mrs. Jefferson thought it was too late for that. The TB Gangsters had made it clear to her they wanted Tyrone and Latanya dead, and they were going to find them and kill them.

Mrs. Jefferson knew the TB Gangsters well, and she knew how they operated, so there was no way she'd have her children come back to the city. There was so much pain in her voice I couldn't help but feel sorry for her, and if there had been any other way, I wouldn't be asking her to do this. But there was no other way.

She was crying, and she begged me once more to leave her and the children alone. Again, I told her I couldn't do that, and she asked me why not. I told her because an innocent man who was trying to protect her son would go to jail for a crime he hadn't committed, and I couldn't let that happen. One way or the other, Tyrone was going to face up to what he had done, and it would be better for him if he did it voluntarily.

Mrs. Jefferson took a couple of deep breaths, wiped her eyes, and I believe she resolved herself to the fact I wasn't going to let this thing go. I say that because she asked me how it would work, and what would happen to Tyrone.

I explained that I couldn't represent Tyrone, but I would help her get a good lawyer for him. Under the circumstances I was confident there would be no charges brought against him. He had acted in defense of his sister who, but for his intervention, would have been raped by Lover Boy. Michael Costanza would corroborate both Tyrone and Latanya's testimony, and that would be more than enough to establish the truth.

I told Mrs. Jefferson when the children came back, I'd try to find a place for all of them to stay far away from the housing project and the TB Gangsters. But I felt obligated to caution her that afterward there was no way I could assure her that she and the children would be safe in New York. I wasn't surprised when she said she knew that, and had already decided to move to Longs to be with her sister. She hadn't planned on having the children come back, but she knew now they had to.

Mrs. Jefferson made us coffee, and while we drank it, she called her sister. We had decided the children should stay there until I made all the arrangements in New York, then Tommy would bring them up. Just to make sure I wasn't promising something I couldn't deliver, I called Joe Benjamin and got his approval for all the arrangements.

What we were doing was very unusual, but this was an unusual case from the start. Joe said the 18B Panel would pick up the expenses to bring the children back to New York, and to house them and Mrs. Jefferson somewhere safe until everything had been resolved. Then he surprised me and said he'd approve paying for the whole family's airfare down to Myrtle Beach after the matter was over. It was much later I found out a good deal of the money for all of this came out of Joe's pocket and not from the 18B Panel funds.

With the details taken care of, there was nothing left for me to do, but figure out how to get out of the housing project alive. Mrs. Jefferson, much relieved to have her problems solved, offered to walk me out, but she was still a target of TB Gangsters, so I couldn't let her.

Looking out her living room window, we could see the middle square and there was a dozen or so teenagers hanging out on the benches. To make matters worse, Mrs. Jefferson said they were all TB Gangsters, and there was no way I could go out of the building without being seen. Whatever bravery I had shown when I came into the building was officially gone.

I was thinking of calling the cops, or asking Mrs. Jefferson if she had a spare bedroom I could use, when she said she had an idea. Her idea turned out to be her neighbor, Gus, a six-foot, six-inch, three-hundred thirty-pound mountain of a man who worked in the project's maintenance department.

Gus knew the layout of the building but, more importantly, he had keys giving him access to the locked areas in the basement. These were areas leading to a rear door that exited near the end of the south side pathway. My escape route to safety.

I thanked Mrs. Jefferson and told her I'd be in contact soon, then I followed Gus out into the hallway and down to the elevator. I wasn't sure taking the elevator was wise, but I wasn't about to argue with Gus.

As it turned out, I had nothing to worry about because when we stopped on the second floor, Gus stood in front of the doors virtually blocking both access and sight into the elevator. When the doors opened, I couldn't tell who was standing there because I couldn't see around Gus' huge body. But whoever it was must have been an unwanted passenger because Gus pushed hard with his right hand saying "Full. Take another one." Then I heard a loud thump as whoever was on the receiving end of Gus' shove hit the floor.

When the elevator reached the basement and the doors opened, Gus got out and told me to follow him. He didn't have to say that because I had no intention of doing anything else. We were in what seemed to be a vacant laundry room with a dozen or so washing machines and dryers, all of which were rather mangled. Gus, noticing my quizzical look, volunteered that none of the machines worked because the "bastard gangbangers" vandalized them trying to get to the coin boxes. The city had replaced the machines a couple of times, but had apparently given up.

From the laundry room, we went into a larger room that Gus said had been a room with storage areas for the tenants, except there was nothing stored there. The individual storage areas were separated by a heavy duty cyclone wire fence, but all the wire had been cut and rolled back. Gus' comment, "Bastard gangbangers!"

We came to a big iron door with four locks and a padlock. Gus patiently picked out keys from a large key ring that hung on his belt and opened each lock. Inside was the boiler room and at the other side of the room was a doorway. Hopefully, my doorway to freedom. When we reached the other side of the room, Gus unlocked the door and opened it slowly, letting in the night air that confirmed I was about to leave the building.

Outside the door was a ramp up from the basement level to the walkway at the south side of the project. At the top of the ramp was a railing and sitting on the railing were a couple of kids who looked to be maybe ten or eleven years old. When Gus saw the kids, he yelled that he wanted to talk to them and, of course, they took off running. Gus's comment, "Dumb little bastards."

With the path cleared, Gus walked me the remaining few yards out of the project, all the way to the safety of East Broadway. I offered him a twenty-dollar bill for his help, but he turned it down saying he did it for Maria, who I took to be Mrs. Jefferson.

My heart rate and breathing had returned to normal once we hit East Broadway. I called Gracie just to let her know I was okay, and told her I'd see her the next day because I was too beat to get over to her place. Then I called Tommy and, after telling him about my visit with Mrs. Jefferson, I told him to sit tight and wait for my instructions.

At the start of our conversation, Tommy had been pissed off with me because I had gone into the housing project alone. But he got over it by the time I finished telling him how it all worked out. Besides, I told him that I had Gus, and he was better than a gun. Tommy being very much like me asked, "You remember Indiana Jones?"

At least I had another reason to be grateful, and this time it didn't involve a taxi ride.

CHAPTER 66

The next few days were busy ones. The morning after talking with Mrs. Jefferson, Connie and I spent an hour looking for an out-of-the-way hotel to keep the Jeffersons and Carlos until we had the legal end all wrapped up.

With ten-thousand-dollar bounties on Latanya and Tyrone's heads, I had to believe every TB Gangster was out hunting for them. Of course, I wanted to protect the kids, but the callous truth was I had to protect them for Michael's sake, as well as their own. If, God forbid, the scumbags got to Latanya and Tyrone before they gave sworn statements to the DA, Michael was doomed.

Connie and I were looking for a hotel or motel that was somewhere the gangbangers weren't likely to look for the Jeffersons if they found out Latanya and Tyrone were back. We lucked out and found a new Motel 6 in a former industrial area of Long Island City right next to the railroad tracks. Without any residential buildings nearby, there wouldn't be much foot traffic and no reason for the gangbangers to look there.

Once we had the location, now I had to figure out how to get everyone there. We checked the airline schedule and found out it was too late for Tommy and the crew to make the afternoon flight, so we booked the morning flight for the next day. I called Mrs. Jefferson, told her the plan, and asked her to call her sister in Longs to make the necessary arrangements, so Tommy could pick up the kids.

Twenty minutes later, Mrs. Jefferson, who told me to call her Marie, called back. She had spoken with her sister, and the kids would be ready to go with Tommy and Carlos the next morning. I called Tommy and gave him final instructions. He was to pick up the Jefferson kids in Longs, and then all of them would fly back on the morning Spirit Airline flight out of Myrtle Beach to LaGuardia Airport. Tommy would rent a car and take the Jefferson kids and Carlos to the Motel 6, and check in everybody, including himself, under false names. Then he was to wait for my call.

I called Maria back and we worked out her escape plan. Her neighbor, Gus, would escort her out of the project and over to East Broadway. From there she'd take a taxi to my office. She'd only take a minimal amount of clothes and personal items for the time being. We'd arrange to collect the rest of the family's things once everything else was worked out.

Things were starting to fall into place. I was tempted to call Marion Marshall, and tell her what was happening, but I decided to wait until I had everybody where I needed them. There was no need to rush now.

I called Joe Benjamin who was thrilled with the

progress we were making. So thrilled he promised to take Gracie and me to dinner when this case was over. He said he'd take us to the best restaurant in New York City, the Olive Garden. Then he laughed and said he was kidding. Not about taking us to dinner, but about the Olive Garden being the best restaurant in New York City. I'd known Joe for over twenty years, and it was the first time he'd ever joked about anything. That gives you some idea of how much Michael's case meant to him.

On a serious note, I did ask Joe if the 18B Panel could provide legal counsel to Tyrone Jefferson. I wasn't sure counsel could be appointed for an indigent defendant before they actually became a defendant, but I figured it was worth exploring. The idea puzzled Joe as well, but he went out on a limb, and said he'd try to get Andy Feldman to represent Tyrone.

Andy is a damn good criminal lawyer who I've known for a long time. Andy is one of those rare guys who handles 18B cases strictly as a public service. It would be great to have Andy representing Tyrone, and I hoped Joe could make it happen.

I didn't have much else to do for the rest of the day, so I went to an AA meeting, then I went up to Kirby, and spent some time with Michael just shooting the breeze. Dr. Najari recommended that I not talk to Michael about Tyrone. He felt it could create a conflict in Michael's mind that might trigger a setback. It was better to wait for the outcome, which hopefully would be a happy one for all concerned.

Michael seemed more relaxed during our visit. I wasn't sure if it was because his mental state was improving or because we weren't talking about the events under the bridge. Whatever it was, I was just happy his state of mind had improved.

After I was done chatting with Michael, I went back and sat with Dr. Najari. I asked what was going to happen to Michael when the charges against him were dropped. Obviously, he would no longer be under an order of detention at Kirby, but could he stay if he wanted to? Dr. Najari said unfortunately no. Kirby was a maximum security facility strictly for patients in the justice system. The best place for Michael to continue his treatment was at a VA Hospital, and Dr. Najari was working on a plan to make that happen.

While at dinner the same evening, I mentioned to Gracie that until this case, I had no idea how many men had been so badly traumatized by the Vietnam War, and we were neglecting a lot of them. Whether you agreed with the war or not, it didn't matter. We owe something to the men and women who fought in it. I was grateful there were people like Joe Benjamin and Dr. Najari who went out of their way to help people like Michael. Gracie said I should include myself in that group, but I couldn't. I was a newcomer to all of this, and my record was hardly worthy of praise.

On balance, I had to admit there were more things in my past that I was ashamed of than there were things I was proud of. I will give myself some credit and say most of what I am proud of happened since I got sober, and just about all that I'm ashamed of happened when I was drinking alcoholically. That's not an excuse, just an explanation.

Gracie said I was being too hard on myself and maybe I was, but I kept thinking about the inequity of the whole thing. I had suffered shame and humiliation, but it had been at my own hand. It was punishment that I deserved for the choices I'd made.

But Michael suffered shame and humiliation not for anything he had done wrong, but because he had done something right. He had answered his country's call and willingly put himself in harm's way for the benefit of his country. And what did that get Michael? He came home a hero and we spat on him and cursed him and accused him of terrible things. Then when he needed our help, we turned our backs on him and left him to die in the streets.

I only hoped we had learned our lesson, and we wouldn't treat the vets from Desert Storm, the Iraq War and the Afghanistan War the way we treated the Vietnam War vets. I know I had learned my lesson, and I planned on doing whatever I could to make sure everyone else did.

Gracie said she was proud of me, and even though I had lost my way for a few years, she had always seen the good in me. Whatever good in me there might be, it was put there by my mother, and sadly I had tried to drown it. Gracie said I was being morose, so she took me home and cheered me up. That meant we had sex.

I made up my mind to be morose more often, so Gracie can cheer me up. I owe it to the both of us, and the best part is I don't have to eat sushi first.

CHAPTER 67

The next morning, I was up bright and early. I had a quick cup of coffee with Gracie, then headed to the office. It was going to be a long day and an important one.

On the way to the office I picked up a copy of the New York Post with the headline, "BIG DRUG BUST." Suspecting I knew something about it, I stopped in Columbus Park and read the article. According to the report, a joint task force of DEA Agents and NYPD cops had raided fourteen Columbian drug cartel storage facilities, and the homes of ten of the cartel's top bosses. Drugs with a street value of more that $900 Million had been seized, along with over a thousand weapons, and cash in an unmentioned amount. It was one of the city's largest and most successful drug raids in ages, and it likely crippled, if not destroyed, the Columbian drug cartel's operation in New York.

Pablo had gotten his revenge in spades, and I wondered if the cartel bosses realized how it had happened. I hoped for Pablo's sake they had.

I didn't have time to savor the article. I had to get to the office and work out the rest of the day's details. Once Tommy and the kids arrived at LaGuardia Airport at around 11:30, there was going to be a lot going on.

The first item on the day's agenda was getting Marie Jefferson out of the housing project safely. As soon as I was settled in the office, I called her on her cell phone to make sure we were still on schedule. Gus was there, and she was packed and ready to go. She was keeping an eye out for traffic in the square and everything looked quiet, so she could leave anytime. I figured there was no sense waiting when the coast was clear, so I said to go now.

Then Joe Benjamin called with bad news and good news. The bad news was he couldn't assign Tyrone's case out as an 18B case until Tyrone was arrested and booked, and his case was turned down by Legal Aid. The good news was Andy Feldman had agreed to take on the case pro bono, meaning for free. Andy was expecting my call to work out the details.

It was still a little early, but I took a chance and called Andy's office. He had just arrived and would call me back in twenty minutes. I used the time to call Tommy to make sure he was on schedule. He was. He and the whole crew were at the Myrtle Beach Airport early awaiting their flight. The airport information board showed the flight was on time, so they should be arriving at LaGuardia Airport by 11:30.

While I was on the phone with Tommy, Marie Jefferson arrived, and Connie escorted her into my office. After hanging up with Tommy, I went over the morning's events with Marie, and I was explaining the deal with

Andy Feldman when he called back.

I told Andy that Marie was in my office and suggested I put the call on speaker, so she could listen in. He thought that was a good idea.

I started off by giving Andy a rundown on the case and answering the couple of questions he had about the facts. When we were done with that, Andy asked Marie if she was okay with him acting as Tyrone's lawyer, and if she had any questions. She was fine with Andy representing Tyrone and, so far, she had no questions. Then Andy and I came up with a plan.

Andy would come out to Long Island City, and sit down with Tyrone and Marie that afternoon. Assuming Tyrone confirmed the story, Andy believed Tyrone would be okay. Technically, under the law, he could be charged with intentional murder even though he was only 13 years old. But it was not at all likely to happen. Worst case, he'd be charged as a minor, but it was more likely that no charges would be brought.

Once Andy had been formally retained as the attorney for Tyrone, he and I would meet with Marion Marshall. Andy would try to work out a deal before Tyrone surrendered to the police. Hopefully, we could have a deal in place that would include dismissing the charges against Michael and without charges being brought against Tyrone. Of course, the DA would want to interview Tyrone before the deal was finalized, but that would be easy enough to arrange.

Marie and I were just finishing our second cups of coffee when Tommy called. The troops had arrived, and he was at the car rental counter. If everything continued on schedule, he and the kids would be at the Motel 6 by one o'clock at the latest.

I was beginning to feel confident things were going to work out, and I think Marie was feeling the same way. After talking with Andy Feldman, she seemed more relaxed, and as we sat in my office waiting, she told me about her plans to move to South Carolina.

She had been to Longs many times visiting her sister, and she and the children loved the area. It was just a few miles away from Myrtle Beach, a family resort area right on the Atlantic Coast that was attracting retirees from the Northeast and Midwest. During her last visit, she had explored job opportunities and found several new banks opening in the area that were looking for experienced tellers. She had over ten years' bank experience, and figured she'd have no problem getting a job.

Marie wanted to know about Michael, who he was, what he was like, and why he was protecting Tyrone. I told her as much as I could without breaking any confidences. She hoped she'd have a chance to meet him, so she could thank him for what he had tried to do for her children.

It was strange, but suddenly I thought a lot of good had come out of a bad thing. Lover Boy had tried to rape Latanya and wound up dead. Not a good thing, especially for Lover Boy, but not particularly a bad thing for the rest of us. But after that, many good things happened. Michael got treatment and was on the road to recovery. Claire and Michael had been reunited after years of separation, and the Jeffersons were going to start a new and undoubtedly better life.

The only thing standing in the way of the happy

ending was the TB Gangsters, and that worried me.

.

CHAPTER 68

By two o'clock I was sitting with Tommy in Room 203 of the Motel 6 on Skillman Avenue in Long Island City, and Marie Jefferson was sitting in the adjoining Room 205 with her children and Carlos. Andy Feldman was on his way, and expected to arrive any minute.

Tommy assured me the whole operation so far had been a piece of cake, and he didn't see any problems in the future. I hoped he was right, but I was still worried about the TB Gangsters, and what might happen if they discovered where Latanya and Tyrone were. Tommy laughed and said if they did, there'd be a lot of dead gangbangers, and he pulled back his jacket and showed me his gun.

I liked Tommy's bravado, but I dreaded the idea of gunplay. When guns get drawn, there's no guarantee only the bad guys are going to get shot. It wasn't that I didn't trust Tommy. He had been trained to use his gun, and I know for a fact he went to the pistol range regularly. It was the other guys I worried about. The moron gangbangers with big guns, no training, and no idea how to use them.

Holding semi-automatic pistols sideways seems to be all the rage with these jerks. But when they do, they cut down dramatically on their aiming ability, which accounts in part for all the stray bullet killings. But I do love reading about these jerks getting their thumbs bloodied by the pistol's slide action because they held the gun the wrong way. Or when they get hit in the face with the hot casing ejected from the pistol. But as much as those stories of self-created injuries amuse me, I hate the fact these scumbags have guns, and I was worried for Tommy and the Jeffersons. I didn't mean to leave out Carlos, but I was starting to think of him as one of the Jeffersons.

As a matter of fact, Marie was starting to think that way too. During the taxi ride from downtown to the motel, she started talking about maybe having Carlos move to South Carolina with her and the children. She'd known Carlos since he was a little boy, and he was good kid. He had been raised right by his mother and grandmother, but his mother died a year ago from cancer. And his grandmother who was approaching 90 was in failing health. Marie thought the grandmother might be headed to a nursing home, and she'd probably be happy if Carlos were taken out of the housing project environment.

I pegged Marie Jefferson as a good person the first time we met, and now my impression was confirmed. Apparently, Carlos and his grandmother were good people, too, and I'm sure there were plenty of other good people living in the housing project. People like Gus. But sadly, they live in a community controlled by the gangbangers. Maybe now you can understand why I hate most of my scumbag clients.

But what the hell, I'm not going to rid the world of the scumbags by complaining and dumping all of this on you. I'll just keep doing what I'm doing, and let's see how it all works out.

Andy Feldman finally arrived, and he spoke with Marie, Latanya and Tyrone who were in Room 205, while Tommy, Carlos and I sat waiting in Room 203. The adjoining door between the rooms was closed, so I couldn't hear what they were saying. But I had a pretty good idea how the conversation was going.

About an hour later, the adjoining door opened and Andy and the Jeffersons joined Tommy, Carlos and me. Andy and Marie were smiling, which I took as a good sign. Andy confirmed the facts were as we thought, and we could proceed as we had discussed. I was thrilled with the news, but still cautious. It's not that I'm a pessimist, but I don't like getting too excited until the deal is signed, sealed and delivered.

Andy suggested he and I meet in Room 205 for a few minutes to work out the details.

CHAPTER 69

Marie had formally retained Andy to represent Tyrone and authorized Andy to share information with me on an as-needed basis. Andy had taken written statements from Tyrone and Latanya, but he wasn't prepared to share them with me just yet. He was able, however, to confirm that the facts were as I suspected. Lover Boy Johnson had attempted to rape Latanya, and Tyrone had intervened. Both Latanya and Tyrone said Michael Costanza was not involved in the attack, and only got involved after Johnson had been disabled and presumably killed.

Andy was willing to show me the written statements, but Marie had asked him not to until she had an opportunity to think things over. She and I were on good terms, but I could understand her reluctance to let me see the statements.

The problem was I didn't want to notify the DA's Office about all of this until I was sure of the stories. It wasn't that I didn't trust Andy, but Michael's future was on the line, so I wasn't taking any chances. Andy said he'd talk with Marie again privately, and perhaps we could get everything squared away.

Marie had been in Room 205 with Andy for less than ten minutes when she came out smiling at me, and told me to go in. As soon as I sat down, Andy handed me Latanya's handwritten statement. It wasn't very long, but it was concise and to the point, which meant Andy had helped Latanya prepare it. There is nothing wrong with that, so long as all he did was edit it to keep it concise.

Anyway, here's what Latanya had to say about that all-important day under the bridge.

She and two of her girlfriends had been hanging out in the park across the street from the crime scene when Lover Boy Johnson approached them and suggested they take a walk. She knew Lover Boy was a member of the TB Gangsters, and she didn't like him because he was always chasing after her and trying to kiss her and touch her. She didn't want to go for a walk with Lover Boy, and told him to leave her alone.

Lover Boy started to walk away, but then he called Janet, one of the girls in the park with her, and Janet went over and talked to him privately. Latanya didn't know what Lover Boy and Janet talked about, but she saw Lover Boy give Janet what looked like a bag of crack. After Lover Boy was gone a while, Janet suggested the three girls walk over to the river. Latanya didn't want to go because she didn't like having to cross through the old construction storage site to get to the river. But Janet insisted and Latanya gave in.

As they were passing through the old storage area, Lover Boy was there, and started talking to them. When

Latanya tried to move past him, he grabbed her by the arms and told the other two girls to get lost. Then he pushed her to where there was a mattress on the ground, and he started trying to kiss her on the mouth. He had opened his pants, and he was putting his hands between her legs. She was pushing against him and trying to escape, but he was holding her too tightly. She was trying to get away, and she scratched his face, but he hit her and held her arms down. Then she suddenly felt Lover Boy jerking, and then he fell onto the ground. She saw her brother, Tyrone, standing there with a hammer in his hand. Tyrone had blood all over his face, hands and chest, and he was crying.

She didn't know what to do, but then a homeless man came and took the hammer out of Tyrone's hand and said "Tell them I did it." Then he just walked away. He went to a little hut-like place and sat down. She and Tyrone ran home.

It was quite a story, and now all the pieces fit together and made sense. The inconsistencies in the Forensic Reports were no longer inconsistencies because Tyrone was left-handed, and he was six inches shorter than Lover Boy. Michael's mumblings about blaming him were consistent with Latanya's story. The crime scene photos showing Lover Boy with his pants partially down and his face scratched fit Latanya's narrative. It all fit together, and proved Michael wasn't the killer.

Tyrone's story was also concise and to the point.

He was in the park playing basketball with his friends when he saw Lover Boy approach his sister and her friends. He knew Latanya didn't like Lover Boy, and she was afraid of him, so he kept watching and moved closer to where his sister was. That's when he heard Lover Boy tell Janet to bring Latanya across the street to the storage lot. When he saw the three girls leaving the park, he decided to follow them. He watched them go into the storage lot, and he went in after them. When he saw Lover Boy, he knew there was going to be trouble. After the other two girls left, Lover Boy was grabbing Latanya and hurting her. She was fighting back, but Lover Boy was so much bigger and stronger than she was. He was scared, but he wanted to help his sister. He knew he couldn't fight Lover Boy, so he looked around for something to hit him with. He found a hammer on the ground, ran up behind Lover Boy, and hit him on the head with it. He didn't think Lover Boy had let go of Latanya, so he hit him again and again until Lover Boy finally let go and fell down. He was crying, Latanya was crying, and he couldn't move. Then a homeless man came up to him, took the hammer away, and said "Tell them I did it." After that, he and Latanya went home and she helped him wash the blood off. Then he and Latanya took all his bloody clothes and dumped them in the trash chute.

The two statements were consistent and definitely cleared Michael of the murder charge. If the DA wanted to bust chops, I guess Michael could be charged with conspiracy after-the-fact or obstruction of justice, but I doubted that would happen. In my book, Tyrone and Michael were both heroes, and if the DA wanted to press charges against either of them, I was prepared to go to the press and turn this into a big public fiasco. I could see the New York Post headline, *"Hero Boy Saves Sister - Homeless Vet Protects Boy - DA CHARGES BOTH."*

This wouldn't be the first time I used that tactic. I

had threatened it once before, and it worked. But I was getting ahead of myself.

Andy and I put in a joint call to Marion Marshall. I explained we had significant developments in the Johnson case. The developments were statements from both a witness and the actual perpetrator, who was represented by Mr. Feldman. The significance was obvious, but just to make sure Marion was paying attention, I threw in, "all of which proves Michael Costanza is innocent."

We asked to meet with Marion and anyone else in the office she thought appropriate, as soon as possible to discuss all of this and work out a deal.

Undoubtedly the news was a shock, but Marion seemed to take it in stride, which tells you something about the woman's talent. She'd try to arrange a meeting for the following afternoon, but she warned us that it had better not be some kind of stunt. We assured her it wasn't, and we'd await her word on the time for the meeting.

Half an hour later Marion called back; the meeting was set for two o'clock the following afternoon. She and her boss would be there. There was nothing left for Andy and me to do, so we shared a taxi back into Manhattan while the group in the motel ordered room service and settled in for the night.

I was feeling better than I had in a long time, and I wanted to celebrate, so I called Gracie and told her to make dinner reservations at whatever restaurant she wanted. I figured it would be the sushi restaurant, but Gracie surprised me. She made the reservation at Raoul's, a great little French bistro on Prince Street in Greenwich Village. Gracie and I had a long history with Raoul's, so it

A MURDER UNDER THE BRIDGE

was a night filled with nostalgia, as well as celebration.

As it later turned out, the nostalgia was great, but the celebration might have been a tad premature.

CHAPTER 70

I was in bed with Gracie trying to figure out if we were going to have sex to cap off an already great night, when my cell phone rang. It was just past eleven o'clock and it was Tommy calling. Even before I answered, I knew it wasn't going to be good news.

Tommy had been keeping an eye out the window, and there were six gangbangers he recognized as members of the TB Gangsters hanging around outside of the motel. How the hell did they find out where everybody was?

Tommy sighed; it was Carlos. He had called a friend to let him know he was back in New York, and he must have mentioned where he was staying.

There wasn't anything we could do about it now except make sure everybody was safe. Tommy had already taken some precautions; he took another room under a phony name and paid cash. The room was a big one on the top floor of the motel, and he gathered everybody in one room. He wanted to know if he should call the cops.

If the cops showed up, there wasn't anything they could do, but it would confirm that the kids were there. Instead of calling the cops, I told Tommy to keep an eye out to see what time the gangbangers left. I was pretty sure they wouldn't stay all night. In the morning, Carlos could call his friend and say they had been moved in the middle of the night to a hotel near the Kennedy Airport, but he didn't know the name.

Then Tommy should take away Carlos' cell phone. I liked the kid, but he was a real yenta. That's a Yiddish word commonly used by New Yorkers to describe a gossip or talker.

I should mention Gracie was sound asleep, so sex wasn't likely before the call, and now after the call I had lost the urge. I had to figure out what, if anything, we could do.

The meeting with Marion was at two o'clock the next afternoon, which didn't give us much time to work things out. The plan was for Andy and me to attend, but to have the Jeffersons in my office and ready to appear if needed. Now the plan needed to be changed if the TB Gangsters kept an eye on the Motel 6, despite the effort to throw them off the trail.

There wasn't much I could do at that point except worry needlessly, so I said the serenity prayer and tried to sleep. It didn't work right away, so I turned on the television and put on AMC, American Movie Classics. I watched a great old World War II story, *Best Years of Our Lives*. It's a 1946 classic starring Fredric March, Dana Andrews and Myrna Loy and if you've never seen it, you should try it. It also starred Harold Russell, an actual

World War II veteran who lost both arms in the war. He was great in the movie and won two Academy Awards. One was for Best Supporting Actor, and the other was an honorary Oscar for "bringing hope and courage to his fellow veterans." If you're into trivia, here's a tip. Harold Russell was the only actor to be given two Oscars by the Academy for the same role.

I didn't watch the whole movie. I didn't have to; I'd seen it at least five or six times before. Besides, it's a long movie, almost three hours long. I fell asleep about a quarter of the way into it, then woke up and turned off the TV after it was over.

Over coffee with Gracie the next morning, I mentioned the call from Tommy as I pondered what to do. While I was getting ready to leave for the office, Gracie gave me a kiss and said "Try not to get killed." That's Gracie's way of telling me to be careful. I assured her dying wasn't on my schedule for that day; at least I hoped it wasn't.

CHAPTER 71

I was in a sticky situation, and I wasn't sure how to handle it. Tommy had called earlier; the gangbangers had left around three o'clock in the morning, and Carlos made the call like I told him to do. But now there was a black pimpmobile parked down the street, and Tommy was sure it belonged to one of the TB Gangsters.

I called Andy, told him what was happening and asked if he had any ideas. He suggested we call the cops, or call Marion Marshall to see if she could be of any help. They were good ideas, but I felt they still left us with a problem.

The best the cops could do was run off the pimpmobile and escort our little group to my office, then if need be, to the DA's Office. That would help, but we'd still have a problem. Assuming we could cut a deal that afternoon, it would take at least a day or two to work out the details, and close the case. While that was happening, the Jeffersons would be at risk.

I called Marion Marshall and asked her if she could

arrange protection for the Jeffersons and Carlos until the matter was resolved, and they were all safely out of the jurisdiction. She appreciated the problem and wished she could help, but the DA's Office was already overloaded with witnesses in protective custody. Besides, Marie and Carlos weren't even witnesses, and once a deal was struck, neither was Latanya. Maybe she could squeeze Tyrone into a safe house, but that was it.

I called Joe Benjamin, but he didn't have any ideas, so I was on my own. Then I had a brainstorm.

I called Richie and explained the entire situation, then I asked him for help. Richie congratulated me on my intuitiveness in having figured the whole crime thing out. But it wasn't congratulations I wanted. I wanted Richie and a couple of his off-duty buddies to provide security for the Jeffersons.

NYPD cops aren't allowed to work off-duty security jobs unless they have permission from the Police Commissioner. But if they volunteered their services, that probably wouldn't violate any policies. I knew I was pushing it, especially for Richie who as a Detective, First Grade, would be taking a big risk. But I was desperate, and Richie seemed like my best option.

I told him it would take two or three days at most, and I needed two guys around the clock. I could even come up with some cash if any of the guys wanted a gratuity. Richie said he'd check around and get back to me.

An hour later Richie called back. He had a crew of six, including himself, willing to work the detail. Richie had divided up the watch into eight-hour shifts, so two of them would always be on duty. No one wanted a gratuity; it was all being done gratis.

I was curious as to why. Richie explained the other five volunteers, including a woman Detective, were Desert Storm vets, and that's why they agreed to do the job. Richie, of course, was doing it as a favor for me.

What could I say? I'm not an emotional guy, but to tell you the truth, I was all choked up. Richie said they were doing it for Michael because they owed it to him. We all owed Michael something, but not everybody was as giving as these cops. Maybe it was because they were war vets, or maybe it was because they understood what it was like to put your life on the line every day and not be appreciated. Whatever it was, I was grateful for their help.

Richie and another Detective were taking the first shift and would meet with Tommy at the Motel 6 at one o'clock. They'd escort the group to my office, and stay with them until I gave them further instructions.

We still needed to find a new safe location for the group to stay, so I asked Connie to do a search on the computer. She found a couple of possible locations, and then together we narrowed it down to one. It was in Nassau County, about 25 miles east of Manhattan, in a well-to-do area where a roaming gangbanger would be as out of place as a cat at a dog show.

I called Joe Benjamin and had him make reservations for four rooms in his name, using his credit card. I didn't think the TB Gangsters knew I was involved with the Jeffersons, but why take a chance? After all, I had promised Gracie that I wouldn't get killed that day. It was one promise I hoped to keep.

I called Andy with the details, and we agreed to meet in his office at one o'clock. That left nothing for me to do until then but worry. Since I got sober, I'm better at worrying than I used to be. When I was drinking heavily, I worried a lot, but only about one thing, getting drunk. Not that I worried because I was getting drunk. No, I worried I wouldn't be able to get drunk. I didn't give a shit about anything else, so what was there to worry about besides getting drunk?

Being sober, I have a lot of things to worry about, and I could probably drive myself crazy worrying. But I learned the Serenity Prayer and use it all the time. If it doesn't work, I call Doug which is what I did that morning. After talking with Doug, I felt better, but I was still a little tense. So I decided to take a long walk before meeting up with Andy.

I had about an hour and half to kill, so I headed north on Mott Street toward Little Italy. By the way, Little Italy is getting smaller as Chinatown moves northward. When I got to Hester Street, I turned left and saw Puglia Restaurant, one of my favorite places for pizza, so I decided to drop in. At Puglia's they have the traditional brick ovens and they make a Puglia Special, with sliced tomato, prosciutto and basil. They don't sell it by the slice, and I can't eat a whole pie by myself, but I ordered it anyway. I figured that I'd box up what I couldn't eat and take it to Andy.

Lunch was followed up with an espresso coffee, and the walk to Andy's office on Broadway did the trick. By the time I sat down in Andy's office, I was relaxed and ready to meet with Marion and whoever else she had with her. As it turned out, it was good that I was relaxed.

CHAPTER 72

Richie and his partner, Patty McKenna, showed up at the motel right on schedule and, together with Tommy, transported the Jeffersons and Carlos to my office. Richie, Patty and Tommy would stay with them awaiting my instructions.

At two o'clock Andy Feldman and I arrived at the DA's Office at One Hogan Place, and were escorted into a conference room where Marion Marshall was sitting with her boss, Martin Boyarsky,

I knew Martin. He started working at the DA's Office during my last year there. A year marked with a great deal of controversy and heavy drinking. I recalled a particularly regrettable incident involving Martin, and if I remembered it, I was sure he did as well.

At the time of the incident, I was a hotshot litigator trying an armed robbery case, and Martin was a new attorney second seating the case. Second seat meant he was supposed to sit in his chair, keep his mouth shut and learn. We were doing well, getting along fine until, for some reason, during the defense lawyer's examination of the arresting officer, Martin took it on himself to stand up and object.

Now I admit at the time I was probably a bit drunk and maybe missed something, but I don't think so. Anyway, I was annoyed at Martin and grabbed at his jacket to pull him down into his chair. Somehow my hand went under his jacket and grabbed the waistband of his pants.

Back then the rage was suspenders and Martin was wearing a pair clipped to his pants. I didn't know at the time that Martin didn't have much in the way of hips or an ass. I think you know what's coming next. Except it's worse than you think.

I must have pulled really hard on Martin's pants because the suspenders ripped free, and the button that closed his pants popped off. As I pulled back and downward, the only thing coming down was Martin's pants. Martin, apparently reacting instinctively to the backward pulling force, leaned forward so when I let go of his pants, he fell across the counsel table.

There he was, his pants around his knees, and his skinny ass covered by his BVDs sticking up in the air. I tried to apologize, but I'm not sure he could hear me over the laughter. Martin righted himself, pulled up his pants and holding them up with one hand, marched out of the courtroom. I don't recall seeing Martin again after that.

There wasn't much I could do about it, so I just shook Martin's hand and tried to ignore the obviously hateful look in his eyes. But I must give the man credit. He didn't let our past interfere with his duty, at least not in the end. At the start of negotiations, he was a real pain in the ass, but as we worked through the issues, he became more reasonable. I still had a feeling that if he was given the chance, he'd yank my pants down, and I wouldn't blame him if he did.

But I digress again. Andy Feldman did most of the talking. He explained the situation and gave Martin and Marion copies of Latanya's statement. Tyrone's statement would stay in his briefcase until we were at least close to a deal.

The first offer from Boyarsky was to put Tyrone on trial as an adult, and to reduce the charges against Michael to conspiracy in the first degree, a Class A-1 felony and criminally negligent homicide, a Class E felony. All those charges were ridiculous and we all knew it. There was no way Boyarsky could prove either charge against Michael, and there was little chance a judge would allow Tyrone to be treated as an adult. Boyarsky was just being a hard ass, and I could tell from the look on Marion's face that she didn't agree with his position.

I was tempted to threaten to pull Boyarsky's pants down, but thought better of it, and let Andy reply instead.

Andy said the offer was unacceptable, and I said simply it was unacceptable to me as well. Boyarsky, of course, relented and said he might agree to charging Tyrone as a juvenile in Family Court, and dropping the conspiracy charge against Michael. That still left the criminally negligent homicide charge, a felony. The charge is a catch-all the DA throws in when the conduct of the defendant won't support any of the other homicide charges.

Andy said calmly and simply, no deal. But I couldn't hold my tongue any longer. I told Boyarsky to charge Michael with whatever he liked, and we'd see what the public thought when they read in the Post that the DA was needlessly charging a war hero with homicide. Then I stood up ready to leave the meeting. Boyarsky realized what I had in mind, and I knew there was no way in hell he was going to let me go to the press with the story. I had him boxed in, and he had no choice but to ask me to stay and talk some more.

Having gotten our alpha dog routine out of the way, we were able to get down to business and after an hour we worked out a deal and committed it to writing. It was a three-step process beginning with Latanya being interviewed under oath by Marion about the events leading up to Lover Boy's death. If Latanya's account under oath was consistent with the account in her handwritten statement, we'd move on to step two. In step two, Tyrone would be interviewed under oath by Marion to confirm Latanya's story. So long as he confirmed Latanya's story, no charges would be brought against him, and we'd move to step three. In step three, Tyrone's sworn testimony would be entered in the record in Michael's case and, based upon Tyrone's admissions, the case against Michael would be dismissed.

Knowing we still had a possible problem with the TB Gangsters, we wanted to get the Jeffersons out of harm's way as quickly as possible. Although Boyarsky balked at having the interviews done right away, Marion agreed she'd do it even if it meant staying late. I called Richie and asked him to escort the Jeffersons over to the DA's Office. Carlos would stay in my office with Tommy.

The interviews would take a while and I wasn't needed there, so I went to Gracie's office and sat with her.

At six-thirty they were still working on the interviews. Gracie was tired and wanted to go home, so I went back to the conference room at the DA's Office and sat on a bench outside the door with Marie, Richie and Patty. Marie was understandably happy and thanked me for all I had done. In a rare moment of humility, I told her it was nothing. Richie laughed; I guess he never thought I could be humble.

At seven-thirty, the door to the conference room opened and Andy came out smiling, followed by a smiling Latanya and a smiling Tyrone. The ordeal was over for them, at least the legal part of the ordeal. No charges would be brought and both kids were free to go.

We all swung by my office, and Richie and Patty picked up Tommy and Carlos and they arranged a caravan out to the motel in Nassau County. Knowing I probably wouldn't be seeing the Jeffersons or Carlos again, we did a big good-bye scene with lots of hugging and some crying. After that, I treated Andy to dinner at Shoo's.

When I got to Gracie's place, she had bought some cupcakes and wanted to celebrate my victory. But I told her I couldn't celebrate because I was feeling too remorseful, and maybe she could take care of me. Did you know being hit in the head with a cupcake leaves a mark? But it washes right off.

CHAPTER 73

The next day Joe Benjamin kept his word, and arranged for the three Jeffersons and Carlos to fly to Myrtle Beach to begin their new lives. The two NYPD Detectives who had taken over for Richie and Patty made sure they all got to the airport and on the plane, safe and sound. Then they went back to their normal business.

I went to court that morning and with Marion's help, we had the case against Michael Costanza officially dismissed.

That afternoon I went to Kirby to visit Michael for the last time. We met in Dr. Najari's office, and it was a very happy event. Michael was doing very well, and Dr. Najari was convinced he would fully recover. Claire had volunteered for Michael to live with her once his in-patient treatment was completed. But Michael turned down the offer, at least for the time being. He felt it would be better for everyone if he completed his treatment before any decisions were made on where he would live.

Dr. Najari had arranged for Michael to continue his

in-patient treatment at the Bronx VA Hospital. He was scheduled to move there the next day, and with any luck he'd be out in six months. Dr. Najari did volunteer work at the Bronx VA Hospital, so he'd be able to keep tabs on Michael. I could tell the doctor had developed a true fondness for Michael, and I knew he'd take good care of him.

When it came time for me to leave, Michael gave me a big hug and kiss on the cheek. I'm not big on stuff like that, but I have to confess that I hugged him back and gave him a kiss on his cheek. If you want to know the truth, we were both crying. Of course, if you tell that to any of my clients, I'll deny it. I have a reputation to uphold.

Over the next few weeks Joe Benjamin and I straightened out the financial end. I think after all was said and done, he was out-of-pocket over five grand, and I was out-of-pocket slightly less. Whatever the cost, it was well worth it.

EPILOGUE

It's been a couple years since that happened.

I'm still practicing law on Mott Street, and living part time with Gracie. We still eat sushi more often than I like. And believe it or not, Gracie dragged me to Europe. Maybe someday I'll tell you about it.

The Jeffersons and Carlos are doing great in South Carolina. I hear from Marie occasionally, and I promised her if I ever get to South Carolina I'll look her up. Of course, chances of my being in South Carolina are just about non-existent.

Michael successfully completed his in-patient treatment and got a job in New York working for a Wall Street brokerage firm through a "help the vets" program. He's doing extremely well. He's still in therapy, and will likely be in therapy for the rest of his life. But that's okay with him. We have lunch every couple of months and he spends most of his holidays in Los Angeles with Claire and her family.

Doug's wife, Laurie, is cancer free and doing fine. Doug, well he's still Doug and will always be Doug.

Peter, he's still sober, still my pigeon, and still a pain in the ass. But as long as he stays sober, that's all that matters.

Tommy's business is thriving, and he hired an assistant to work for him. Of course, when I need his help I demand he do the work himself. Sometimes he listens to me. I love the kid.

A MURDER UNDER THE BRIDGE

One thing hasn't changed. That's the plight of our veterans. These brave men and women who volunteer, and put their lives on the line to protect us and our way of life, deserve far better treatment than they are getting. It's our duty not just as citizens, but as human beings to take care of our veterans. When the government fails at the job, we need to stand up and make sure it gets done. Please support our veterans, so stories like Michael's don't become any more common than they already are.

ABOUT THE AUTHOR

Donald L' Abbate graduated from Manhattan College and Fordham University School of Law. After a successful career as a civil litigator at a prominent law firm he co-founded, he retired and began writing novels as a hobby. Encouraged by his wife, he published his first novel, "The Broken Lawyer" in June 2016. This is his second novel. He lives with his wife Rose in South Carolina.

Made in the USA
San Bernardino, CA
18 January 2017